The Book of Other People

The Book of Other People

Edited by ZADIE SMITH

HAMISH HAMILTON

an imprint of

PENGUIN BOOKS

HAMISH HAMILTON

Published by the Penguin Group
Penguin Books Ltd, 80 Strand, London WC2R ORL, England
Penguin Group (USA) Inc., 375 Hudson Street, New York, New York 10014, USA
Penguin Group (Canada), 90 Eglinton Avenue East, Suite 700, Toronto, Ontario, Canada M4P 2Y3
(a division of Pearson Penguin Canada Inc.)
Penguin Ireland, 25 St Stephen's Green, Dublin 2, Ireland
(a division of Penguin Books Ltd)
Penguin Group (Australia), 250 Camberwell Road, Camberwell, Victoria 3124, Australia
(a division of Pearson Australia Group Pty Ltd)
Penguin Books India Pvt Ltd, 11 Community Centre, Panchsheel Park, New Delhi – 110 017, India
Penguin Group (NZ), 67 Apollo Drive, Rosedale, North Shore 0632, New Zealand
(a division of Pearson New Zealand Ltd)
Penguin Books (South Africa) (Pty) Ltd, 24 Sturdee Avenue, Rosebank, Johannesburg 2196, South Africa

Penguin Books Ltd, Registered Offices: 80 Strand, London WC2R ORL, England

www.penguin.com

First published 2007
1

Introduction text and selection copyright © Zadie Smith, 2007
Copyright for individual stories lies with each author © 2007

'Nigora' by Adam Thirlwell, 'J. Johnson' by Nick Hornby, with illustrations by Posy Simmonds first published
in the Guardian, 2007; 'Cindy Stubenstock' by A. M. Homes first published as 'Fair Art' in Exhibit-E, New York;
'Roy Spivey' by Miranda July, 'Magda Mandela' by Hari Kunzru, 'Gordon' by Andrew O'Hagan, 'Puppy' by
George Saunders, 'Hanwell Snr' by Zadie Smith, 'Donal Webster' by Colm Tóibín all first published in the
New Yorker, 2007

The moral right of the author has been asserted

Set in 12/14.75 pt Monotype Dante
Typeset by Rowland Phototypesetting Ltd, Bury St Edmunds, Suffolk
Printed in Great Britain by Clays Ltd, St Ives plc

A CIP catalogue record for this book is available from the British Library

ISBN: 978–0–241–14363–6

www.greenpenguin.co.uk

Contents

Contents

Introduction

The Book of Other People is about character. The instruction was simple: *make somebody up*. Each story was to be named after its character: 'Donal Webster' by Colm Tóibín, 'Cindy Stubenstock' by A. M. Homes, 'Frank' by A. L. Kennedy, and so on. When the commission was sent out, there were no rules about gender, race or species. This freedom resulted in 'The Monster' by Toby Litt and 'Puppy' by George Saunders. Late in the making of this book I tried to make a case for first and last names, for reasons of uniformity. The idea was not popular. Reproduced here is Edwidge Danticat's protest, convincing in its simplicity: 'I think the variety of names is good. It makes it less monotonous-looking. Since people are named different things by different people.' Surnames have not been forced upon Danticat's 'Lélé' or Adam Thirlwell's 'Nigora' or on any others who did not want them. In one case, the omitted last name is the deliberate secret upon which the story hinges. In another – to use a distinction of Simone Weil's – the character is a sacred human being and not a 'person' or 'personality', and his particular name is not important.

There are twenty-three stories in this volume, too many to mention individually. Each is its own thing entirely. The book has no particular thesis or argument to convey about fictional character. Nor is straight 'realism' or 'naturalism' – if such things exist – the aim. The hope was that the finished book might be a lively demonstration of the fact that there are as many ways to create 'character' (or deny the possibility of 'character') as there are writers. It is striking to see how one simple idea plays out in individual minds, the 'character' of the prose itself being as differentiated as the 'other people' with which these stories are nominally populated.

As editor, I have tried to retain the individuality of each piece by leaving them, by and large, little changed.

There is, however, an element of their character that has been removed: the fonts. Publishers standardize fonts to suit the style of the house, but when writers deliver their stories by e-mail, each font tells its own story. There are quite a few writers in this volume who use variations on the nostalgic American Typewriter font (and they are all American), as if the ink were really wet and the press still hot. We have two users of the elegant, melancholic Didot font (both British), and a writer who centres the text in one long, thin strip down the page, like a newspaper column (and uses Georgia, a font that has an academic flavour). Some writers size their text in a gigantic 18. Others are more at home in a tiny 10. There are many strange, precise and seemingly intimate tics that disappear upon publication: paragraphs separated by pictorial symbols, titles designed just so, outsized speech marks, centred dialogue, un-centred paragraphs, no paragraphs at all. It seems a shame to lose these idiosyncratic layouts and their subtle effects. Anyway: I hope what remains will satisfy.

Before leaving you to the stories themselves, I'd like to speak briefly of a technical matter, one that is usually considered to be in bad taste if you are speaking of the 'Art of Fiction': money. This book is a 'charity anthology', which means the editor must ask writers to work for free, knowing full well that a 'story' is like a gas that expands into whatever available space one has. When you begin a story it's impossible to say how much time will pass before you're able to finish it. It might take two hours of your time, or a few days, or four months, or more (this is particularly true for graphic novelists). So it was with this project. I want to thank all the writers for putting time aside – sometimes a great deal of time – to do something for nothing. Traditionally, writers denounce the very idea of writing for no remuneration ('I don't want the world to give me anything for my books,' George Eliot once said, 'except money to save me from the temptation of writing only for money'), but maybe there is also an occasional advantage in writing once again as you wrote in the very beginning, when it was still simply writing and not also a strange breed of employment. It is liberating to write a piece that has no connection to anything else you write, that needn't be squished into a novel, or styled to fit the taste of a certain magazine, or designed in such a way as to please the kind of people who pay your rent. In *The Book of Other People* we find writers not only trying on different skins but also unlikely styles and variant attitudes, wandering into landscapes one would not have placed them in previously. I recommend them to you with the proviso that their order is simply alphabetical (by character). Each reader should line them up as they like.

The beneficiary of this book is 826 New York,* a non-profit organization dedicated to supporting students aged six to eighteen with their creative and expository writing skills, and to helping teachers inspire their students to write. So *The Book of Other People* represents real people making fictional people work for real people – a rare example of fictional people pulling their own weight for once.

Zadie Smith
6 March 2007
Rome

---

* You can find out more about their work at www.826ny.org.

Judith Castle
David Mitchell

'Hello? Judith Castle?'

'This is she.'

'My name's Leo Dunbar. I'm Oliver's –'

'Oliver's *brother*! Oh, I've heard bucketloads about *you*, Leo!'

'Uh . . . likewise, Judith. Look, I'm –'

'All rapturous, I trust?'

'I'm sorry?'

'What Olly's told you. About little old *moi*. All rapturous, I trust?'

'Look, Judith, I have . . . some, well, some rather dreadful tidings.'

'Oh, I know! And let me tell you, I'm spitting kittens about it.'

'You . . . *know*?'

'It's all over the news, of course.'

'*What?*'

'A national rail strike *is* national news, Leo! The *very weekend* I'm due to come down to Lyme Regis and consummate my relationship with Olly, those bloody train drivers go on strike! It'll be back to the seventies, spiralling inflation, *Saturday Night Fever* and uppity Arabs all over again, mark my words. These things go in cycles. Still, no union bully is going to stand between your brother and me. Now I *do* drive, but motorways bring on my migraine, as Olly has doubtless explained. Are you driving up to fetch me, or is he?'

'Judith, my news was a little different.'

'Spit it out, then.'

'Oliver's . . . dead, actually, Judith . . . Judith? Are you there?'

'But our suite is already booked. A *de luxe* double. The girl at, at, at the Hotel Excalibur took my credit card number. It's all confirmed. I told Oliver yesterday. Olly wasn't dead then. He wasn't even ill.'

'It was a hit-and-run. He went to buy a bag of frozen peas, but never made it back. The ambulanceman said he was . . . the

3

ambulanceman said Oliver would have been dead before he landed.'

'But this is . . . outrageous . . .'

'We can't believe it ourselves.'

'This is . . . well . . . your brother . . . when's the funeral?'

'The funeral?'

'Olly and I were lovers, Leo! How can I not come to the funeral?'

'I'm . . . I'm afraid we've already had the funeral.'

'*Already?*'

'This morning. Very low-key. I tipped his ashes off the Cobb.'

'Off the what?'

'The Cobb. The sea-wall at Lyme Regis.'

'Oh. The Cobb. Yes. Olly promised to take me there . . . for the sunset. Tomorrow night. The sunset. Oh. This is all . . . so . . . so . . . *dead?*'

'Dead.'

'The very least I can do is to come and help out.'

'Judith, you're an angel, and Olly spoke about you in the fondest possible terms, but, if I can be frank, best not to. Everything's very . . . intense. You understand, don't you? There're relatives to be told, an ex-wife, and then the business to be wound up, solicitors . . . mountains of paperwork . . . insurance, wills, powers of attorney . . . a thousand-and-one things . . . it just never stops . . .'

Camilla's holidaying in Portugal with her father and Fancy-Piece. I got through to her voicemail and left the bare bones of my tragedy. Watering my tomato plants calmed me, until I spotted some greenfly. The vile little things got a good drenching with aphid killer. Then it was the turn of those ants who have colonized my patio. Kettle after kettle after kettle I boiled, until their bodies covered the crazy paving like a spilt canister of commas. Suddenly I found myself sitting in the conservatory with *Evita* playing at an unpleasant volume. Olly admitted that Sir Andrew turns out a fine tune. It was one of the last things he said to me. 'Another Suitcase in Another Hall' came on and suddenly my eyes streamed, unstoppably. This weekend was to have been a new beginning. Seeing Olly's studio;

meeting his family; making love with a sea-breeze caressing the curtains. After so many limp introductions and dashed hopes, here, at last, was a man whose faults could be mended. Some brisk walks to flatten that paunch. A tactful word to get him to ditch that moustache. Some musicals to oust his 'electric folk' tendencies. That Olly and I were intellectual equals was no surprise: *Soulmate Solutions* don't let any old Tom, Dick and Harry sign up. But at our rendezvous in Bath, he couldn't hide how utterly *enchanté* he was with little old *moi* on a carnal level. Once over fifty, most British women go to seed, leaving the rest of us to arise, like roses in a bombsite.

I swerved my Saab into the last parking space at the clinic, to the fury of some Flash Harriet who thought she had a prior claim. Water off a duck's back. To my dismay, my bookshop was open but devoid, apparently, of all life. Winnifred was in the stock room, busy with a sneezing fit, so I manned the till and started sifting the morning's post: three invoices; one tax form; two CVs from great white hopes after Saturday jobs; a letter informing the recipient that he has won a mansion in Fiji via the lottery – for every blatant scam, there are a thousand halfwits who refuse to understand that nobody gives money away – and a postcard from Barry from Grainge-over-Sands, the asylum-seeker's detention centre of the soul. An Australian came in and asked for *The No. 1 Ladies' Detective Agency*, so I got chatting, and soon persuaded Milly from Perth to buy the Alexander McCall Smith box set. She left, and Winnifred saw fit to put in an appearance. Winnifred is a lesbian myopic vegan Welsh homoeopathic Pooh Bear sort of a woman.

'Judith! What can we . . . do for you today?'

'Re-order the Ladies' Detective Agency box set, for starters. We're still a martyr to our hayfever, aren't we?'

'But . . . you do remember, Judith, don't you . . . that, actually . . .'

'That actually *what*, Winnifred?'

'. . . you aren't actually employed here . . . any more. Not as such.'

5

'*Some*one has to keep on top of things, with Barry swanning off while the town is swimming with holidaymakers. If that last customer had been one of those gypsies – whoops, it's "travellers" nowadays, isn't it? – you'd have an empty shop by now. Think on.'

'But . . . Barry's probably not . . . expecting . . . to actually pay you.'

'Am I *dressed* like I worry about next week's rent?'

'Judith . . . Barry did say that if you came in, I should ask you to –'

'Oliver's dead, Winnifred.' The words burst out of me. 'My . . . my beau. Dead.'

Winnifred took a step back. 'Oh, *Judith!*'

'My soul-mate.' A sob swallowed me whole. 'Hit-and-run.'

'Oh, *Judith!*'

'Really, the irony is too much to bear. Olly was going to introduce me to his family, *tomorrow*. Show me how to hunt fossils together. Share ice-cream on the Cobb. Consummate our relationship. Such . . . dreadful tidings . . . I wasn't sure to whom I could turn . . .'

'Oh, Judith. Sit down. I'll fetch a cup of tea.'

'The theatre committee need me in thirty minutes, but I *could* find a little time for a sympathetic ear . . . Earl Grey, then, with a slice of lemon, if it's not too much trouble.'

My Amateur Dramatics Society is putting on Sir Andrew's *The Phantom of the Opera* in October, so rehearsals are well under way. Our director, Roger, gave the lead to June Nolan, wife of Terry Nolan. All Lions Clubbers together. Very cosy. Never mind that June Nolan has all the operatic elegance of a dog-trainer. I turned down a minor role, and focused on stage-management. Let others grapple for glory. My job is thankless, and hectic; like I told Olly, if Muggins here didn't do it, the whole place would fall apart in a week.

Tears welled up again as I unlocked my little theatre. Olly was to visit me for *Phantom*'s opening night. *Everyone, this is Oliver Dunbar, a very dear friend. Runs a studio in Dorset, but he's exhibited*

*in New York City, no less. Oh, ignore Mr Modesty! Olly's photography is
very highly sought after.*

In the kitchen, silence swelled up. Butterflies fussed on the
nodding buddleia outside. A divine July, but *someone* hadn't put the
window key back where it lives, so I couldn't air the place. I began
a round of pelvic-floor exercises. Somewhere nearby, a car alarm
was going on and *on* and on and *on* and on and *on*, like an incurable
migraine. God, I des*pise* people who can't set their car alarms
properly. I despise Fancy-Piece's pleased-to-see-you smile. I despise
liver cooked in cream.

Where the hell *was* everyone?

'June, where the hell *is* everyone?'

'Who is this and where the hell is who?'

What sort of actress doesn't know her *who*s from her *whom*s?

'Judith, of course. Doesn't your mobile tell you who's calling?
Didn't have you down as a technophobe, June. Let me show you
how. Then you'll always know who's trying to reach you.'

'I know perfectly well how to do it, thank you, Judith. Your
number isn't programmed in, for some bizarre reason.'

'Well, I'm here at the theatre and not a *soul* has shown up for
the meeting, and if people think they can put on a musical worthy
of the name with *this* level of commitment, they –'

'The meeting was yesterday.'

'I *beg* your pardon?'

'The meeting was yesterday.'

'Since when were *Phantom* meetings held on a Thursday?'

'Since last meeting. Nadine couldn't make it this Friday, so Janice
switched it to Thursday. Don't you remember?'

'No *wonder* people get muddled, if days get swapped around at
the drop of a –'

'Nobody else managed to get muddled, Judith.'

If June Nolan weren't such a Lady Muck – Terry's a big nob at
the cider factory in Hereford better known for an outbreak of
Legionnaires' Disease than for cider – I'd never have let it slip.

'Well, I *am* a tad distracted. My lover has died. It's rather thrown me for a loop, I confess.'

'Oh.' *That* made Lady Muck change her tune. 'How . . . did it happen, Judith? Were you very close?'

'A hit-and-run. The police are still hunting the killer. Oh, I'm not sure if *anyone* could understand *how* close Olly and I were. It was beyond closeness. We were one, June. One. I shall never be whole again.'

When June Nolan *finally* let me go, Muggins here cleaned up the needlessly made tray of coffees, locked up my theatre and headed back towards the clinic car-park. That car alarm was *still* blaring. Outside the clinic stood a young family, which sounds sweet, but this one made my heart sink. *She* was about sixteen, fat, dressed like a sporty tramp, and holding a newborn baby in one hand and a giant sausage roll in the other. *He* looked about eleven, had a lip stud, a rice-pudding complexion, and that hairstyle where strands drip over the criminal forehead. He was a two-thirds scale model of one of those English yobs you see littering European street cafés since budget air-travel came to the masses. Right outside the clinic, *right next* to his own baby, this boy-father was *smoking*. Had it been any other morning I might have passed by, but the universe, via Leo, had just sent me a message about the fragility of life.

'How *dare* you smoke near that baby!'

The boy-father looked at me with dead eyes.

'Haven't you heard of lung cancer?'

Instead of yelling abuse, he inhaled, bent over his baby and blew out cigarette smoke *straight* into the poor moppet's face.

Is *that* family the future of Great Britain?

Yes? Then perhaps eugenics is due a rethink.

A care home spies on the clinic car-park. Yvonne, an aromatherapist I was briefly friendly with, told me that on average its inmates last only eighteen months. The elderly wilt when transplanted. Queen Elizabeth opened this very building a few years ago. I made sure I got to shake the royal hand. She's smiling at me, in our photograph. Thankful for my assurance that not *all* her loyal subjects think she organized poor Diana's assassination. Mind you, I'd put nothing past that Duke of Edinburgh. Told her that, too. A subject has a duty to tell her monarch what's what.

A janitor-type was peering into my Saab with a knotted-up face.

I realized the offending alarm was, in fact, mine.

With a crisp 'Excuse me', I nudged him to one side.

The janitor reared his bulk at me. 'Is this *your* car?'

Without responding, I unlocked my car and disabled the alarm.

'Is this' – in the sudden silence he was shouting – 'is this *your* car?'

'Do I *look* like a joy-rider?'

'*Thirty minutes*, this sodding alarm's been going. Nobody over there' – he gestured at the care home's windows, each framing a pale wispy face with less than eighteen months to live – 'could hear themselves *think*!'

'I doubt much thinking goes on there. Shouldn't *you* be more concerned about thieves tampering with vehicles under your very nose?'

'Oh, I *very* much doubt there was *ever* any thief!'

Water off a duck's back. 'Oh, so we live in a yob-free oasis, do we? See that midget thug over by the clinic? How do you know it wasn't him? You'll excuse me. I'm in rather a hurry.'

Thankfully, my Saab started first time.

I reversed out of the tight spot.

I found myself heading not homewards, but on the road to Black Swan Green. I very nearly turned around: Daddy and Marion weren't expecting me until Sunday. But the universe had told me to cherish my loved ones, so onwards I journeyed, onwards, until the steeple of Saint Gabriel's and its two giant redwoods sailed closer, closer, over the orchards. Philip and I would explore that graveyard, while our parents chatted after church. How long ago? When Mummy could still go outside, so the late 1970s. Philip found a crack at the base of the steeple. A crack of black. A door to the land of the dead, Philip told me. Left ajar. Philip heard voices, he swore, crying *lonely, lonely, lonely*.

And it occurred to me that Olly wasn't the only victim of that hit-and-run murderer, because the Mrs Judith Dunbar-Castle whom I would have become had also been slain.

No, 'Dunbar-Castle' sounds like a National Trust property.

Judith Castle-Dunbar was a woman in her fifties, though she could pass for her forties. She was content, and contentment is the best beautician, as Maeve, the owner of an organic shop who pulled the wool over everybody's eyes, not just mine, used to say. Olly and I would have pooled our funds and bought a spacious house near Charmouth. The Dunbar family would have embraced me. Unlike that gold-digging Patricia creature, who bled him white. Leo would have been Olly's best man, and Camilla my bridesmaid. Olly's grown-up son would have wept for joy into his champagne. *I don't think of you as a stepmother – you're the big sister I never had.* A chamber orchestra would have performed *Jesus Christ Superstar* for us as, one by one, Olly's friends would have let slip that my husband was on the ropes before he met little old *moi*.

Magpies loitered with intent on Saint Gabriel's lychgate.

Once, I was taller than the beech hedge around Daddy's house. Now it's as high as the car port. When one returns to childhood haunts, one is supposed to find how much smaller everything has become. But in Black Swan Green, I always feel that *I'm* the shrinking one.

'Daddy! So here's where you're hiding!'

'Why would I "hide" in my own greenhouse?' Daddy was bent over a cactus, stroking it with a special brush. He switched off the radio cricket. 'You aren't due until Sunday.'

'I was just passing. Don't switch the radio off on my account.'

'I switched it off because the agony's too much. We're 139 for 8 against Sri Lanka. *Sri Lanka.*'

'That's a gorgeous bloom, Daddy.'

'This, you mean? Mexicans call it the Phoenix Tree. The Yanks call it the Blue Moon. I call it a waste of bloody time. Six years of fussing and fretting, all you get is this mouldy mauve flower and the aroma of cat litter.'

'Oh, Daddy!'

'You can cut me eighteen inches of that twine.'

'Sure. Is Marion not around, Daddy?'

'She's at her book group. You're too old to say "sure".'

'Her book group? Jilly Cooper's got a new one out?'

'They're reading an Icelander. Halldor Laxless, I believe.'

'"Halldor Laxless". My.'

'The only writer I can stomach is Wilbur Smith. All the rest are bloody Nancy boys. Eighteen inches, I said. That's more like two feet.'

'I put a punnet of strawberries on the kitchen sill.'

'They bring me out in a rash. You're staying for lunch, I suppose.'

Mummy used to complain that Daddy loved his greenhouse more than his real house. Neighbours' children's frisbees and shuttlecocks would get confiscated for landing too near it, never mind that they ganged up on *me* to vent their displeasure. And no silky mistress was ever cared for as much as the green velvet lawn upon which Daddy lavished vitamins and weedkiller. I remember the day Philip was shown how to mow it. *It's a man's job, Judith. Women are congenitally incapable of straight lines. End of story.* A lesser woman would still be bitter.

'Did Philip's birthday card ever arrive, Daddy?'

'Philip has to lick the Adelaide office into shape.' With tweezers and a surgeon's delicacy of touch, Daddy tied a droopy cactus limb to a bamboo splint. 'I raised that boy to see a job through. Not to ponce around with cards and Interflora and ghastly ties.'

'So nothing's come of his plan to make it over this summer?'

'Philip's the project-leader.' Daddy measured out a cup of cactus feed. 'He has too much responsibility just to drop everything.'

'Oh, dear. Still no *Mrs* Philip Castle on the horizon?'

'How the bloody hell should *I* know, Judith? *You'll* be the first to find out when he *does* get hitched, via your global intelligence network.'

'Only asking, Daddy. Only asking. I see you got the CCTV installed around the front.'

'And the back. The Old Vicarage had a break-in. I'd get myself a couple of lurchers – teach 'em to bite first and ask permission later, like my father in Rhodesia – but Marion isn't having it. We booked that kayaking trip in Norway, so you're on the garden-watering detail in September.'

'If I'm around, I'll be delighted to oblige.'

Daddy gave me a significant look.

I held it. You mustn't let Daddy intimidate you, or he'll turn you into Mummy. 'A new development on the Glebe, I see.'

'"Development"? Don't get me started. Once upon a time, this village *was* a village. These days, *any* Paddy O'Speculator can slip those human turds at the council a few quid and knock up a dozen houses overnight for seven hundred grand apiece. Ah, Marion's back. I can hear her car.'

'*Such* a shock!' Marion poured the coffee while I stacked her gold-edged tableware in the dishwasher. 'So much life ahead of him! Poor, *poor* man. And poor, *poor* Judith.'

'I died with him, Marion. That's how it feels.'

'A photographer, you mentioned?'

'Ha!' Daddy dunked his biscuit. '*That* old chestnut.'

'A *very* highly regarded one. His gallery's in Lyme Regis. Daddy, what is so amusing about Lyme Regis?'

'Nothing whatsoever.'

Marion gave him a glare like Mummy never would. 'The police are *bound* to catch the driver sooner or later, aren't they?'

'The police won't shift their comfy arses an inch,' muttered Daddy, getting up. 'Not if it's not about blowing up airports. Not these days.'

'The sergeant told me the rain washed the clues away.' I sat back down and sipped Marion's excellent coffee. She replaces her machine every year, whether it needs replacing or not. Mummy used a percolator only once in her life. She put three filters in instead of one, and the kitchen floor was flooded. She cried about it for three nights running.

Marion had reconditioned yew boards laid everywhere after she married Daddy. A hanging stitched by one of her sponsored African children adorns the Afrikaner fireplace: *Happiness is not a Destination, it is a Method of Life.* As long as flies aren't drinking from your eyes, I suppose that's true. A lesser woman would be upset at how Daddy has let all trace of Mummy disappear from her home. What would Mummy's ghost recognize now? The alpine rockery, installed years ago to keep up with the Taylors; the cactii and their greenhouse of course; Mummy and Daddy's honeymoon photograph on the dresser, bleached blue by four decades; the summer house Daddy built for her, in the vain hope it would help with her agoraphobia; the chill in the downstairs loo. That's her lot. I haven't been upstairs here for years. Nor do I care to. Marion and Daddy's love-life is doubtless conducted on some space-age double mattress. They *do* have a love-life. I sense these things.

'If your engagement was an open secret,' Marion was saying, 'Olly's family must want you there for the funeral.'

'They wouldn't dream of burying him without me. Olly's brother told me the dreadful tidings before he told Olly's ex-wife.'

'So, when is the service?'

Daddy turned the kitchen radio on. ' *– has announced that indus-trial action threatening rail travellers with chaos and misery this weekend has been averted, following the rail union's acceptance of a 4.9 per cent pay increase over two years, with an enhanced system of bonuses. Officials say –* '

Daddy fiddled the dial, in search of cricket, grumbling in-coherently.

But the universe had spoken loud and clear.

'My train leaves tomorrow. Crack of dawn.'

The taxi-driver at Axminster Station flicked his cigarette away and heaved my suitcase into his unwashed cab. 'Cheer up, love. May never happen.' I replied, tartly, that 'it' already *had* happened. 'I am

here to bury my husband. He lost his long battle with leukemia.'
My words wove an instant magic. Off went his trashy local radio
station, away went that 'love' and on came a proper air of respect.
As he drove me down to Lyme Regis through the drizzle, he made
attempts at informed conversation about his son's school and the
Ofsted table; about a proposed site for a low-security prison, shouted
down by outraged locals; about a Victorian mansion once owned
by Benny Hill and, rumour has it, home to all sorts of goings-on,
obscured now by leylandii of gigantic height. My responses were
polite but minimal. Widows should not be chatty, and I had my
pelvic-floor exercises to run through.

'Hope the weather picks up for you,' he said, as I paid, 'madam.'

It was the same at the Hotel Excalibur. 'Business or pleasure, is
it?' asked the bouncy creature in that cud-chewing Dorset accent.
'Neither,' I told her, with courage and dignity. 'I am here to bury
my husband. Iraq. I'm not at liberty to tell you any more.' Before
my very eyes, she transformed into a real receptionist. She checked
if a quieter, more spacious room, away from the conference wing,
was available. Lo and behold, it was. 'At no extra charge?' I verified.
She was pleasingly shocked. 'We wouldn't dream of it, madam!
You'll be more comfortable there, Mrs' – she glanced at my form –
'Mrs Castle-Dunbar. Would you like a lie-down now? I can send
some tea up to your room.' I'd prefer to stretch my legs, I told her,
and she got me an umbrella. Several 'Made in China' umbrellas
were in the stand – left behind by forgetful guests, doubtless – but
she picked me out a sturdy, Churchillian, raven-black affair.

Yes, there are boxes of tatty junk in Lyme Regis, but also cabinets
of *bona fide* rareties. Nestling between Cap'n Scallywag's Diner and
Wildest Dreams Amusement Arcade you'll find Feay's Fossils and
Henry Jeffreys Antiquarian Maps. From a florist on Silver Street, I
purchased twelve ruby roses. In a jeweller's on Pound Street, a pearl
necklace caught my eye. £395 is not small change, but one doesn't
bury one's soul-mate every day of the week, and I negotiated a
discount of £35. I got the elderly proprietor to snip off the tag so I

could wear it now. 'Very good, madam,' he replied. England would be a superior country if everyone in shops spoke like that.

Then I came to the Cobb.

It curves out into the sea, this ancient stone wall, before dividing into two arms. One arm shelters the modest harbour. The other lunges into open water. Judith Castle-Dunbar followed the latter, cutting a swathe through a platoon of German pensioners. She booted their backsides into the briny drink, or imagined doing so, so vividly that she heard their cries and hearty Teutonic *plop!*s. Sir Andrew's *Requiem* – more sublime than Mozart's, who never knew when to stop – thundered over the water, for her, for the soul of Oliver Dunbar. Beadlets of mist clung to her overcoat. She reached the end. Judith Castle-Dunbar gazed towards France, obscured today by an inconsolable sky of tears. *An inconsolable sky of tears.* Judith Castle-Dunbar flung one red rose into the funereal waters below her. And another, another, another, sinking into the fathoms. Rest in peace. The widow has an uncanny sensation of being in a film.

Gulls are her familiars. Damp tourists, anglers, local hoodies and drug addicts, bored rich Germans, spiteful June Nolans, soya-milk Winnifreds and bronzed Marions, holiday admirals in their afford-able yachts . . . they watch on, wondering, *Who is that woman? Why is her sadness so deep?* She will remain anchored in the inlets of their memories, long after today. This woman moves in a separate realm. A Meryl Streep sort of realm. A realm which ordinary people can glimpse, but never inhabit.

Tucked up on the toppermost shelf of the town, Oliver Dunbar Photography was open for business as usual. A bell greeted me: the very bell Olly must have heard every day of his working life here. Right here. I must obtain it, and have it rigged up to my door at home. Inside, a man was speaking on the telephone. Leo! I recognized him by his voice. Leo is a touch beefier than Olly, but he has those sensuous Dunbar eyes, and that Jeremy Irons bone structure. His black clothes – obviously he'll be in mourning for weeks yet –

suited him well, and what pluck, I thought, to keep the show on the road at a time like this. Doubtless the Dunbars are rallying round. Despite my discreet enquiries, Olly never mentioned Leo's wife or girlfriend, and all ten fingers were free of rings. With the receiver still wedged between his ear and his manly shoulder, Leo smiled apologetically and gestured that I should make myself comfortable. An electricity passed between us. I sense these things. Why should it not? He is my dead lover's brother. I am one of the family. Closing my umbrella, I stood it in a bucket, and withdrew into a side-gallery to give Leo some privacy. His conversation wasn't worth overhearing, anyway: arrangements for wedding photographs at the council offices. Olly and I were to have married in a stone circle.

The side-gallery was walled with portraits. Some faces are windows, others are masks. What jokes had Olly told to coax out those smiles? What gentlenesses? Whatever they were, they outlived Dear Olly, and, in these portraits, my dear man's humour and compassion will outlive us all. Diamond-anniversary couples; babies on rugs; sisters in easy poses, extended families in stiffer groups; matriarchs amidst tribes of grandchildren; shiny newly-weds; surly, softened adolescents; a Sikh family even, here in Dorset. What a miracle it is, how two faces become one in their children's.

Families, I decided, come in three types.

First, families who participate in each other's lives.

Second, families who merely *report* their lives to each other.

Third, families who don't even do that.

We Castles, I suppose, are type two. Philip has his sights on type three, which is his lookout. But my fondest aspiration is to belong to the first type of family. To belong to a family who won't push you away for the crime of desiring intimacy! Even if I suggest to Camilla, my *daughter*, that I visit her in London, it's *No, Mum, this week's no good*; or *Sorry, Sinead's having a party this weekend*; or *Later in the summer, Mum, work's gone* mental *right now*. Then August arrives and she clears off to Portugal with her father and Fancy-Piece. How am I supposed to feel? So Muggins here does her best at the bookshop, the drama society, my England in Bloom Committee, and what do I get? The likes of June Nolan dubbing me a 'busybody' of course, that's all water off a duck's back, but where's the sin in wanting to be needed? In telling one's loved ones those home truths they need to hear?

Everything would have changed, post-wedding. Everything. Olly, his sisters, Leo here, *plus* better halves, *plus* toddlers, gather at their parents' home every weekend. I'd be a peace-broker, a soft-shoulder, a mucker-inner, a washer-upper. *We swear, Judith, we don't know how we got by without you.*

'*So* sorry to keep you,' said Leo. 'You wouldn't believe how –'

The phone rang.

'Not *again!*' Leo rolled his long-lashed eyes. 'Do you mind?'

'Go ahead.' Judith Castle-Dunbar's voice is armoured in self-belief, and brings to mind the huskiness of Margaret Thatcher. I like it. 'You must have so much to sort out.'

'This is too rude, and *you* are too kind.'

'Not at all.' I toyed with my pearls, wondering if he'd guessed the identity of little old *moi*. 'You're holding up valiantly.'

Leo smiled his roguish smile and answered the phone in his masculine way. I perched on a bottom stair and did some pelvic-floor exercises. 'Jimbo!' Leo muffled his voice this time, speaking low and turning away. 'Olly's not here, no . . .'

An acquaintance had yet to hear the dreadful tidings, doubtless.

'He's not answering the phone for a day or two.' Leo spoke low, but my hearing is excellent. 'He met this woman on the Internet, right – yeah, I know, how dodgy is that? So they meet up, just the once, just a week ago, right, in Bath – and *in* sink those female talons . . . Nah, she said "mid-forties" but Olly reckons it's more "mid-sixties" . . . It's not that, though. After *just one meeting*, right, she books herself in at the Hotel Excalibur no less to – exact words, I josh not – to "consummate our relationship"! "*Consummate our relationship*"! Couldn't make it up, could you? So Olly comes on his knees to me, right, to phone her up and tell her he's dead. It's not funny! No other way to get her off his back . . . Whassat? . . . I dunno . . . some tragic menopausal hag. Like she's *desperate* to be loved, but she pounces on anyone who *might* love her, so desperately, so hungrily, they run a mile! What? . . . Oh, that's the funniest part. I *meant* to say he'd had a heart attack – nice and clean, see, no complications – but when the crunch came, right, out came this garble about a hit-and-run driver . . . Stop laughing! *Then*, of course, Miss Hormone Replacement Therapy demands a starring role in the funeral, right, so *then* I have say he's already been cremated, and I tipped his ashes off the Cobb myself . . . Look, Jimbo, got to run, a customer's waiting. Olly'll be down the Lord Nelson later. Get the gory details off him yourself. Yep. Bye.'

An ice-cream van crawled by in the hissing rain.

Its chimes played that famous pop-ballad. About love, and Robin Hood.

What's that song called? Top of the charts, it was, one summer.

One long hot summer, when Camilla was little.

Oh, *everyone* knows that song.

Justin M. Damiano

Daniel Clowes

JUSTIN M. DAMIANO

#477171

MOTION PICTURE ASSOCIATION of AMERICA

CLAP CLAP CLAP CLAP CLAP

CHIEF FILM CRITIC FOR
WWW.JUSTINMDAMIANO.COM

A CRITIC IS A WARRIOR, AND EACH OF US ON THE BATTLEFIELD HAVE THE MEANS TO GLORIFY OR DEMOLISH (WHETHER A FILM, A CAREER, OR AN ENTIRE PHILOSOPHY) BY INFLUENCING PERCEPTION IN WAYS THAT, IF HEARTFELT AND TRUTHFUL, CAN HAVE FAR-REACHING REPERCUSSIONS.

JUSTIN!

PRESS SCREENING

JUSTIN!

WHAT DID YOU THINK?

I--

DIDN'T YOU LOVE THE SCENE WITH THE BIDET? I CAN'T BELIEVE A MAN WOULD THINK OF SOMETHING LIKE THAT!

MARION PUTMAN-ZEIRING, FREELANCE

ARE YOU GOING TO THE JUNKET? I HEAR HE'S GOING TO BE THERE BUT HE'S NOT DOING ANY WEB OR RADIO STUFF, AND NONE OF THE ACTORS ARE IN TOWN. STILL, I'M DEFINITELY GOING.

ARE YOU HUNGRY?

NOT ESPECIALLY.

C'MON, I'M STARVING.

HE SO PERFECTLY GETS HOW WE'RE REALLY ALL LIKE THESE ALIENS WHO CAN NEVER HAVE ANY MEANINGFUL CONTACT WITH EACH OTHER BECAUSE WE'RE ALL SO CAUGHT UP IN OUR OWN LITTLE SELF-MADE REALITIES, YOU KNOW?

M OST CRITICS WILL GIVE ANY MOVIE THREE AND A HALF STARS IF IT FLATTERS THEIR SELF-IMAGE. I TAKE IT MUCH MORE SERIOUSLY. HAVE YOU EVER NOTICED HOW MOST CRITICS USUALLY DISAGREE COMPLETELY WITH THE PUBLIC? THAT SHOULD TELL YOU A LOT ABOUT CRITICS.

HA HA HA HA HA

WE REALLY HAVE TO HELP THIS ONE OUT. THERE'S NO WAY THE STUDIO'S GOING TO SPEND A DIME ON IT.

GOOD. I HOPE IT FAILS.

YOU DO?

I HAVE NO MORE PATIENCE FOR DIRECTORS WHO HAVE TO DWELL ENDLESSLY ON SOME IVORY TOWER VISION OF "SORDID HUMANITY," "OH, EVERYONE IS SO IMMORAL EXCEPT FOR ME!" BLAH BLAH BLAH!

IF I WANTED TO SEE REALITY, I'D WATCH "TRADING SPOUSES"!

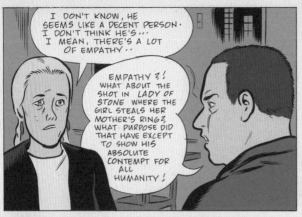

I DON'T KNOW, HE SEEMS LIKE A DECENT PERSON. I DON'T THINK HE'S... I MEAN, THERE'S A LOT OF EMPATHY..

EMPATHY?! WHAT ABOUT THE SHOT IN *LADY OF STONE* WHERE THE GIRL STEALS HER MOTHER'S RING? WHAT PURPOSE DID THAT HAVE EXCEPT TO SHOW HIS ABSOLUTE CONTEMPT FOR ALL HUMANITY!

HONESTLY, SOMETIMES I THINK I'M THE ONLY PERSON IN MODERN ALTERNATIVE FILM CRITICISM WHO ISN'T THOROUGHLY BRAINWASHED.

I GUESS I DON'T REMEMBER THAT.

WELL WATCH IT AGAIN!

JUNKET

HE'S DOING A ROUND TABLE BUT ONLY FOR THE BIG GUYS. NO NET STUFF.

I HEARD.

ROY EPPLEY, CINEMATOPOLIS.COM

I LOVE THESE PUBLICISTS - THEY ALWAYS SPRING FOR GOOD BAGELS INSTEAD OF USING THE SHITTY ONES FROM ROOM SERVICE.

THEY THINK WE'RE THE SAME AS THE NEWSPAPER GUYS. THEY DON'T GET THAT WE'RE NOT GOING TO BE INFLUENCED BY ALL THIS BULLSHIT.

EVERY CRITIC, EVEN THE MOST MAINSTREAM HACK, THINKS OF HIMSELF AS A "REBEL." BUT IN A CULTURE OF SELF-INDULGENT EXPERIMENTALIST NAVEL-GAZING, A REAL REBEL BELIEVES IN TRULY SUBVERSIVE IDEAS LIKE "ESCAPISM" AND "UNIVERSALITY."

SPEAK FOR YOURSELF!

SO WHAT DID YOU THINK? NOT HIS BEST, BUT STILL PRETTY AMUSING, I THOUGHT.

READ MY REVIEW.

HE'S TRASHING IT!

THAT'S VERY INTERESTING, BECAUSE JUST LAST NIGHT I HAPPENED UPON AN ARTICLE IN AN OLD *KINO-KULTURE* IN WHICH HE WAS REFERRED TO AS "THE ONE GREAT DIRECTOR OF THE NINETIES" BY A CERTAIN "J. MICHAEL DAMIANO."

REALLY?

HOW OLD WERE YOU?

ACTUALLY IT WAS PRETTY WELL WRITTEN. A LITTLE OVER THE TOP MAYBE, BUT-

I WAS YOUNG. YOUNG AND STUPID.

HEY JUSTIN!

GUESS WHAT? HE SAW YOUR NAME ON THE LIST AND HE SAYS HE REMEMBERS SOME ARTICLE YOU WROTE ABOUT HIM OR SOMETHING. ANYWAY, HE SAYS YOU CAN SIT IN FOR MANOHLA AFTER LUNCH IF YOU WANT!

COURTNEY HEISLER, ASSISTANT, NIXON AND WHITE PUBLICITY, INC.

AS MOST OF YOU KNOW, MY SITE DOESN'T USUALLY FEATURE INTERVIEWS, AND I WASN'T REALLY PREPARED TO GO AFTER HIM IN THIS SETTING (NOT THAT THE PRINT GUYS WOULD EVER LET ME TALK ANYWAY).

I COULDN'T HELP BUT THINK ABOUT THE 22-YEAR-OLD JUSTIN AND HOW OVERJOYED HE WOULD BE TO LEARN THAT HIS HERO HAD READ THAT ARTICLE. IF ONLY HE WERE SITTING AT THIS TABLE INSTEAD OF ME!

I FOUND I WAS OVERCOME WITH MEMORIES OF THAT SHITTY APARTMENT IN WASHINGTON HEIGHTS. I REMEMBERED HOW MUCH ELLEN AND I LOVED *THE DEVIL'S ROWBOAT* (STILL HIS ONLY DECENT FILM) WHEN WE FIRST SAW IT, AND HOW DESPERATELY I WANTED TO IMPRESS HER WITH THAT ARTICLE.

SO HOW WAS IT?

FINE.

DID YOU ASK HIM ABOUT THE SHOT?

WHAT SHOT?

THE LADY OF STONE, DUMB-ASS!

I DIDN'T HAVE -

WELL NOW'S YOUR CHANCE!

C'MON, LET'S GO!

IF YOU DON'T, I WILL!

NO, THAT'S

LOOK, I

OKAY, I'M GOIN

AND SO:

THAT WAS... THE DISTRIBUTOR CUT OUT AN ENTIRE SCENE THAT EXPLAINED WHY SHE DID IT. SHE WAS SUPPOSED TO BE A VICTIM. IT WAS... I WEPT WHEN I SAW THAT CUT.

SOMETIMES A CRITIC HAS TO MAKE SOME VERY TOUGH DECISIONS. HERE I HAD WRITTEN A DEVASTATING ATTACK, BUT SOME NAGGING VESTIGE OF GUILT KEPT ME FROM UPLOADING IT. WAS HE EVEN TELLING THE TRUTH WITH HIS LITTLE EXCUSE? DID IT MATTER?

ELLEN USED TO MAKE FUN OF MY TASTE IN MOVIES. SHE SAID I WAS A "ROMANTIC SAP" WHO PREFERRED ART CREATED BY FOCUS GROUPS AND COMMITTEES OVER THE IDIOSYNCRATIC NUANCE OF A SINGULAR VOICE. AND OF COURSE SHE WAS RIGHT.

REVIEW

ALL I CAN SAY IS THAT SHE CRIED AT THE END OF TITANIC AND I FELL ASLEEP DURING LE MÉPRIS.

I BELIEVE IN THE TRANSFORMATIVE POWER OF CINEMA. IT IS ONLY THROUGH THIS SHARED DREAM-EXPERIENCE THAT WE CAN TRANSCEND THE OPPRESSIVE MINUTIAE OF DAILY EXISTENCE AND FIND SOME SPIRITUAL CONNECTION IN THE DEEPER REALITY OF OUR MUTUAL DESIRE.

HOW OFTEN HAVE WE WATCHED A MOVIE AND WISHED WE COULD FEEL THOSE EMOTIONS IN OUR REAL LIVES? BUT WHAT'S STOPPING US? WHY CAN'T WE REJECT THE MUNDANE AND EMBRACE THE POSSIBILITIES OFFERED BY A CINEMA OF PLURALISTIC WISH-FULFILLMENT?

UM, WE KIND OF HAVE THIS NEW POLICY THAT YOU'RE NOT SUPPOSED TO SIT AT A TABLE FOR MORE THAN TWO HOURS.

WHEN ELLEN FINALLY LEFT, SHE SAID SHE FELT AS THOUGH SHE DIDN'T EVEN KNOW ME. SHE SAID I LIVED ENTIRELY INSIDE MY OWN HEAD. I CAN SEE HER POINT, AND I OFTEN WONDER IF SHE'S EVER SEEN MY SITE. THEN SHE'D KNOW THE REAL ME.

AND SO I HIT THE UPLOAD BUTTON AND LAUNCHED FIFTY UNSTOPPABLE MEGATONS OF JUSTIN DAMIANO INTO THE ETHER.

DC '06

Frank

A. L. Kennedy

The cinema was tiny: twelve rows deep from the blacked-out wall and the shadowed doorway down to the empty screen, which had started to stare at him, a kind of hanging absence. How did they make any money with a place this small? Even if it was packed?

Which it wasn't. Quite the reverse. There was, in fact, no one else here. Boy at the door had to turn the lights on just for him, Frank feeling bad about this, thinking he shouldn't insist on seeing a film all by himself and might as well go to the bigger space they kept upstairs which had a balcony and quite probably gilt mouldings and would be more in the way of a theatre and professional. In half an hour they'd be showing a comedy up there.

Or he could drive to a multiscreen effort: there'd been one in the last big town as he came round the coast – huge glass and metal tower, looked like a part of an airport – they'd have an audience, they'd have audiences to spare.

Although that was a guess and maybe the multiplex was empty, too. The bar, the stalls that sold reconstituted food, the toilets, the passageways, perhaps they were all deserted. Frank felt that he hoped so.

And he'd said nothing as he'd taken back his torn stub and walked through the doorway, hadn't apologised or shown uncertainty. He'd only stepped inside what seemed a quite attentive dark as the younger man drifted away and left him to it.

Four seats across and then the aisle and then another four and that was it. The room wasn't much broader than his lounge and it put Frank in mind of a bus, some kind of wide, slow vehicle, sliding off to nowhere.

He didn't choose a seat immediately, wandering a little, liking the solitude, a whole cinema of his own – the kind of thing a child might imagine, might enjoy. He believed he would move around later if no one else appeared, run amok just a touch and leave his phone turned on so he could answer it if anybody called.

Then behind him there came a grumble of male conversation, a blurry complaint about the cold and then a burst of laughter and the noise of feet – heavy steps approaching and a softer type of scuffling that faded to silence. Frank was willing to be certain that Softer-foot was the kid from the door: lax posture and dirty Converse All Stars with uneven wear – product of a careless home, a lax environment – probably he'd padded in close again and then headed back out to the foyer – that's how it sounded, but you never could tell.

At least one person was still there, still loitering, and for a moment this was almost unnerving. Frank being alone in a cinema, that was all right – alone in a muddle of people in a cinema, that was all right – just yourself and one other, two others, strangers at your back as the lights dim and the soundtrack starts to drown out everything – that might not be good. Silly to think that way, but he did.

For a moment.

Then he focused on being irritated, his nice privacy broken when it had extended so very far by now, right up to the black walls that melted when you studied them, disappeared down into the black carpet and left you adrift with nothing but the dull red shine of plush seats and a sense of your skin, your movement, fidgets of life.

It was fine, though. Nobody joined him. The heavy steps withdrew, closed themselves up, Frank guessed, inside the projectionist's box, along with another, more ruminative laugh. After that a regular, clattering slap started up and he supposed this to be the sound of loose film at the end of a reel, but he couldn't imagine why it was simply rattling round again and again.

He waited, the clatter persisting, his feet and fingers beginning to chill. One punter, apparently, didn't merit heating. Even if he did still need it. Simply needing didn't mean you'd get. Little vents near the ceiling breathed and whispered occasionally, but that would be the wind outside disturbing them. The night was already roaring out there and set to turn worse, rain loping over the pavements, driven thick, and a bitterness underlying it that ached your teeth, your thinking. Warmth had drained from his shins where his trousers were soaked and the coat he was huddled into was only a fraction less damp.

Frank put on his hat.

The rattle of unattached film continued. And he believed he'd heard a chuckle, then a cough. Frank concentrated on his head, which felt marginally warmer, because of the hat. Good hat: flat cap, proper tweed and not inexpensive. A man should have a hat, in his opinion. Beyond a certain age it will suit him and give him weight, become a welcome addition to his face, almost a trademark. People will look at his hat as it hangs on the back of a chair, or a coat hook, or rests on the edge of his desk, and they will involuntarily assume – *Frank's here, then. That's his hat. Frank's old, familiar hat.* Through time, there will be a small transfer of emotion and people who are fond of him will also like his hat, will see something in it: a sense of his atmosphere, his style – and they'll be pleased.

His own transfers were largely negative. For example, he truly detested his travelling bag. This evening it would be waiting inside his hotel room, crouching by his bed like the guard dog in an unfamiliar house. It always was by his bed, no matter where he was sleeping, neatly packed for when he'd have to leave, fill it with his time and carry it the way he'd enjoy being carried, being lifted over every obstacle.

Never thought he would use it on his own account – the bag. Never thought he'd steal his days from everyone and run away.

Not his fault. He didn't want this. She forced his hand.

He'd been in the kitchen, preparing soup. Each Friday he'd make them both a big vegetable soup: beans, leaves, potatoes, celery, lentils, tomatoes, bits of pasta, seasonal additions, the best of whatever he found available. Every week it would be slightly different – less cabbage, some butternut squash, more tamarind paste – but the soup itself would be a steady feature. If he was at home that evening he would cook. It would be for her. It would be what he quietly thought of as an offering – *here I am and this is from me and a proof of me and a sign of reliable love.* She would open some wine, maybe, and watch him slice: the way he rocked the knife, setting a comfy rhythm, and then the onions and garlic would go on the heat to soften and the whole house would start to smell domestic and comforting and he would smile at her, tuck his ingredients into the pan, all stripped and diced, and add good stock.

He'd been in the kitchen, slicing, no one to watch. French knives, he had, sharp ones, well balanced, strong, a pleasure to work with, and she'd been late home so he'd started off without her. The blade had slipped. With squash you've got to be careful because it's always tough and can deflect you, slide you into an accident. But he hadn't been paying attention and so he'd got what he deserved.

He'd been in the kitchen alone. Funny how he didn't feel the pain until he saw the wound. Proximal phalanx, left ring finger, a gash that almost woke the bone. Blood.

He'd been in the kitchen and raised his hand, had made observations, considered his blood. It ran quickly to his wrist, gathered and then fell to the quarry tiles below, left large, symmetrically rounded drops indicative of low velocity and a perpendicular descent, and haloing every drop was a tiny flare of threads, of starring. The tiles were fairly smooth, but still confused his fluid into throwing out fine liquid spines. Glass would be better, holding his finger close over glass might give him perfect little circles: the blood, as it must, forming spheres when it left him and the width of each drop on impact being equal to each sphere's diameter. You could count on that.

He'd been in the kitchen, being with the blood. He'd allowed the drops to concentrate at his feet, to pool and spatter, patterns complicating patterns, beginning to look like an almost significant loss. Twenty drops or so for every millilitre and telling the story of someone standing, wounded, but not too severely and neither struggling nor in flight.

He'd been in the kitchen and laid his own trail to the French windows. Tiny splashes hazed a power point in the skirting board, dirtying its little plastic cover – white, the kind of thing you fit to stop a child from putting its fingers where they shouldn't be. No reason for the cover, of course, their household didn't need it – protection from a danger they couldn't conjure, an impossible risk.

He'd been in the kitchen marking the reflections with his blood. Then he'd paused for a few millilitres before he needed to swipe his whole arm back and forth in mid air, blood hitting the dark glass of the doors in punctuated curves, the drops legging down before they dried, being distorted by motion, direction, gravity. He'd pumped his fist, then tried to cup his hand, catch some of his flow, then cast it off again, drive it over his ghost face and the night-time garden outside, the dim layers of wind-rocked shrubs, the scatter of drizzle, thinner and less interesting than blood. He'd thrown over-arm, under-arm, tried to get a kick out of his wrist until the hurt in his hand felt anxious, abused. Then he'd rubbed his knuckles wetly across his forehead before cradling them with his other palm, while his physiology performed as could be predicted, increased heart rate jerking out his loss, building up his body of evidence. Read the blood here and you'd see perhaps a blade that rose and fell, or the clash of victim and attacker: blows and fear and outrage, shock.

He'd been in the kitchen and she had come in. Never even heard her unlock the front door, nor any of the usual small combinations of noise as she dropped her bag and shed her coat, made her way along the corridor and then stood. He'd only noticed her when she spoke.

'Jesus Christ, Frank. What have you done. What the fuck are you doing.'

He'd turned to her and smiled, because he was glad to see her. 'I'm sorry, the soup's not ready. It'll be . . .' He'd glanced at the clock and calculated, so that she'd know how to plan her time – she might want a bath before they ate. 'It'll be about nine. Would you like a drink?' He could feel a distraction, a moisture somewhere near his right eyebrow.

'What the fuck are you doing.'

He'd smiled again, which meant that he might have seemed sad for the second or two before. 'I know, but nine isn't too late.' He needed to apologise and uncover how she was feeling – that would help their evening go well. Time spent paying attention to people is never wasted. 'Unless you're really hungry. Are you really hungry?' Her hair had been ruffled, was perhaps damp – a pounce of bad weather between her leaving the car and reaching their doorstep had disturbed it. Skin paler than normal but with strong colour at her cheeks, as if she was cold. Her suit was the chocolaty one with this metallic-blue blouse, a combination which always struck him as odd but very lovely. 'You look tired.' It was the fit of the suit. So snug. It lay just where your hands would want to. 'Would you like a bath? There'll be time. Once it's ready, it doesn't spoil.' She'd kept her figure: was possibly even slimmer, brighter than when they'd first met. 'I got some organic celeriac, which was lucky.' He seemed slightly breathless for some reason and heavy in his arms.

'What if I'd brought someone back with me. What if they'd seen . . . you.'

'I didn't . . .' and this was when he'd remembered that his finger was really currently giving him grief, extremely painful. He'd felt confused. 'I didn't think you were bringing anyone.'

At which point she'd lifted up a small pot of thyme he kept growing near the sink and had thrown it towards his head and he'd bobbed down out of the way so it had broken against a wall behind him and then hit the tiles and broken again. Peat and brownish ceramic fragments were distributed more widely than you might think and the plant lay near his feet, roots showing from a knot of earth as if it were signalling distress. Thyme was quite hardy, though, he thought it would weather the upset and come through fine in the end.

'It's all right. I'll get it.' Frank wondering whether the pan and brush were in the storm porch or the cupboard underneath the stairs. 'It'll be fine.' He couldn't think where he'd seen them last.

'It's not all right. It won't be fine.' And she walked towards him, sometimes treading on his track, her shoes taking his bloodstains, repeating them, until she stopped where she was close enough to reach up with her right hand – she wasn't right-handed – and brush his forehead, his left cheek, his lips. This meant his blood was on her fingers, Frank softly aware of this while she met his eyes, kept them in the way she used to when he'd just arrived back from a trip, a job – this was how she'd peered in at him then, seemed to be checking his mind, making sure he was still the man he'd been before.

After the look she'd slapped him. Fast. Both sides of his jaw. 'It's not all right.' Leaving and going upstairs. He didn't follow because he was distracted and he shook his head and tasted metal against his teeth and felt he might have to accept that he no longer was the man he'd been before.

Not that he'd been anybody special.

And this evening he was apparently even less: the sort of man who'd sit in a cinema but never be shown a film.

The projection box had quietened, the rattling stilled. There had been a few ill-defined thumps a while ago and then silence and the sensation of being watched. Frank was quite sure the projectionist had decided not to bother with the movie and was waiting for Frank to give up and go away.

But that wouldn't happen. Frank was going to get what he wanted and had paid for. Overhead, deep mumbles of amplified sound were leaching through the ceiling, so the other feature had begun. Still, he suspected that no one was watching upstairs, either – he'd not heard a soul in the foyer.

Half an hour, though – if the comedy had started, that meant he'd been stuck here for half an hour.

He removed his hat and then settled it back on again.

Being left for half an hour was disrespectful, irritating. Any longer and he would be justified in growing angry and then making his displeasure felt.

He coughed. He kicked one foot up on to the back of the chair in front, followed it with the other, crossed his legs at the ankle. He burrowed his shoulders deeper into the back of the seat. This was intended to suggest that he was fixed, in no hurry, willing to give matters all the time they'd take. The next step would involve conflict, tempers, variables it was difficult and unpleasant to predict.

Only then a motor whirred and the lights dimmed further then evaporated and the screen ticked, jumped, presented a blurry certificate which adjusted to and fro before emerging in nice focus and showing him the title of his film, the entertainment he had picked. Silently, a logo swam out and displayed itself, was replaced by another and another. Silently, a landscape appeared and displayed itself, raw-looking heaps of brown leaves, blades of early mist between trees, quite attractive. Silently, the image altered, showed a man's face: an actor who'd been famous and attractive some decades ago and who specialised these days in butlers, ageing criminals, grandfathers, uncles. Silently, he was looking at a small girl and silently, he moved his lips and failed to talk. He seemed to be trying to offer her advice, something important, life-saving, perhaps even that. But he had no sound.

The film had no sound. What Frank had thought was an artistic effect was, in fact, a mistake – perhaps a deliberate mistake.

He kept watching. Sometimes, when he'd been abroad, he'd gone to the cinema in foreign languages and managed to understand the rough flow of events. He'd been able to enjoy himself.

But this was an artistic piece, complicated. People seemed to be talking to each other a good deal and with a mainly unreadable calmness. As soon as the child disappeared, he was lost.

So he stood, let the chair's seat bang vaguely as it flipped out of his way, and strode up the incline of the invisible floor towards the invisible wall and its hidden doorway.

Outside, the projectionist's box was clearly labelled and its door was, in any case, ajar, making it very easy to identify – an unattended projector purring away there, a dense push of light darting out through the small glass window, thinning as it spanned the cinema and then opening itself against the screen. It was always so cleanly defined: that fluttering, shafted light. Frank briefly wondered if the operator had to smoke, or scatter talc, raise steam to make sure it stayed that way, remained picturesque.

In the foyer, there was the boy with the dirty shoes, leaning against a pillar and looking drowsy.

'There's no sound.'

'What.'

'I said, there's no sound.'

The boy seemed to consider saying *what* again before something, perhaps Frank's expression, stopped him.

'I said, there's no sound.' Frank not enraged, not about to do anything, simply thinking – *no one helps and you ask and it doesn't matter because no one helps and I don't know why.* He tried again. 'I can't hear. In the normal way I *can* hear. But at the moment I can't. Not the film. Everything else, but not the film. That's how I know there's something wrong with the film and not with me.'

The boy was eyeing him, but didn't seem physically strong or apt to move abruptly.

Frank believed that he felt calm and was not at risk. He continued to press his point. 'There is a problem with the film. The film is playing, but there's no sound.' And to explain what he'd been doing for all of this time: 'It's not been started long and it has no sound.' Although this maybe made him seem foolish because who would have normally waited more than half an hour in a cold, dark room for a film to start?

'There's no sound?' The boy's tone implied that Frank was demanding, unreasonable.

Frank decided that he would like to be both demanding and unreasonable. If he wasn't the man he had been, then surely he ought to be able to pick the man he would be. 'There's no sound.' Frank swallowed. 'I would like you to do something about it.'

This wasn't a tense situation, he'd thought it might be, but he'd been wrong. His potential opponent simply shrugged and told him, 'I'll go and find the projectionist.'

'Yes, you should do that.' Frank adding this unnecessarily because the boy had already turned and was dragging across the foyer carpet.

Something would be done, then.

Frank sat on the small island of seats provided, no doubt, for short periods of anticipation – people expecting to be joined by other people, parties assembling, outings, families, kids all excited by the prospect of big pictures, big noise, a secure and entertaining dark. The door to the larger auditorium was open and he could see a portion of the screen, the giant chin and mouth of a woman. There were also figures in some of the seats, film-goers. Or models of film-goers, although that was unlikely. They must have been stealthy, creeping in: or else they'd arrived before him, extremely early. Either way, he'd not heard them, not anticipated they'd be there.

That was surprising. Frank prided himself on his awareness and observation and didn't like to think they could fail him so completely. In a private capacity this would be alarming, but it would be disastrous in his work. He was resting at the moment, of course. Everybody who'd said that he ought to rest had been well intentioned and well informed. He'd needed a break. Still, there would come a day when he'd return and then he'd need his wits about him.

Expert. That's what he was.

'There are other things you can do.'

She hadn't understood. When you're an expert then you have an obligation, you must perform.

'There are other things to think about.'

She'd never known the rooms he'd seen: rooms with walls that were a dull red shine, streaking, hair and matter; floors dragged, pooled, thickened; footprints, hand prints, scrambling, meat and panic and spatter and clawing and smears and loss and fingernails and teeth and everything that a person is not, should not be, everything less than a whole and contented person.

Invisible rooms – that's what he made – he'd think and think until everything disappeared beyond what he needed: signs of intention, direction, position; the nakedness of wrong; who stood where, did what, how often, how fast, how hard, how ultimately completely without hope – what exactly became of them.

Invisible.

At which point, his mind broke, dropped to silence, the foyer around him becoming irrelevant. A numbness began at the centre of his head and then wormed out, filling him with this total lack of anything to hear. He tried retracing his thoughts but they parted, shredded, let him fall through into nowhere. And the man he'd been before was gone from him absolutely, he could tell, and whatever was here now stayed suspended, thoughtless.

No way of telling how long. Big numb space, not even enough to grip hold of and start a fear. Maybe mad. Maybe that's what he was. Broken or mad. Broken and mad.

Then in bled a whining: a thinner, more pathetic version of his voice and his mind seemed to catch at it, almost comforted.

No one helps.

It felt like a type of mild headache.

No one ever helps. I just stay at home and the light bulbs die and the ceilings crack and everything electrical is not exactly as it should be – there are many faults – and I call the help lines and they don't, I call all kinds of people and they don't help, I spend hours on the phone and I get no answers that have any meaning, I get no sense – there are constantly these things going wrong, incessantly, every day, and I want to stop them and I could stop them but no one helps and I can't manage on my own.

Like that evening with the blood – he couldn't very well have been expected to deal with those circumstances by himself.

He'd done all he could, waited in the kitchen and kept the soup on a low heat so that it would be ready for her. Except that wasn't the main point.

His finger was the more important detail. He washed that under the tap and then wound it round with an adhesive dressing from the first-aid kit. He'd used the kit in the hallway cupboard rather than go and maybe disturb her in the bathroom.

The bathroom, that was more important than his finger. He'd

been guessing she was in the bathroom, because the hot water was running, he could tell from the boiler noise, and she'd probably be in there adding bath oil, enjoying the steam, getting the temperature right for steeping in – he hadn't known. He never had seen her bathing, the details.

The bathroom was connected with his finger because he'd bound his injury downstairs so as to avoid her and had possibly not done this well, maybe he should have taken better steps to close the wound, because the scar that he'd eventually grown was quite distinct. If anyone examined his hands closely they would see it – an identifying mark.

Then – a key detail – he'd noticed that his shirt was bloody and he should change it, padded upstairs, and that had meant changing his plans and going upstairs, sneaking into their bedroom, pulling out any old sweater and wrestling it on.

The smell of her in the bedroom. Same thing you'd get when you hugged her, or rolled over on to her pillow when she wasn't there. Frank had seen men hug their wives, the way they'd fit their chin down over the woman's shoulder and there would be this smile, a particular young-seeming grin with closed eyes – always made him think – *bliss*.

That one soft word, which in every other context he did not like or use.

Going up to the bedroom had been a risk – she might have been there, too, resting on her pillow, or undressing and having some kind of large emotion that she didn't want to be observed. But he'd been careful to listen at the bathroom door as he passed it and had heard the sound of her stirring in the bath, a rise and fall of water, some kind of smoothing motion.

Somehow, that was another point to emphasise. It should not be forgotten, that moment of leaning beside the door and listening to a movement he could not see and imagining his wife's shoulder, side of the breast glimpsed, her cheek, the lift of her ribs – always a slim girl – and a glimmer of water chasing over and down, being lost.

Once he'd put on his sweater, Frank thought he was hungry and so he'd gone down to the kitchen, cut into the bread he'd baked – a moist, yeasty loaf made with spelt, which was a little difficult to get, but worth the effort – and he'd ladled out some soup. When he took the first spoonful, though, it tasted salt, peculiar, and a fierce weakness of his arms and throat disturbed him and he ended up throwing his soup away.

It wasn't that he didn't realise she was upset.

He did know her and did understand.

She'd brought no one home and they had no children, no child, and she was the only person who'd seen him, just her, and they were married, had been married for years, so that should have been all right. But her feelings did exist, of course, and should be considered. She was upstairs bathing and having emotions. Undoubtedly the most important thought that he could have, should manage to have, would be that she had feelings. These feelings meant she didn't like his soup, or his bread, or his hat, and she blamed him for terrible things, for one terrible thing which had been an accident, an oversight, a carelessness that lasted the space of a breath and meant he lost as much as her, just precisely as much.

He wanted to go to her and say: *I've watched this before, been near it – the way that a human being will drop and break inside, their eyes dying first and then their face, a last raising of light and then it goes from them, is fallen and won't come back. They walk into our building and whatever they think and whatever we have told them, there is a person in their mind, a living, unharmed person they expect to greet them and return their world. Then our attendants lead them to the special room, to the echoing room, and they see nothing, no one, no return, a shape of meat, an injury. Some of them cry, some accept the quiet suggestion of tea and the plate of biscuits we set down to make things seem homely and natural and as if life is going on, because it is, that is what it does – picks us up and feeds us with itself, drives us on until we wear away. Some of them are quiet, inward. Some I can hear, even in my office. They rage for their lovers, their loves, for their dead love, their dead selves. And they rage for their children. And they fail to accommodate their pain. And they leave us in the end, because they cannot stay. They go outside and fall into existence. Our town is full of people running back and forth in torn days and every other town is like that, too. Our world is thick with it, clotted in patterns and patterns of grief. And, beyond this, I know you're sad. I know your days are bleeding, too. And I know I make you sad. I don't understand how not to, but please don't bring in more of the grief, don't add to it. If there is more, then I won't be able to breathe and I'll die.*

And I miss her, too.

And I miss her like you do.

The no one who comes home with you holding your hand.

The girl who isn't there to mind when I hurt myself.

'That'll be okay, then.'

Frank saw the young man's sneakers, the intentionally be-draggled cuffs of his jeans. Frank looked at them through his fingers, keeping his head low. 'I'm sorry.' This emerging less as a question than a statement, a confession. He rubbed his neck, his helpless sweat, and said again, more clearly and correctly, 'I'm sorry?'

'The projectionist's just coming back. You can go in and wait.'

Oh, I know about that, I've done that. Wait. I can do that. Past master.

Frank swallowed while his anger crested and then sank. These spasms were never long-lasting, although they used to be less frequent. That could be a cause for concern, his increased capacity for hatred.

'Are you okay?'

The boy staring with what appeared to be mild distaste when Frank straightened himself and looked up. 'No. At least, yes. I am okay. I have a headache, that's all.'

Standing seemed to take an extremely long time, Frank trying not to fall or stagger as he pressed himself up through the heavy air. He was taller than the boy, ought to be able to dominate him, but instead Frank nodded, holding his cap in both hands – something imploring in this, something anachronistic and disturbing – and he cranked out one step and then another, jolted back to the doorway of the cinema and through.

The dark was a relief, peaceful. He felt smoother, healthier as soon as it wrapped him round, cuddled at his back and opened ahead to let him pad down the gentle slope and find a new seat.

It was actually good that his film had been delayed. This way, his evening would be eaten up – back to the hotel after and head straight for bed. Double bed. Only one of him. No need to pick a side: her side, his side. He could lie where he wanted.

She preferred the left. He'd supposed this was somehow to do with the bedroom door being on the right. Any threat would come in from the right and he would be set in place to meet it. Frank had thought she was letting him guard her while she slept: Frank who was perfectly happy on whatever side was left free, who might as well rest at the foot of the bed like a folded blanket. It didn't matter. He didn't mind.

Really, though, she didn't expect Frank to defend her. Her choice had nothing to do with him. In fact, they'd had other bedrooms with the door in other places and with windows that could be climbed through, you had to consider them, too – their current window was to the left – and she'd still always lain on the left. She was left-handed, that was why. Easier to reach her book, her water glass, her reading lamp if she was over there.

She hadn't read on their last night, at least he didn't think so. He'd waited for her in the kitchen with the soup and she'd never come down. He'd cleaned up his blood and repotted the plant and listened to the sound of the water draining from her bath and her naked footsteps on the landing, not moving towards the stairs. Then he'd decided his first cleaning hadn't been thorough and he'd scrubbed the place completely – work surfaces, floor, emptied out the fridge and wiped it down, made it tidy. The cupboards needed tidying, as well. That took quite a time. Finally, he decanted the soup into a container, washed the pot, looked at the container, emptied it into the bin and washed the container.

It was two in the morning when he was done.

And when he had slipped into bed he had expected her to be sleeping, because that would be best.

'What were you doing?' Only she wasn't asleep, she was just lying on her back without the light on and waiting to ask him, 'What were you doing?'

'I . . . cleaning.'

'What's wrong with you.'

And Frank couldn't tell her because he didn't know and so he just said, 'I understand why people look at fountains, or at the sea. Because those don't stop. The water moves and keeps on moving, the tide withdraws and then returns and it keeps on going and keeps on. It's like –' He could hear her shifting, feel her sitting up, but not reaching for him. 'It's like that button you get on stereos, on those little personal players – there's always the button that lets you repeat – not just the album, but the track, one single track. They've anticipated you'll want to repeat one track, over and over, so those three or four minutes can stay, you can keep that time steady in your head, roll it back, fold it back. They know you'll want that. I want that. Just three or four minutes that come back.' Which he'd been afraid of while he'd heard it and when he'd stopped speaking she was breathing peculiarly, loudly, unevenly, the way she would before she cried. So he'd started again, because he had no tolerance for that, not even the idea of that. 'I want a second, three, four seconds, that would be all. I want everything back. No stopping, I want nothing to stop.' Only he was crying now, too – no way to avoid it. 'I want her to be –' His sentence interrupted when she hit him, punched out at his chest and then a blow against his eye causing this burst of greyish colour and more pains and he'd caught her wrists eventually, almost fought her, the crown of her head banging against his chin, jarring him.

Afterwards they had rested, his head on her stomach, both of them still weeping, too loudly, too deeply, the din of it ripping something in his head. But even that had gone eventually, and there had been silence and he had tried to kiss her and she had not allowed it.

That was when he had taken his bag and left the room, the house, the town, the life.

I miss her, too.

Behind Frank, the projector stuttered and whirred, light springing to the screen and sound this time along with it. He fumbled into his pocket and found his phone, turned it off. That way he wouldn't know when it didn't ring, kept on not ringing.

Frank tipped back his head and watched the opening titles, the mist, the trees, the older man's face as it spoke to the small girl's, as he spoke to his daughter, while the world turned unreliable and salt. And the film reeled on and he knew that it would finish and knew that when it did he would want nothing more than to start it again.

Gideon

ZZ Packer

You know what I mean? I was nineteen and crazy back then. I'd met this Jewish guy with this really Jewish name: Gideon. He had hair like an Afro wig and a nervous smile that kept unfolding quickly, like origami. He was one of those white guys who had a thing for black women, but he'd apparently been too afraid to ask out anyone, until he met me.

That one day, when it all began to unravel, Gideon was working on his dissertation, which meant he was in cutoffs in bed with me, the fan whirring over us while he was getting political about something or other. He was always getting political, even though his Ph.D. had nothing to do with politics and was called 'Temporal Modes of Discourse and Ekphrasis in Elizabethan Poetry'. Even he didn't like his dissertation. He was always opening some musty book, reading it for a while, then closing it and saying, 'You know what's wrong with these fascist corporations?' No matter how you responded, you'd always be wrong because he'd say, 'Exactly!' then go on to tell you his theory, which had nothing to do with anything you'd just said.

He was philosophizing, per usual, all worked up with nervous energy while feeding our crickets. 'And *you*,' he said, unscrewing a cricket jar, looking at the cricket but speaking to me, 'you think the neo-industrial complex doesn't pertain to you, but it does, because by tacitly participating *blah blah blah* you're engaging in *blah blah* commodification of workers *blah blah blah* allowing the neo-Reaganites to *blah blah blah* but you can't escape the dialectic.'

His thing that summer was crickets, I don't know why. Maybe it was something about the way they formed an orchestra at night. All around our bed, with the sky too hot and the torn screen windows, all you could hear were those damn crickets, moving their muscular little thighs and wings to make music. He would stick his nose out the window and smell the air. Sometimes he would go out barefoot with a flashlight and try to catch a cricket. If he was successful, he'd put it in one of those little jars – jars that once held gourmet items like tapenade and aïoli. I'd never heard of these things before, but with Gideon, I'd find myself eating tapenade on fancy stale bread one night, and the next night we'd rinse out the jar and *voilà*, a cricket would be living in it.

Whenever he'd come back to bed from gathering crickets, he'd try to wedge his cold skinny body around my fetal position. 'Come closer,' he'd say. And I'd want to and then again I wouldn't want to. He always smelled different after being outside. Like a farm animal, or watercress. Plus he had a ton of calluses.

Sometimes I'd stare in the mid-darkness at how white he was. If I pressed his skin, he'd bruise deep fuchsia and you'd be able to see it even in the dark. I was very dark compared to him. He was so white it was freaky, sometimes. Othertimes it was kind of cool and beautiful, how his skin would glow against mine, how our bodies together looked like art.

Well, that one day – after he'd railed against the Federal Reserve Board, NAFTA, the gun lobby and the neo-industrial complex – we fed the crickets and went to bed. When I say went to bed, I mean, we made love. I used to call it sex, but Gideon said I might as well call it rape. Making love was all about the mind. One time, in a position that would have been beautiful art, he said, 'Look at me. Really look at me.' I didn't like looking at people when I did it, like those tribes afraid part of their soul will peel away if someone takes a picture of them. When Gideon and I did lock eyes, I must admit, it felt different. Like we were – for a moment – part of the same picture.

That night, we did it again. I couldn't say for sure if the condom broke or not, but it all felt weird, and Gideon said, 'The whole condom-breaking-thing is a myth.' But we looked at it under the light, the condom looking all dead and slimy, and finally he threw the thing across the room, where it stuck to the wall like a slug, then fell. 'Fucking *Freestyles*! Who the hell buys fucking *Freestyles*?'

'They're free at the clinic,' I said. 'What do you want, organic condoms?' We looked it over again but that didn't stop it from being broke. Then Gideon made a look that just about sent me over the edge.

I had to think. I went in the bathroom and sat on the toilet. I'd done everything right. I hadn't gotten pregnant or done drugs or hurt anybody. I had a little life, working at Pita Delicious, serving up burgers and falafel. Almost everything there was awful, but the falafels weren't half bad. It was at Pita Delicious that I first met Gideon with his bobbing nosetip and Afro-Jewish hair. The Syrian guys who owned the place always made me go and talk to him, because they didn't like him. The first couple of times he came in he'd tried talking to them about the Middle East and the Palestinians and whatnot. Even though he was on their side, they still hated him. 'Talk to the Jew,' they said, whenever he came in. Soon we were eating falafels on my break, with Gideon helping me plot out how I was going to go back to school, which was just a figure of speech because I hadn't entered school in the first place.

When I came back to bed, Gideon was splayed out on top of the blanket, slices of moonlight on his bony body. 'All right,' he said. 'Let's get a pregnancy test.'

'Don't you know anything? It's not going to work immediately.'

He made a weird face, and asked, 'Is this the voice of experience talking?'

I looked at him. 'Everyone knows,' I said, trying to sound calm and condescending, 'that it's your first missed period.'

He mouthed *Okay*, real slowly, like I was the crazy one.

When my period went AWOL, I took the pregnancy test in the bathroom at Pita Delicious. I don't know why. I guess I didn't want Gideon hovering over me. I didn't even tell him when I was going to do it. One pink stripe. Negative. I should have been relieved, relieved to have my lame life back, but the surprising thing was that I wasn't. Then I did something I never thought I'd do, something unlike anything I've ever done before: it was really simple to get a pink marker, and take off the plastic cover and draw another little stripe. *Two stripes,* the test said, *means you're pregnant.*

When I got back home, I told him the test was positive, and flicked it into his lap: 'What do you care?'

I told him that I didn't know what I was going to do – what *we* were going to do. He paced in front of the crickets for a while. Then he put his arm around me, like I'd just told him I had AIDS and he'd mustered the courage to give me a hug.

'What're we gonna *do?*' I asked. I don't know what I expected – whether I thought I'd catch him in a lie, or he'd say something about not wanting the baby, or what – I forgot. All I knew was that something was pressing down on me, drowning me. If he'd said anything, anything at all, I would have been fine. If he'd start talking about the dialectic or about mesothelioma or aïoli or how many types of cancer you could get from one little Newport menthol – I'd have been all right. Even if he cursed me out and blamed me and said he didn't want the baby – I'd have understood.

But he didn't say anything. I saw everything he was thinking, though. I saw him thinking about his parents – Sy and Rita – growing worried in their condo's sunny Sarasota kitchen; I saw him never finishing his thesis and going to work for some grubby non-profit where everyone ate tempeh and couldn't wear leather and almost had a Ph.D.; I saw him hauling the kid around to parks, saying it was the best thing he'd ever done. Really. The best.

I walked out of that room, out of that house he rented with its really nice wood everywhere. I kept walking away, quickly at first, then so fast that the tears were the only thing keeping me from burning myself out like a comet. I wasn't running from Gideon anymore, but even if he was following me, it was too late. Even with no baby, I could see there'd be no day when I'd meet Sy and Rita, no day when I'd quit Pita Delicious before they quit me, no day when I'd hang around a table of students talking about post-postfeminism, no day when Gideon and I would lock hands in front of the house we'd just bought. Anyone could have told him it was too late for that, for us, but Gideon was Gideon, and I could hear him calling after me, hoping the way he always did that the words would do the chasing for him.

Gordon

Andrew O'Hagan

1. Pride

They say Gordon nearly lost an eye in the 1950s, playing football by a slagheap on the edge of Kirkcaldy. 'Never mind,' said his father on the walk back from the Infirmary. 'We're all half blind in the face of Divinity.' Gordon felt a painful nip under the nurse's bandage and saw a presentation of cold stars in the road's tarmac. Years later he remembered that walk home and the way he had felt proud at the perfect ordinariness of his school shoes. 'That's a likeable person, that doctor,' his father had said with a cough as Gordon walked out in front. 'He knows how to be a doctor. He believes every man must suffer a little damage.'

2. Romance

There was a linoleum factory up on the main road and Gordon could see it smoking from his room at the manse. He always had that strange ability – one emboldened by his reading of books and plays – to conjure some kind of high romance out of an industrial scene, though neither of his brothers had time for books, being busy all the while with haircuts and phone calls. Gordon would memorize quotations and say them to himself under the bathwater with his ears crowding around with noise. His eye was better by then and his father was deeper in league with the Lord. Gordon would stand in the talcum-powdered air of the bathroom muttering calculations and strange moral sums about the cause of Hamlet's unhappiness. His mother knew her second son was bound for Edinburgh when he came down one evening with a sullen face.

'The problem in *Hamlet* is the ghost,' he said. 'He's imprudent. He's unwise. You can't command a person's conscience. And by forcing a family into action you kill them all.'

3. *Value*

Baked beans became a subject for a while. Gordon worked out that each bean had a certain value to the world, but he felt it curious that some beans were eager for their own preferment. On toast, some of those beans had a truly remarkable orange lustre, and it seemed the biggest beans exactly understood – in a way the pulpy and burst ones certainly did not – what their role might be in the perfect meal. At his student flat in the Grassmarket, the dishes were known to pile up in the general desolation of a Belfast sink, but Gordon was busy accommodating the facts of life to a nourishing vision of the future. He never got drunk because he feared more than anything a loss of control, and so, on Friday nights, as the squads of local boys went skidding up the Lothian Road fuelled by pints of lager, Gordon would be inside the Cameo watching old movies about blind pianists or soldiers mangled by war and self-consciousness. He often picked up a bag of chips amid the broad, late-night fraternity of the Grassmarket, and would cradle them up the tenement stairs to have with his beans. That was the essence of his student years: the vapour of warm newspaper soaked in patches of vinegar.

4. *Reason*

That's a terrible black sloshing out there in the North Sea. The very idea of people being trapped on those oil rigs for weeks at a time began to unsettle Gordon's sense of the perfectly deployed and the reasonably useful life, but then again the 1960s offered a vista of possibilities for the modernizing of Scotland, and it looked as if oil might certainly have its part to play in all that. It was just, to

Gordon, that the substance itself seemed to be so little separate from the conditions of its retrieval. Dark, I mean. All dark. And he couldn't get away from that notion of living men with healthy bones using machines to suck out the dead carbon liquor of the earth. 'Wasn't that a wee bit on the savage side?' He said this several times to a girl he met for coffee at the George Hotel, and she paid close attention with her beautiful green eyes before saying she had better get going or she was liable to miss her bus.

5. Form

He saw copies of his first book in the window of a leftist bookshop in Glasgow and had to admit he felt a tear forming in the corner of his better eye. He had captured – as was readily admitted by the *Greenock Telegraph* – the often under-described lives of Scottish old-age pensioners in the second half of the century, and had done so in a prose of untrammelled epic beauty. He had invented a fragmentary style that was best suited to capture the frayed lives of his subjects, and the *Dundee Courier*, having caught Gordon presenting his findings to a formal gathering of accountants at the rear of Milne's Bar, was ready and indeed very able to form the view that the author showed considerable form as an orator.

6. Sensibility

Gordon was forever finding restaurant receipts in the pockets of his suits or stuffed in his wallet. Sometimes they weren't receipts exactly but yellow Switch carbons, indicating how much he'd spent and whether service was included but not particularly saying what had been ordered. Over recent years he had developed an active resentment against fizzy water. When the taxi brought him back one night to Millbank, he pondered that Islington drink, and watched the news with a growing sense of hatred.

7. Enlightenment

There is a statue of Adam Smith that stands in a fork in the road across from the church where Gordon's father once presided. The son always thought of the memorial as a thing covered in snow, though in truth the Scottish sun was always more likely to pour down its benisons on that noble pate, that head with the world-sized mind within, the very image of it leading out the brilliant and patient sons of Kirkcaldy. Gordon went back to look at the statue after his father's death in 1998. It was indeed snowing that particular day, and Gordon looked at the stone Adam Smith as if he might discover some marks on that famous countenance left there by his own former scrutiny. Gordon fancied the tenets of the Enlightenment might in fact offer a suggestion about how to live. He saw too little of himself in Smith's face, but felt the statue looked altogether smaller than how he remembered it back in the days of the school certificate and the worries of Higher English. There was no one about at that early hour, but Gordon instructed his driver to go if he would and see if he couldn't bring a ladder from the church hall.

8. Politics

London is a smear of buses and chances in the afternoon. How colourful too is the capital city, how full of the foreign arts. Right at the opening to Horse Guards Parade a soldier stands on his horse wearing the helmet and red tunic, his sword resting on his right shoulder, the tourists taking their pictures and laughing at duty. A blonde girl from Athens, Georgia, and her friend threaten all of a sudden to climb up and draw on the guard with lipstick. They whisper to one another about how it is against the rules for him to speak and about how he can't move too much either. The guard simply stands there as if their dreams were none of his business.

The guard can hardly hear them in fact, and he merely feels tired at the base of his spine and is gagging for a pint. He wonders if his wife made it to the supermarket, and isn't there a great offer on those stubby bottles of German beer? As his thought fades into the wan, persistent, Shakespearean sun, the guard looks up to see Gordon passing in the Whitehall traffic, his head against the window and his one good eye on the road.

Hanwell Snr

Zadie Smith

Hanwell Snr was Hanwell's father. Like Hanwell, he existed in a small way. Not in his person – he was a 'big personality', in that odious phrase – but in his history, which is partial, almost phantasmagoric. Even to Hanwell he seemed a kind of mirage, and nothing pleasant about it. A feckless and slapdash man – worse, in many ways, than a cruel man. Those who have experience of such people will understand. Cruelty can be righteously opposed, eventually dismissed. A freewheeling carelessness with your cares is something else again. It must teach you a sad self-sufficiency, being fathered like that, and a brutal reticence of the heart. A reluctance to get going at all.

Hanwell Snr came to Hanwell like a comet, at long intervals. He was there when Hanwell was born, surely, and six years after that on a beach in Brighton, holding Hanwell by the armpits and dangling him over a pier. Hanwell Snr spent that evening away from his family, to whom he gave a little money with the generous idea of a round of fish and chips. It didn't stretch as far as that. A boyo, with charm in spades. That sounds antique, but 'boyo' was the word one would have used at the time. First to raise a glass and last to put it down – very much hail fellow, well met – although he was never a drunk, and never incompetent. The type to sing along with those far worse gone than himself, with the idea of gaining advantage over them in their weakness. Back at home, he had a machine he put tuppence in and a fag came out, like in a pub. Also, an eye for his wife's nearest neighbour, a widow, Sue Boyd – Sue, Sue, I'm very much in love with you, to the tune of a famous ballad of the time, catching her round the waist and waltzing her from the back door to the gate, Mrs Hanwell smiling helplessly on from the window.

A big man physically, far bigger than Hanwell. And then later, maybe that same year, maybe the next, on November the fifth, suddenly at the back door in the blackness with the gift of some penny bangers. He didn't stay to light these with Hanwell. Then gone again. 'Went out for a pack of cigarettes and never came back': a common enough refrain in England, then and now. Only, Hanwell Snr was one of the periodic returnees. This makes it worse, as previously discussed. Leaving Hanwell standing in the blackness in short trousers holding bangers. This was never forgotten. It persists, a fleck of the late 1920s. It is recorded here by a descendant of Hanwell Snr of whom he could have had no notion, being as unreal to him as broadband or goblins. No one can explain the process by which these things are retained while much else vanishes – a lot of sentimental rubbish is written on the subject. Hanwell himself kept faith with scientific explanations. He knew nothing whatsoever of science. Dimly, he imagined chemical flare-ups in the brain chemistry, arresting moving images (his analogy came from photographic film, of which he had some experience), and that these 'flare-ups' are random in their occasion and unobservable at the moment they happen. Of course, the writing of this is also a kind of 'flare-up', albeit of a sadder, secondary and parasitic kind.

In the mid-thirties, Hanwell Snr went to Canada, an attempt to make his fortune in logging. Hanwell was given a brief, thrilling tour of the ship before it sailed, although not by his father; a crewman put a candle on a thick brass rail and thus demonstrated to Hanwell how crosswise scratches turn orderly and concentric in thrown light. Three years later Hanwell Snr returned, still with no money. He was now able to roll a cigarette with one hand the way the cowboys did. Hanwell was not especially impressed. Subsequently, Hanwell Snr became a conductor on the buses. Then came the war, from which he never really returned, having fallen for a middle-class lady who drove an ambulance. Turned up once at Hanwell's own barracks, with a new name – 'Bill' – and the affectations of an Irishman. It was eerie to witness. Words held no security with Hanwell Snr, served as no anchor, bore no relation to the things of the world. A darker shade of this same tendency is called 'psychopathy'. He took out a few filthy photos from the Far East and told amusing, believable anecdotes set in Kerry. This, to a stranger, would appear to fit well with the copper-wire hair and the close eyes. Hanwell wished himself more of a stranger. As it stood, he could only wince inwardly at this second, false personality, while making a good show of laughing along as Bill made a friend of all the young soldiers whom Hanwell himself had not yet managed to befriend. 'Good sort, your old man! Lively, good for a laugh!' Said approvingly, and probably true (Hanwell tried hard to be generous in his interpretations), if you happened not to be his son. If you happened not to be his son. Bill walked out two hours later, merry as Christmas. Wasn't seen again by Hanwell for twelve years.

It was August of 1956. Hanwell got word that his father was nicely set up with a little business in an obscure village in the county of Kent. Without any real expectation – or none he could confess to himself – Hanwell got on his bike. This time, he would appear. It was nothing to him, back then, to ride from London to Kent. He was young, relatively speaking, though he wouldn't have thought himself especially so, with a young family already. He did not know then that a second family lay in wait for him, not yet sprung, coiled in his future.

A roasting August day. Hanwell had devised a water carrier out of an old plastic kerosene bottle and strapped it to the crossbar – an invention a little ahead of its time. He powered along a newly built stretch of the A20, wherever possible nipping off and taking byroads through the villages, feeling that the air was purer there. I hope I can say 'hedgerow' and it will be clear that I don't mean to be poetic, but only historically accurate. Hedgerow, thick and briary, caught his shirt twice and made it ragged round the elbow. He had it in his mind – as I have it in mine, with equal stubbornness, when I am writing at length – not to stop before a certain point; he would eat at his destination and not before. One more mile, one more chapter, one more mile, one more chapter. The village was in a little valley; Hanwell swooned round the bends and rolled into town, stopping at the village green, which was all the village there was. Two establishments stood nearby: a redbrick pub with pretty clumps of lavender growing in the window pots and, on the other side of the green, a luridly painted fish-and-chip van. Hanwell knew better than to hope. He got off his bike and pushed it with a sure touch round the perimeter, the faintest pressure of left hand to saddle. It was four o'clock – the van was shut up. He leaned the bike against gypsy-red lettering outlined in gold: HANWELL'S FINEST FISH AND CHIPS. He went to sit in the grass, beneath a tree, overlooking the cricket pitch and the marshy land near the ponds. He was unable to absorb these various lessons in the colour green. Instead, there was smell: sear-leaved, blowzy roses, last of the summer. Collect them, give them to your sister, 1931.

Recipe for Irene Hanwell's Lady's Perfume

Six roses (*stolen, petals removed*)
Water from the tap
Empty milk bottle
Squish petals in fist to release the odour. Put in bottle. Fill with water.

His feet stank. He took off his shoes. At home he had a wife who was not well, not well in a manner he could do nothing about nor understand, but, as he sat here now in the sun, the tense, resistant nub of flesh inside his back resolved itself for the first time in months. He lay down. His spine pressed into the soil a notch at a time, undid him. Upside down was a land of female legs. He was fond of these new bell-shaped skirts, wide enough to crawl under and be kept safe, and wished he had waited to marry, or married differently. He thought, What if I stayed here? Let the sun swallow me, and the orange dazzle under my eyelids become not just the thing I see but the thing that I am, and let the one daisy with the bent stem and the rose smell and the girl upside down on the pub bench eating an upside-down ploughman's with her upside-down friend be the whole of the law and the girth of the world. Wasn't it the work of moments, of a little paint, to change HANWELL'S FINEST to HANWELL & HANWELL?

Note: I have reconstituted Hanwell's thoughts for you, as seem likely to me, and as sound nicest. In the novel *Middlemarch*, we find the old adage of a man's charity growing in direct proportion to its distance from his own door. This is reminiscent of all the dutiful grandchildren and great-grandchildren lingering over deathbeds with digital recorders, or else manically pursuing their ancestors through the online genealogy sites at three in the morning, so very eager to reconstitute the lives and thoughts of dead and soon-to-be-dead men, though they may regularly screen the phone calls of their own mothers. I am of that generation. I will do anything for my family except see them.

It was 1956, as mentioned above. There was nothing but the sun, and Hanwell and the sun. Lying in a patch of long grass, Hanwell dreamed a conversation:

HANWELL SNR: (*lying beside Hanwell*) So you found me, then.

HANWELL: Yes, Alf. Wasn't I meant to?

HANWELL SNR: Now, look: have a smoke – don't get ahead of yourself.

HANWELL: (*taking a Senior Service from its packet*) Thank you.

HANWELL SNR: So, boy. How are you? I'm doing all right for myself, as you can see.

HANWELL: Ah, yes, indeed, and even so. Thus is it much liketh the great novel by George Eliot –

HANWELL SNR: Oh, don't talk guff, boy. You always do that – pretend you're something you're not and never have been. You never did read any of that. Anyone'd think you'd been up to the university, talking like I don't know what.

HANWELL: (*sadly*) We couldn't afford the uniform for the grammar. I passed the eleven-plus, but we couldn't afford it.

HANWELL SNR: (*laughing till he cries*) Still telling that old chestnut? Dear, oh dear. Bit antique that story, isn't it? I'd rather call a spade a spade, let everything come up roses. Well, whatever floats your boat, Hanwell, I'm sure.

HANWELL: (*sung*) I put a chestnut in a boat . . . I rowed it with a spade . . . A rose I gave my love that day.

HANWELL SNR: You've gone soft.

'Whose bike is this?'

Hanwell sat up and was greeted – not with any particular surprise, although with a little sheepishness – and offered the first chips out of the fryer, which he accepted.

'I've a little fold-up table somewhere here . . .'

Hanwell watched Hanwell Snr struggle with the household bric-a-brac and shabby furniture piled up in the back of the van. A tall lamp with a tasselled shade and a coat stand lay across each other: a coat of arms for the house of Hanwell. The ambulance driver, Bunty, who might have kept things clean for him, had died the year before – her money had bought this little concern. Maybe she had cooked him his greens, too, and watched his drink, and it was only now that the ghastly bloat took hold, and the blood vessels broke and dispersed beneath the skin of the nose and cheeks, and the orange whiskers grew wild and laced with grey. It was a shock. Historically, Hanwell Snr was physically superior to Hanwell: Sit on my back – go on, sit on it! You won't break me! Usually said to a lady, and then when she was settled like the Buddha he'd do a press-up or two, sometimes five. Now he turned, holding the little table upside down against his vast belly, and this soft thing, more than all the rest, announced him as a man deserted by women.

'There we are' – his great arse pressed on the tabletop; the cast-iron legs sunk deep into the lawn – 'I don't believe in standing and eating.'

He brought out two little stools, and Hanwell sat on the one handed to him. For a time, Hanwell Snr made his own reluctance to sit appear quite natural, busying himself with the hot oil and dismissing certain chips as not fit to be thrown in the fryer if his only son was to eat them. When the fuss of frying was over, Hanwell realized the obvious: his father couldn't stand to look at him. They remained looking out on the meadow beyond the green, Hanwell Snr leaning against the van, despite his beliefs, with his sweaty cone of newspaper and chewing each chip a long time. He looked across Hanwell if Hanwell spoke, but never at him.

Of their conversation, Hanwell could retain practically nothing, finding it quite as unreal as their dream talk earlier. While Hanwell silently pursued a series of unlikely but longed-for confessions (*Well, son, the thing is . . . To tell you the truth, I regret terribly . . .*), in the real, thick ripple of the air Hanwell Snr was sweating and rambling about the Suez business and the Araby bastards and other matters of the world that Hanwell – the least political of men, a man for whom the world was, and could consist only of, those people he saw or spoke to every day, fed, washed or made love to – could not comprehend. At last the topic turned to the people who concerned Hanwell – Hanwell's wife, Hanwell's daughters. Hanwell shyly described his current difficulty, making use of the doctor's careful and superior phrases ('mental disturbance' and 'a tendency toward hysteria'). Hanwell Snr drew a hankie from his back pocket, worked it round the grime on the back of his neck. He took his time folding it back into quarters. Hanwell saw at once that his father thought it entirely typical of Hanwell to marry a woman who was broken in some way, and now felt much the same satirical disgust he'd expressed when the boy Hanwell, instead of laughing at being dangled from a pier, took it in his head to cry.

'Well, I'll say this,' he said, finishing his lecture about Hanwell's ineptitude at choosing things right and seeing the way of things, and moving on to the more general subject of 'women', which allowed, at least, the concession that Hanwell's trouble might not be Hanwell's fault alone: 'They rewrite history – can't let a man be himself. Always telling you what you would be and should be and might be, rather than what you are. And what they're offering in return for all that isn't half as good as they think it is – or I've never found it so. But maybe you've done better – Lord knows, they look a damn sight better these days than in my day . . .'

Twenty yards from where they sat, two young women in sundresses were helping each other achieve a handstand. Hanwell Snr nudged Hanwell in his gut, and Hanwell felt strongly the implicit insult to his own mother, who still lived, and still wore her flapper curls – white now – close to her forehead, and the same heavy felt cloche caps and Harold Lloyd glasses, perfectly round and thick-rimmed. He said nothing. He ate his chips as the blonde, peaky-looking girl firmed her body in preparation for the arrival of the lovely thick ankles of the brunette, well fed as they never were ten years earlier, and when this brunette overreached, and her breasts pressed tight against the cotton of her yellow dress and her legs went backwards, and the crinoline frothed over her blonde friend's narrow shoulders, Hanwell and Hanwell watched them laugh and shake together and fall, finally, in a human heap on the grass. Soon after, Hanwell Snr gathered the two empty paper cones and pressed them into a soggy ball in his hands, and said he'd better open the shutters, as it was teatime and folk would be wanting their food. Hanwell never saw him again.

On a date in 1986, one that only the record office would remember now, the phone rang in Hanwell's kitchen as he cooked. He was making pizza with homemade dough for the young children of his second family, and his topping was a loose, watery, fresh tomato sauce, laced with anchovies and black olives, so piquant and delicious you could eat it by the spoonful and forgo the crust altogether. It is possible only I liked to do that. I extrapolate my feelings too generally.

'Yes, I see – thank you . . . it was good of you to let us know,' said Hanwell in a voice a shade more posh than his own. He put down the phone and left the room. After the pizza was finished, he came back in, pale, but composed. He said his father had died, a sentence that required us – my mother, my brother, and me – to invent a whole human in one second and kill him off the next.

Hanwell had said nothing to prepare us. He had known weeks earlier that his father's death was imminent – he did not go to him. Twenty years later, Hanwell's son would not go to Hanwell when his hour came. It happens that in the course of my professional duties I am often found making the statement 'I don't believe in patterns.' A butterfly on a pin has no idea what a pretty shape it makes.

'He never settled,' said Hanwell, 'and now he's come to the end of the road,' a quaint metaphor, like those that Borges enjoyed, and we, equally, interpreted it literally, thinking of Brighton pier, Brighton being Hanwell country for us, and the place where Hanwell's people generally died. When I was a kid, I had a dream – never forgotten! – of the cool, flat Brighton pebbles being placed over my body, as the Jews place stones on top of their dead; piled up and up over my corpse, until I was entirely buried and families came to picnic over me, not knowing, for I was Brighton bedrock now, as Hanwells had been (in my dream logic) since there were Hanwells in England. There have always been Hanwells in England. But I am a female Hanwell and lost my name when I married.

J. Johnson
Nick Hornby,
with illustrations by Posy Simmonds

A Writing Life

JAMIE JOHNSON was born in 1955, in Southend, Essex. He studied English at Cambridge University, and has contributed to the *TLS*, the *Literary Review*, the *Independent* and *Mojo*. This is his first book. He lives in North London.

JAMIE JOHNSON is the author of JUST CAN'T GET ENOUGH, a memoir about sex addiction, which was shortlisted for the *Guardian* First Book award. He was born in 1955 in Southend, Essex, and has contributed to *Esquire*, *Playboy* and *Nuts*. He lives in Essex with his wife and two children. (CAN'T GET NO) SATISFACTION is his first novel.

JAMES JOHNSON rereads the poems of John Donne every year. He is the author of two previous books, and has been shortlisted for the *Guardian* First Book award. He has contributed to the *TLS*, the *Literary Review* and the *Independent*. He is currently a Visiting Writer at Essex University, and lives just outside Shoeburyness with his wife and four children. HOW DRY A CINDER is his second novel.

JIM JOHNSON is the author of several books for adults, including HOW DRY A CINDER, a historical novel about the last years of the poet John Donne, which was longlisted for the John Donne Prize. He lives in Hartlepool in the North-East of England with his wife, five children, two cats, one dog, two gerbils called Romulus and Remus, and Dylan the goldfish. This is his first children's book.

ANNIE GREEN is an artist, and the illustrator of the much loved Elvis the Elephant series. She too lives in the North-East of England, with a large menagerie including a snake. She drives an old 2CV called Poppy.

J. THOMAS JOHNSON is the author of several books. He has worked as a bartender, lumberjack, nightclub bouncer, pearl-fisherman, police-dog trainer, professional wrestler, private detective, Nepalese tour-guide, assassin, and writer-in-residence at a number of British universities. He has been fascinated by the Alaskan wilderness ever since he was a child. He lives with his partner, the illustrator Annie Green, just outside Hartlepool in the North-East of England.

Five things you didn't know about **JIMMY JOHNSON**:
1) The first single he bought with his own money was 'Bridge Over Troubled Water'!
2) The uncle of his best friend at school used to play bass with the Starlight Vocal Band!
3) He had a ticket to see the Sex Pistols play at the Screen on the Green in Islington – but he didn't go!
4) He has an iPod – but his kids have to download the music for him!
5) JOHNSON'S POP MISCELLANY is his eighth book – but the first one to mention Gilbert O' Sullivan!

BRIAN BRITTEN used to play for Reading, Millwall, Leyton Orient, Southend United, Walsall, Tranmere Rovers and Hartlepool. He was once described as 'the best defender never to have played in the top two divisions'. He claims to have kicked 'at least six' future England internationals.

JIMMY JOHNSON is a professional writer. FOREIGN NANCY BOYS is his twelfth book. He lives in – and supports – Hartlepool.

THANKS TO: THE LORD GOD ALMIGHTY (love You, and everything You do for us), Sharon Osbourne (DA BOMB!), Simon Cowell (I've nearly forgiven you!), David and Victoria, Wayne and Coleen, Mum and Dad, baby bruvva, everyone in the Barnet Posse except Nicola Braithwaite, everyone at the Pink Coconut in Bushey. And yo Mr Osbourne! I wrote a book! Even after all what you said about me when I left school! A big shout-out to Jim Johnson for his help in putting this together. Top man.

Lélé
Edwidge Danticat

It was so hot in Léogâne that summer that most of the frogs exploded, scaring not just the children who once chased them into the river at dusk or the parents who hastily pried the threadbare carcasses from their fingers, but also my 39-year old sister Lélé, who was four months pregnant with her first child and feared that, should the temperature continue to rise, she too might burst. The frogs had been dying for a while, but we hadn't noticed, mostly because they'd been doing it quietly. Perhaps for each that had expired, one had taken its place along the river bank, looking exactly the same as the others and fooling us into thinking that a normal cycle was occurring, that young was replacing old and life replacing death, sometimes slowly and sometimes quickly, just as it was for us.

'This is surely a sign that something terrible is going to happen,' Lélé said, as we sat on the top-floor verandah of my parents' house one particularly sweltering evening. Even though my father, the former justice of the peace of the town of Léogâne, had died more than ten years ago, and my mother five years before that, I've never been able to stop thinking of the place that I, and now my sister, called home as theirs. The dollhouse façade of our wooden ginger-bread had been meticulously sketched by Papa, who'd spent his nights after work updating and revising each detail as their home was built from the ground up. He and Maman had driven to the capital to purchase the corrugated metal and bordered jalousies, a journey which at the time, before my sister and I were born, took several agonizing hours in an old pick-up truck that they'd inherited from my half-French grandfather, the previous justice of the peace. The shell of the truck was still out there somewhere among the dozens of almond trees that dotted our three hectares, its once thunderous engine rusting into the earth, like the neglected memorial it was.

The air on my verandah was just slightly cooler than it was in either of the two bedrooms where my sister and I slept, just as we had as children, surrounded by shelves lined with leather-bound notebooks filled with the concerns and complaints that had consumed the days, and sometimes nights, of our father and grandfather. Last year, I decided to read all their notebooks before I moved them to the courthouse archive in town. And now, despite her current condition, my sister, who was in the middle of a separation from her husband, was helping me sort through them.

'In all of their notes,' Lélé was saying, 'I've not seen one mention of frogs dying like this.'

Before becoming pregnant, Lélé had been a heavy smoker, and sometimes when she made some pronouncement – for she had one of those voices with an air of always seeming to be making a pronouncement – she sounded a bit out of breath. This was further aggravated by the fact that she now had a baby pressing on her lungs, I'm sure, but, come to think of it, she had spoken that way even when she was a child, sometimes purposefully emphasizing a lisp that strangely enough made her sound even more certain.

'I've talked to a few people about it,' I told her. 'I even called some doctor friends in Port-au-Prince.'

'What would doctors know about dead frogs?' she promptly cut me off. 'You need world specialists, people who study the earth.'

Throwing her head back, three long plaits bouncing in the evening air, Lélé tapped her palm for emphasis and said, 'Mark my words. The summer won't pass before there's a catastrophe here.'

Living only a kilometer or so from the river, I thought that the eventual smell of rotting frogs might be at least one potential catastrophe, but, in the days that followed, there was no smell at all. As soon as the burnished skins and tiny organs were exposed to the sun, the shredded frogs dried up, vanishing into the river bed.

This was a lucky thing for Lélé, who at this stage of her pregnancy was still willowy and trim, in part because she didn't have much of an appetite. The smell of most things sent her retching, except the moldy fragrance of ancient ink and dissolving paper, which she relished so much that I frankly suspected her of nibbling away at small fragments of the town's judicial legacy.

A week after Lélé made her prediction, the frogs were no longer even a problem. A few inches of rain had fallen somewhere up in the mountains, and the river overflowed, drowning the remaining frog population and depositing a tall layer of sandy loam far beyond the river's banks, crushing, among other things, the field of vetiver that I, like my father and grandfather before me, had faithfully planted at the beginning of every year. Some years I had actually made a profit from my vetiver, which was not only good for the soil but also very much sought after by perfume-company suppliers. Those years, I'd used the money to plant a few more almond trees near the section of our property that nearly merged with the open road. Lélé loved the almond trees, and before she was pregnant, whenever she and her husband Gaspard came to visit, they'd both spend hours crushing the fibrous fruits with river stones to dig out the kernels.

The morning Gaspard came to see Lélé, I had to run off to court. I was a judicial witness in the case of a former priest who was suing for medical expenses for his psychiatric care. The priest claimed that he'd been forced by the police chief to offer extreme unction to some prisoners whom the police chief had then ordered executed before they could appear before a magistrate. I had been called by the priest's niece, with whom he was living after being expelled from his parish, to take a statement about her perception of the priest's mental health, and all I planned to do in court was reiterate what was already obvious: that for one reason or another the priest was now insane. The magistrate, who had no patience for cases in which there were no possibilities for bribes, would probably dismiss the case outright. However, since there were two local radio journalists expected, he had no choice but to put on the charade and pretend to listen to all of us before making up his mind.

I have no formal training in the law. All I know I learned by shadowing my father. His approach had always been the same. We are there only to witness, not participate, he'd say, to grant a piece of paper, an affidavit, a notarized statement, which might be helpful to someone in some later legal proceeding or action. If we are required to speak before a judge, we need state only what we've seen. We do not conjecture or make guesses. We speak only when asked.

This is the approach I was taking with Lélé and Gaspard. As Gaspard's four-wheeler pulled up in front of the house, I purposely accelerated mine in the other direction. I would probably have to be in court at their divorce proceeding. There would be enough time to take sides.

Neither the priest nor his niece showed up, so the magistrate dismissed the case. During the ten years I'd been doing this, I'd found that more people don't show up than do. Many simply wanted the benefit of the initial hearing, in the field or in my office, where I took most of my notes. The rest already knew the likely outcome of their cases or were too scared to present themselves.

Gaspard's car was still out front when I returned home for lunch. Gaspard was a small man, shorter even than my sister in her bare feet. He was handsome, though, with a dark-brown elfin face and a wide grin that he seemed unable to restrain even when he was angry. He was from a family of tailors and dressed very well, lately favoring airy white embroidered shirts and loose cotton pants.

Lélé and Gaspard were sitting on opposite sides of the living room when I entered, Gaspard on our sixty-year-old fleur-de-lis-print chaise longue and Lélé in a rocking chair by the louvered doors overlooking the now crushed vetiver field.

Marthe, who had been with us long enough to have delivered both my sister and me, sauntered over with a small shiny tray to collect an empty glass from Gaspard. I had an image in my mind of Gaspard having sat there all morning, sipping a single glass of

Marthe's tasty, vanilla-essence flavored lemonade while staring at Lélé's expressionless profile. Even though I had hired a younger girl to help her, Marthe still preferred to do most of the light work around the house herself, including receiving our guests. Marthe was in her late sixties, about the age that our mother would have been if she were alive. She also had the same moon-shaped face and stocky frame. Growing up, I thought Marthe and my mother were sisters. I'm still not convinced that they weren't.

I waited for Marthe to leave the room, then, rubbing my hands together, said, 'So, *les amoureux*, have we reconciled?'

Gaspard looked up at me, his uncontrollable grin momentarily menacing. For once, while smiling, he almost appeared to be gritting his teeth.

'She hasn't told you?' he asked.

I raised my shoulders and shrugged, looking over at my sister, whose eyes never wandered from the devastated vetiver field.

'We have to clean up that field,' she finally said. 'And we should do it sooner rather than later. There might still be something worth saving there.'

'Sometimes, there's nothing to save,' Gaspard said.

He stood up and quickly breezed past me, but, as he reached the doorway, where he was closest to my sister, he walked back and laid a hand on my shoulder.

'Sorry, brother,' he said. 'You shouldn't have seen that.'

I shook my head, not sure what to say. It seemed like all the cards were in Lélé's hand. It was her move.

I waited until I heard Gaspard's car start up. When his tires scratched the driveway gravel, I asked my sister, 'Are you sure this is the right time for irreconcilable differences?'

She got up from the rocker, pulled the louver doors shut, considerably dimming the room.

'I don't want to talk about it,' she said, plopping herself down on one of the old divans by the closed fireplace.

'Is he cheating on you?' I asked. 'If he is, I can find some way to have him thrown in jail.'

'He's not cheating,' she said.

'Are you cheating?'

She popped her eyes real wide in response, then pointed at her belly.

'Is it his baby?' I said, sitting down on the floor at her feet.

'You fool,' she said.

Placing my head on her knee, I felt like I did when I was a boy and would run home, devastated, after going with my father to record a death.

'You can't do this type of work if you cry at the scene,' my father had said, slapping the back of my head in front of his witnesses. Once, even after I had seen the severed body of a beheaded man. The man's own brother had taken a machete to his neck during a dispute over a plot of land. That night, Lélé had let me sleep in her bed, but most importantly she'd let me cry.

'You sure you don't want to tell me?' I asked.

'Maybe in good time,' she said.

'Have we ever used this fireplace?' I said, pointing to the only concrete part of the house, a square cave that Lélé had recently filled with giant decorative candles.

'Marthe would know better,' she said, 'but I only remember us using it once, the night you were born. It filled the whole place with smoke and nearly burned down the house.'

The next day I was taking an affidavit for an actual divorce when it began to rain. I was nervous about the river overflowing again, this time pushing past the vetiver fields and the almond trees. Ours was now the only place that close to the river. The others, newer and shabbier, had been taken downstream in flash floods, many with entire families inside. I had been meaning to tell Lélé that we should do something about the house. I had refrained from discussing it with her only because I hadn't decided myself what to do. Should we sell it to someone to whom we would be passing on the same problem we now faced? Should we destroy it and rebuild on higher ground? Should I move somewhere else and use it only during the dry season? I was sure Lélé would already have a solution, about which she felt a hundred per cent sure, so I wanted to make up my mind before speaking to her. Still, as it continued to rain and more passers-by sought shelter on the front gallery outside my office, I saw myself becoming more and more walled off from Lélé.

For years now, I had been holding quarterly meetings with the peasants in the villages, especially the villages upriver from us, telling them that the river was raging in response to the lack of trees, land erosion, the dying topsoil.

'What do you want us to do?' they'd ask me in return. 'Give us something to replace the charcoal and we'll stop.'

Sometimes in my attempts to get them to not cut down young trees, I'd reach for the basest metaphors, the most melodramatic pleas. 'It's like killing a child,' I'd say.

'If I have to kill a tree child to save my own child, I'll kill the tree child,' they'd say.

Now, thanks to their stupidity, or rather the stupidity of their needs, our parents' house might soon be under water. We might wake up floating above our beds and have to climb on top of a roof to wait for the current to die down. My sister might give birth in a tree.

'*Merde*,' I said to the complainant in front of me. 'Why do you want to divorce your wife anyway?'

'Because she's ugly,' he said, his face looking as deadly serious, though perhaps not as anxious, as mine.

'When did she get so ugly?' I was shouting at him, but he didn't even seem to notice.

'After the children,' he said. 'She lost some teeth and she's no longer kind.'

'What type of kindness are you expecting from her?' I asked.

'All kinds,' he said, winking. 'You know.

'How many children do you have?'

'Ten,' he said.

I lowered my pen and stopped taking notes. I felt like hitting him the way my father had hit me.

'Be a man,' I wanted to say. 'This is your life.'

I wanted to have with him the talk I might soon need to have with my sister, convince him that, in abandoning his family, he was acting like a coward. However, when I looked up, it was perfectly sunny outside again. Those who had sought shelter from the rain on the front gallery outside my office were now making their way back into the street. The cars were circulating again too, splashing muddy water everywhere.

'Come back tomorrow,' I told the unhappy husband. I planned to make him come to see me at least ten times before I would type his statement, as the law required me to do, and file it for him.

It turned out that it had not rained near the house and the river had not overflowed. It was rare that it overflowed in the daytime anyway, which made me all the more anxious. All the deadly flash floods had taken place at night. Perhaps my fear was slightly irrational. Yet, the previous summer, the country's fourth largest city had been submerged under water for weeks. I could no longer chance it.

When I got home, I immediately wanted to approach the question of the house with Lélé. I found her in her old room sitting in the middle of a large mahogany canopy bed that our parents had had constructed for her when she was a teenager. From the house she and Gaspard had shared for the last twenty years, she had brought a large mosquito net, which she'd draped over the canopy, making her appear as though she were trapped in a colorless dream. Our father's notebooks were spread out, open, all around her. On her lap was her own composition notebook. She was scribbling furiously, flipping through page after page while jotting things down.

I walked out to her terrace, where she kept, among her many potted plants, a wicker chair on which she sat out every morning, draped in one of her bed sheets, watching the sun rise over the mountains. I pulled the chair inside and propped it in front of the armoire across from her. As I sat down, she looked up, momentarily acknowledging me, then turned her attention back to the notebooks.

'Do you work the same way they did?' she asked.

'What do you mean?' I said.

I was speaking to her through a veil, but neither of us made any effort to change that. If anything, it made me feel a bit more comfortable, braver.

'Do you keep your notes like Grand-père and Papa did?' she asked.

'Sure,' I said. 'They're all in the archives in town, which is where these should also be. We kept them much too long. They don't belong only to us. They belong to Léogâne.'

'They do belong to us,' she said. 'Listen.'

Leaning over, she stretched out her arm and grabbed one of the notebooks by her knees. She must have pressed too far down on her belly, for she snapped her head back, dropped the notebook and began rubbing her stomach.

'Are you all right?' I asked.

'Give me a minute,' she said. She went on rubbing her stomach, closing her eyes, whispering to herself.

'Did you hurt yourself?' I asked.

'I'm fine,' she said, opening her eyes again. 'Let me read this to you.'

She seemed composed, nearly herself again, when she raised one of my father's notebooks to her face.

'Here, he has some notes about the theft of a cow. Livestock stolen, etc. . . . it said, but in the margin, he wrote, "Lélé born today. We named her Léogâne. Hope she doesn't think entire town belongs to her."'

Reaching over, she picked up another notebook. '"Lélé first in school,"' she read. '"Told me in my ear after dinner that she wants to follow me in work as justice of the peace."'

I wanted to ask her if he had written anything like that, or anything at all, about me, in case I had missed it, hadn't seen it. But I knew he hadn't. And she did too.

'You could have been,' I told her. 'We both could have done the job.'

'I suppose,' she said, 'thirty years ago, you couldn't bring a little girl around with you documenting the ills of the town. Both he and Maman told me as much.'

'Look,' I said, trying to cheer her up, 'they gave you their whole world, which was this town. They gave you its name. They were very proud the day of your marriage. They loved Gaspard. They were sad that you couldn't have children. They'd be so happy now.'

She turned the notebook pages, closing them all. I thought she was going to raise the mosquito net and crawl out, but she didn't.

'Speaking of Gaspard,' I said.

'You want to know when I'm going back?'

I felt like I was talking to one of the people who came to file their complaints. I needed specific locations, dates, and times.

'Why?' she asked.

'Because I am thinking of selling the house.'

'No,' she said, 'not the house.'

'It's starting to seem foolish to live here so close to the river,' I said. 'I'm beginning to feel like it's a death trap.'

I wanted to climb in there with her and tell her that everything was going to be okay, that it was all right now for us to try to forge our own paths, to move away from the past. Instead she gathered the notebooks in a pile and slid towards the edge of the bed away from them. She raised the mosquito net so fast that in an instant our faces were nearly touching. I was so unprepared for it that I had to slide the chair back a bit.

'You want to know why I left Gaspard?' she said. 'It's because of the baby.'

'What about the baby?' I asked.

'It's sick,' she said.

'Sick?'

'Is that how you remember all the things people say to you?' she asked. 'Do you simply repeat what they say?'

'What do you mean the baby's sick?' I asked.

Just then, Marthe walked in, announcing lunch. 'Lélé, you haven't eaten all day,' she said, wagging a scolding index finger. 'You have to eat to keep that baby strong.'

'We'll be down soon, *chérie*,' Lélé said.

'Okay,' said Marthe, 'but we're not going to let the food get cold. You know how much I hate cold food.'

'Do you realize how long she's been telling us that?' Lélé said when Marthe left the room.

'Probably our whole lives,' I said.

'Do you realize how astonishing that is?'

'Tell me about the baby,' I pressed.

'I didn't want to do it,' she said, 'but Gaspard insisted because of my age, so we went to the hospital, L'Hôpital Sainte Croix, and had it done.'

I'm not sure I grasped everything she said. There was a test with pictures, an ultrasound. The baby, determined to be a girl, had a large cyst growing from the back of her neck, down her entire spine. If she lived long enough to be born, she would probably die soon after.

'What happened?' I asked. 'What caused that?'

'A stroke of bad luck,' she said. 'No one knows.'

Both the doctor and Gaspard thought she should abort while she still could. She wanted to see the whole thing through, to carry full term.

'This is your beheading,' I said.

'What?' she said.

'I'll do what I can to help,' I said.

'There's nothing to do,' she said. 'That's the point.'

'Have you thought about the birth?' I asked.

'Marthe will do it,' she said. 'Marthe will deliver her here, just like she did us.'

That night after dinner, it was too hot to stay inside and we sat out on the verandah again, listening to sounds we had neglected on other evenings: the wailing of cicadas, the crowing of disoriented cocks, the hushed laughter of distant neighbors cutting through our property. Unlike the summers of our childhood, when, in spite of the heat, we would have been running around half dressed, we heard no stirring in the trees around us, no birds settling in for the night. And we heard no croaking frogs splashing in and out of the river. We heard no frogs at all.

Already, my sister's baby felt like an absence too, something we should grieve while ignoring. Every now and then, I would see her twist her body from side to side. Then she would rise up momentarily from her chair as the baby roused inside her for what seemed to me like a series of first times. Looking down at the gentle crescent curve of her body, she did not touch her stomach, nor did she invite me to touch it or lower my ear to it. And I did not dare ask.

Gaspard came by the house again early the next morning. It was a shockingly beautiful morning. Not yet sultry or overcast, but intensely bright, almost dazzling. It was the type of morning that evaporated all my other fears about living in a river's path, the type of morning that would probably keep me in Léogâne forever, planting my vetiver and almond trees.

I was leaving for work when I saw Gaspard sitting in his car, his front wheels facing Lélé's terrace. I tapped on the window, and he reached over and opened the door for me. Sliding into the passenger seat, I gave his shoulder the type of light squeeze he liked to give mine, as a greeting, an apology. Sitting there quietly, we took turns looking down at the gravel pathway leading through the almond trees towards the open road. When we were children, Lélé and I had often raced each other from the house to the road. Our dash had always seemed endless, exhausting, but we were extremely proud of ourselves when we made it to the end, either in front of or behind the other. Looking up at Lélé's terrace where she sat every morning wrapped in a blanket watching the sun rise, Gaspard and I saw only her feet peeking out over the edge, encased in the lace-shaped clerestory trim.

'I'm not going to leave her,' he said. 'After the baby's born, we'll see where we can go.'

He raised his hands as if to wave in Lélé's direction, but she was looking past us, towards the mountains, framed by a halo of indigo sky.

'She wants to bury the child here,' he said. 'She wants it to have spent its whole life here in your parents' house. I suppose she feels that if she'd never left, none of this would have happened. She'd be here like you, alone, but safe from the things you document so well.'

'It's still questionable how well I do with the documenting,' I said.

'She admires you,' he said, 'and she thinks you do well.'

When I said nothing else, he added, 'Among the trees. She wants to bury the child among the almond trees.'

Just then I noticed that he was not speaking to me at all. He was speaking to Lélé. She had turned her gaze away from the mountains and was looking straight at him, at us, her gaze unwavering, almost like a challenge, a dare.

'It's a fungus,' Gaspard said.

'I thought you didn't know what caused it,' I said.

'Not the baby,' he said, 'the frogs.'

The day before, when he'd been visiting with Lélé, she had told him to try to find out for her what could have killed the river frogs. He'd gone back home and telephoned several people including one of his childhood friends, a Haitian–Canadian botanist who had told Gaspard that, given the descriptions and circumstances, he could only imagine that the frogs had probably died from a fungal disease that's caused by the hotter than usual weather.

'Is there anything we could have done for them?' Gaspard had asked his friend.

'No,' the friend had said. 'We all have our paths to tread and this was theirs.'

The Liar

Aleksandar Hemon

The crowd is whirring in a cloud of brazen afternoon dust; they have waited too long already. Finally, the Procurator steps down to the penultimate stair, spreads his feet and installs his arms akimbo to assume a routine pose of authority. His impressively rotund belly is outlined under the sweaty toga, the shadow of the navel at its center. He scans the crowd with contempt, the eye of the navel following his gaze as he turns a little to the left, a little to the right. The din dies down. With their swords, the soldiers push forward two tattered men – the men's shackles rattle as they totter – and position them on each side of the Procurator, who doesn't even glance at them. It all looks like a well-rehearsed performance.

'People!' the Procurator shouts. 'People! Look at me!'

The crowd has been looking at him all along, but now it tightens, as if each man were a blood vessel and the air has just become colder. The dust is slowly settling down, coating their bodies, biting their eyes.

'These two caitiffs here have violated the laws of the Empire,' the Procurator thunders. 'They ought to be punished with the utmost severity. But they are just men and the Empire is merciful – one of them shall live.'

The crowd rumbles with excitement. The Procurator points at the man on the right: he is scrawny, with long, narrow arms and broken teeth, his left eye turgid with blood and pus. 'This man is a thief,' the Procurator says. 'He has robbed men of their sustenance. He has sneaked up on them at night. He has stolen their meager property. Fathers have become destitute, mothers have wept, because of this scoundrel.'

The thief looks at the crowd with as much innocence in his right eye as he can muster. The crowd knows his ilk, they recognize his sinewy greed, but they can also see the bruises on his forearms; they can see the crusty gullies of blood stretching from his nostrils along the curly curve of his mustache to disappear in his beard.

'People,' cries the thief with a cracked, screeching voice. 'I was hungry, my children were hungry. I was hungry!'

A soldier smacks the thief across the face with the back of his hand and a fresh spring of blood sprinkles the thief's beard. The crowd mutters, excited by blood promising more blood.

'This one,' – the Procurator points at the man on the left – 'this one is a mountebank, a liar. He has uttered many a humbug. He has spread calumnies, lies, false stories, besmirching honest men and the Empire. For him, nothing is sacred. He has transgressed against the truth, my friends, not just the Empire – the truth. And the truth is the mother of law and order.'

The crowd turns its attention to the man on the left: his hands are tied behind his back; his shoulder blades are sticking out like fins; his kneecaps are as bare as baby skulls; his flocculent beard is sagging with sweat, as if he were shriveling – but he has no bruises, other than the shackle blisters on his ankles. He confessed to the guards whatever they wanted to hear, and then told them what they didn't ask for, freely embellishing so as to make them agreeable – they just listened, shaking their heads in disbelief, yet unable to stop listening or beat him. The liar looks back at the crowd innocuously: there are the bloodthirsty, law-loving brutes, ever picking their asses in the first row; and there are the handy pick-pockets pilfering their pockets; and over there, safely on the flanks, the citizens of good standing, disgusted and scared by the spectacle, shouting down a drunkard whining about his unfaithful wives. He recognizes the children with pockmarked faces and tawny teeth, who scuttled after him and pulled his donkey's tail not so long ago; and there is the drunk harlot with her green eyes filling up with tears, as though he were her husband. He spots the spies watching the crowd from within the crowd, pricking up their ears for a nefarious word about the Procurator or the Empire.

He knows he should be calm and dignified and serene. He knows he could turn the crowd and make it love him – he has done it before. He could just look them straight in the eye, lock the harlot's gaze, or touch the hairy brute, and tell them one of the tales he picked up roaming the land, or a parable Joseph told him, or the story he dreamt up last night. But the Procurator would never let him speak; and, even if he did, the crowd desired blood, not words. A strange panic possesses him, as if his whole being sneezed – a painful, shattering, humiliating desire to live and breathe in this body, now and forever. So he begins twitching his head to the right, throwing his glance at the thief like a tether, saying with his body, because his suffocating voice would not do it, saying: 'Take him! Take *him!*'

The crowd is bedeviled by a sudden change in the liar's demeanor. His face is madly taut; his neck keeps cramping; his eyes are bulging out sideways, as if trying to sneak out of the sockets. They see now that the liar is not just a liar, but that he is overtaken by evil spirits; they can see he is a bad seed. The thief does nothing, conscious that something good for him is beginning to happen.

'Let the thief go,' they shout. 'Let him go.'

'Let him go,' the Procurator orders the soldiers.

The liar drops his head to his chest, as if all the neck tendons suddenly snapped, and closes his eyes. The crowd stands in silence for a moment, enjoying the moment of his recognition, but then they start fidgeting and shuffling their feet, and the dust is aroused again, darker this time, as the sun has begun to set.

And the soldiers load a huge wooden cross on the liar's back – a handful of splinters immediately pierces the skin on his right shoulder, releasing lush blood streams. He drags the cross through narrow streets teeming with people, wiping the sweat off their faces, waiting for him to drop and die. But he keeps on going, and in a hallucinatory moment sees the thief's tranquil face in the crowd, as if what has just happened never happened.

The cross slips from his shoulder, scraping off a large swath of skin. The soldier marching next to him lifts the cross and loads it back on, but puts it down on his left shoulder, slowly. 'There,' the soldier says. The liar is panting, nearly oblivious to the pain, but still manages to utter a grateful world to the soldier. The crowd thickens around them, so the soldiers have to spread it, beating it back with spears and the flat sides of their swords.

'This does not bode well,' says the liar to the soldier.

The soldier says nothing.

'You know,' the liar says and coughs up a flock of blood drops, 'I am the son of God.'

The soldier says nothing.

'I am,' the liar says. 'I have been told.'

'Verily you are,' says the soldier. 'And I am Virgil.'

And the procession moves on, up the hill, on top of which most of the crowd is already waiting. The liar looks up toward it, hoping against hope that the voices in his head have told him the truth.

Jordan Wellington Lint

Chris Ware

Jordan Wellington Lint

to the Age 13.

C. Ware.

September 12th, 1957.

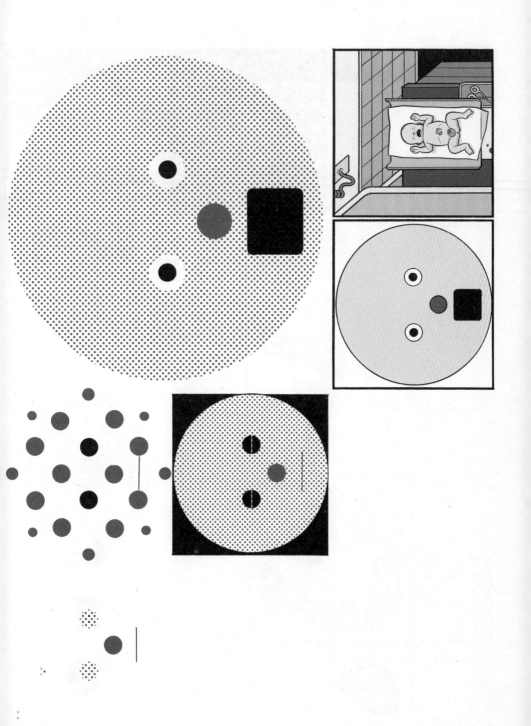

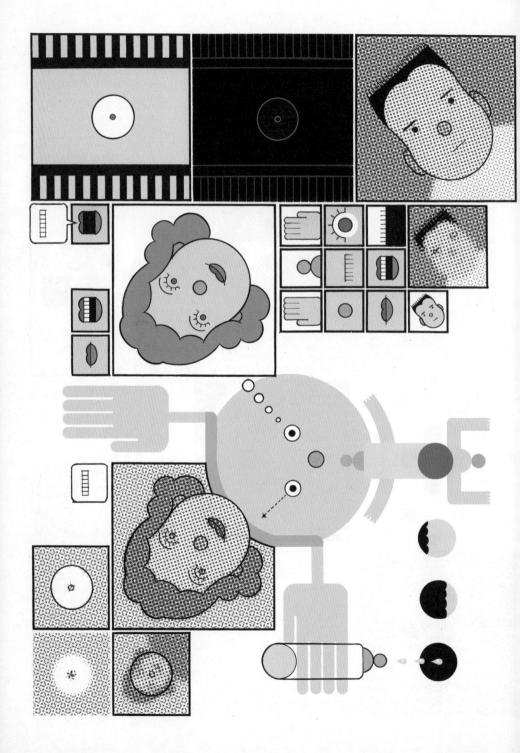

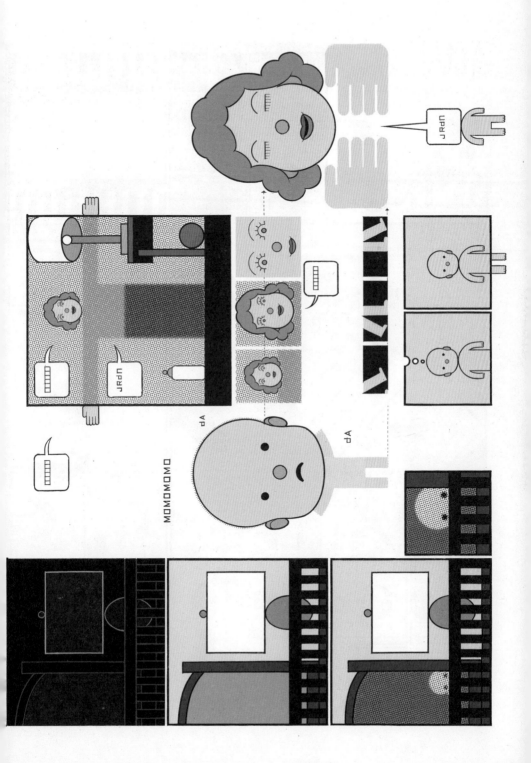

February 12th, 1960.

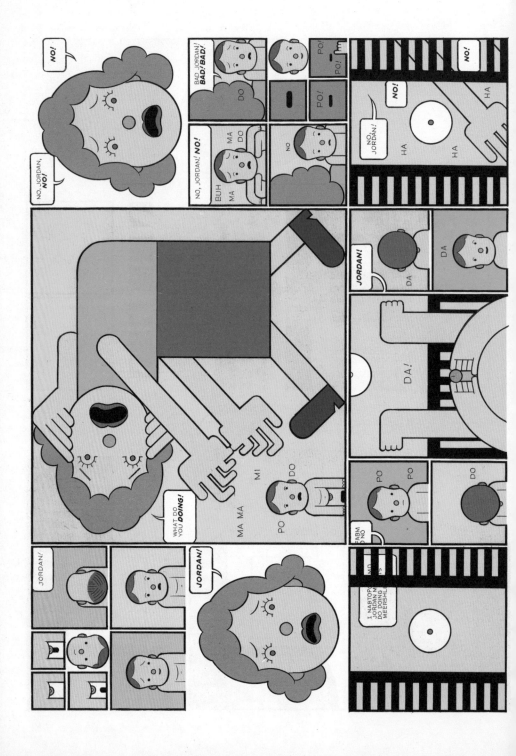

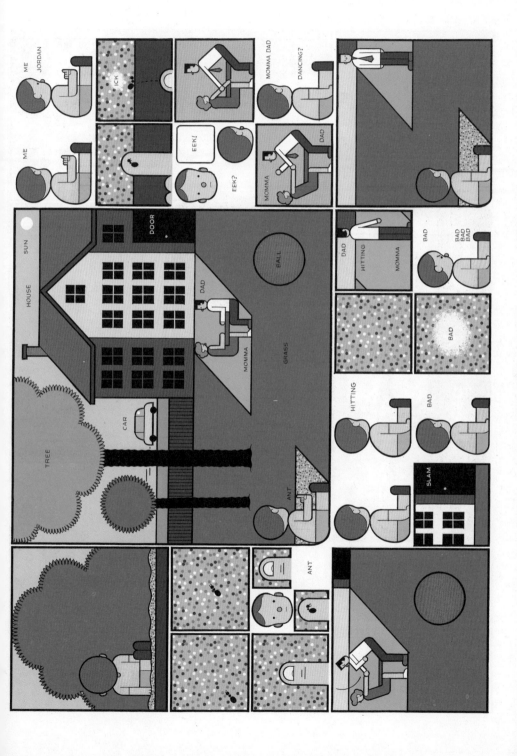

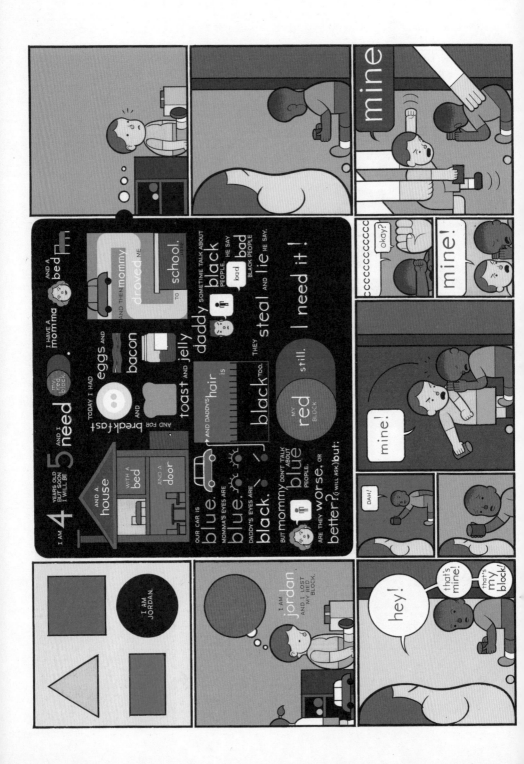

May 23rd, 1963.

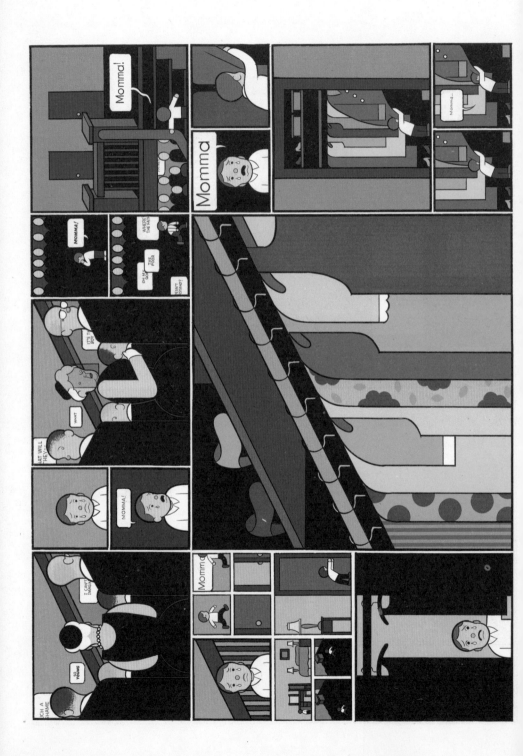

October 14th, 1965.

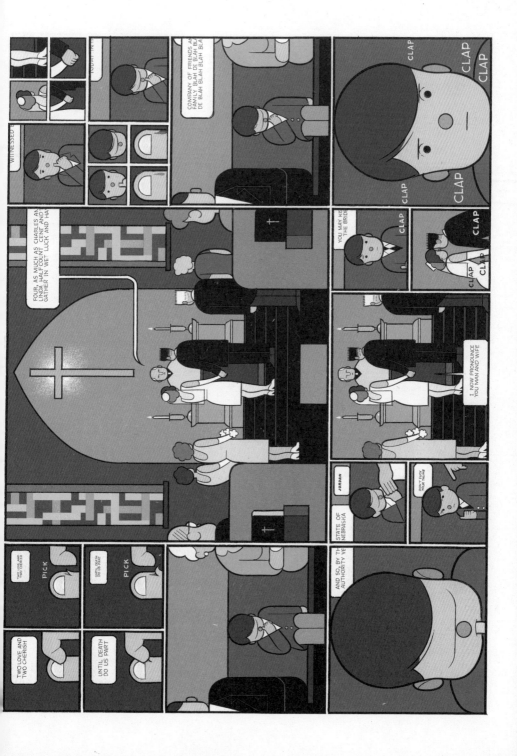

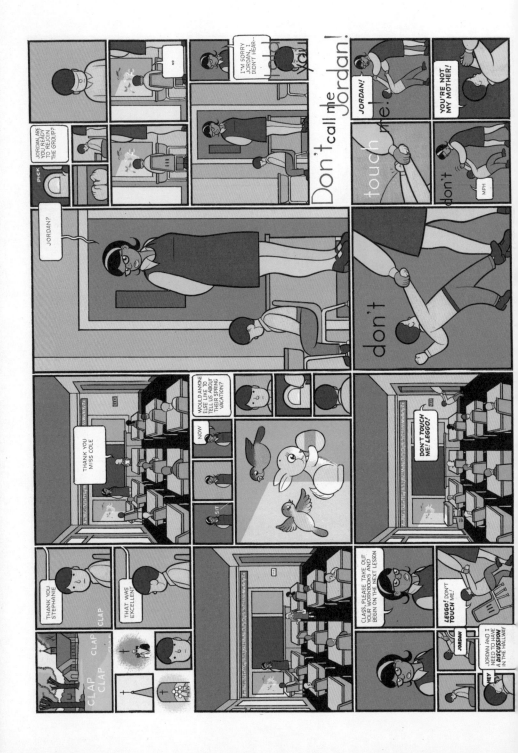

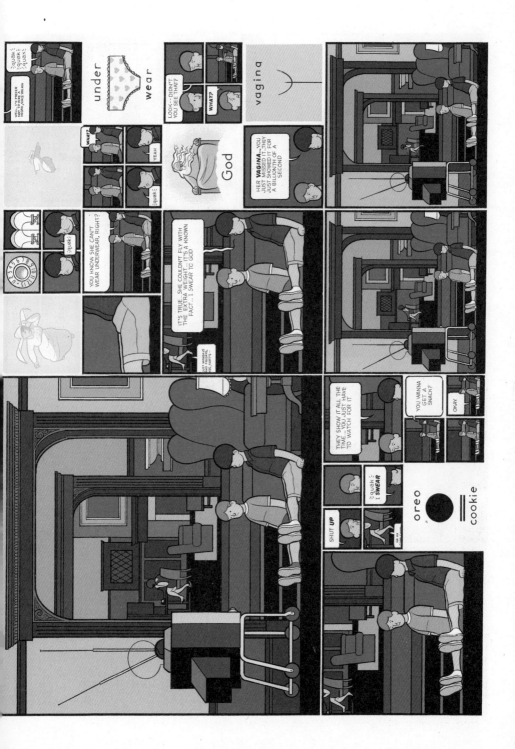

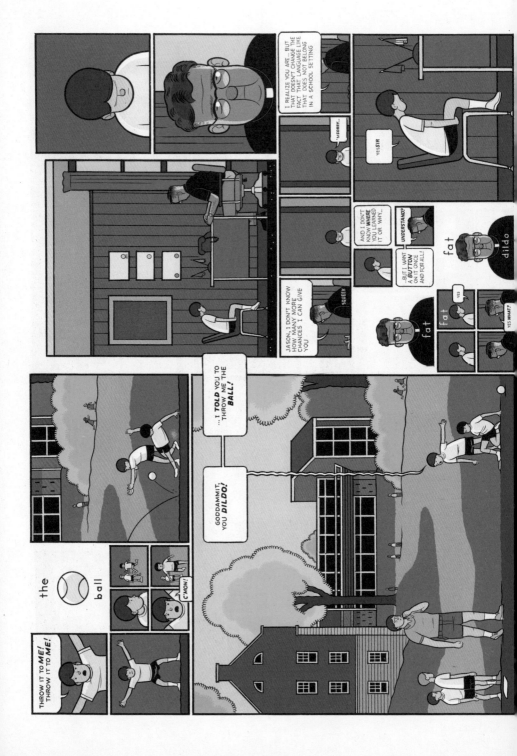

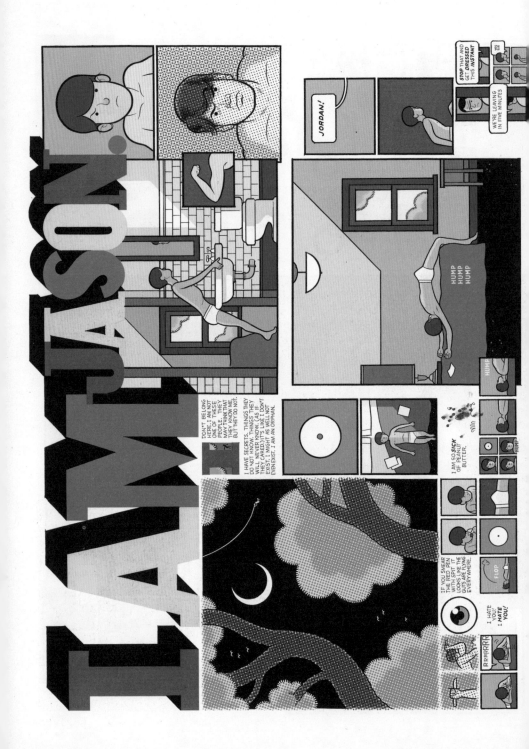

Magda Mandela
Hari Kunzru

It is 4.30 am and Magda would like us, her neighbours, to know that she is a very talented woman, a woman of accomplishments. Magda is a nurse, a qualified pilot, a businesswoman and philanthropist, a gifted and sensitive lover, the holder of certificates in computing and English grammar, a semi-professional country singer and a mother. Yes, a mother! Magda has a daughter. Who came out of this pussy right here.

Right here, she says. Out of this pussy. RIGHT HERE. And all along the street we come to our windows to twitch the net curtains and face the awe-inspiring truth that is Magda in her lime-green thong. She's standing on the top step, the lights of the house blazing behind her, a terrifying mash-up of the Venus of Willendorf and a Victoria's Secret catalogue, making gestures with a beer can at the little knot of emergency service personnel gathered on the pavement below.

One of the younger and less experienced constables has obviously asked her to accompany him to a place where, as an agent of the state, he will feel less exposed. A police station, perhaps. Or a hospital. Anywhere that will tip the odds a little in his favour. Magda has met this suggestion with the scorn it deserves. She knows she outnumbers these fools. YOU KNOW ME, she says. Then, with a sinister leer, AND I KNOW YOU.

Being known by Magda is a messy and unavoidably carnal experience. All of us neighbours are known by Magda. Last time she knew me, she pushed me up against the side of my car. I know you, she breathed huskily. I knew I'd been known.

In their big reflective jackets, the policemen appear crumpled and insubstantial. They are visibly trying to block out the knowledge of her knowledge, no doubt using mental techniques they were taught at the training school: *I am a powerful person. I control my own destiny.* Behind the ambulance, one of the paramedics is taking a quick nip of oxygen.

They don't realize what they're up against. Magda is the daughter of Nelson Mandela, major world leader and saviour of his country. Don't these Day-Glo fools see the resemblance? It's staring them in the face. If they have any doubts, ANY DOUBTS AT ALL, she tells them, they have only to consult the autobiography *Long Road to Freedom*. Read the autobiography! Read page 37 and page 475! They will see. THEN THEY WILL KNOW.

Magda is coated in something that I suspect is coconut oil. She has the air of a woman who has roused herself from titanic erotic exertions to be here with us on Westerbury Road tonight. She has been INTERRUPTED. She has THINGS TO DO. There's no sign of Errol. I hope he's all right. Errol is quite fragile.

Magda lives in Errol's house. This is a scandal on Westerbury Road, because Errol is a widower in his seventies, who brought up a family and was expected to eke away his twilight years on DIY, Sunday church and the occasional tot of Wray & Nephew rum. However, Errol likes Wray & Nephew more than he likes church, and last year (according to Lauren at Number 20) he met Magda at a lock-in at the Victoria Arms, one of the least salubrious pubs in our little corner of East London. I've been to one of those lock-ins. They do get frisky. Magda is at least thirty, possibly forty years younger than Errol. For a while after she moved in, he pottered around with a smile on his grizzled face, raffishly touching the brim of his baseball cap to us neighbours and whistling as he swept the leaves off his front steps. These days he wears the sour expression of a man who's been cheated at cards.

What Errol signed up for was a bit of bounce and warmth and comfort on cold nights. Instead he's been swept into a world of grand operatic passion. Between Magda and Errol there is a love that can spill out in many directions. It has left Magda sleeping in a rolled-up carpet on the pavement and Errol hobbling across the street to take refuge in my kitchen; during Old Testament times, Errol prefers to keep a door between the two of them – and who can blame him for that? Magda's wrath is sharp and terrible. It involves a lot of casting out and smiting. The recently smitten include: Errol (obviously), Lauren at Number 20, the Meals-on-Wheels lady and several council workmen, whom Magda battered with one of the stock of road cones she keeps in the front yard. Magda leaves Errol at least once a month. Sometimes Errol throws her out. Frequently, instead of leaving Errol, Magda punishes him by going to the Victoria Arms and finding a young man to bring home and sit with on the steps. For a day or two, Errol will look grim and spend a lot of time in the betting shop. Then things will go back to normal.

Magda must be excused her foibles, because she is wrestling with the great question of her life: old man or young man? Both have their plus points. Young men have more energy and are less scandalous, unless they smoke crack on the steps or go telling lies to Errol. Old men are more dignified and have houses. Old men are Magda's weakness: I LIKE A OLD MAN. She mentioned her inclinations to my father (seventy this year), when he came to visit the other week. There was a commotion outside, and I found Magda knowing him against a lamp-post. You are a old man, she purred appreciatively, rubbing up and down against his leg. I like a old man.

Old man, young man. Which will it be? For all her turbulence, Magda is concerned about the proprieties. She values the good opinion of us neighbours. The other night she came out onto the steps to explain her relationship with Errol. My neighbours, she said, I must tell you why I am here. We rose from our beds and came to our windows. I AM HIS NURSE. He is a old man. He can't satisfy a woman like me. He is limp and goes to sleep. I need more of a man than such a one. I am a qualified nurse, a gifted woman. He is like a father to me. The problem with you people is this. I will tell you now: You all have dirty minds. Filthy dirty. I think I have said enough. Now fuck off.

As neighbours, we often fail Magda in this way – with our

prurience, our tendency to jump to conclusions. She frequently has to chastise us. Occasionally she does a round of the street and casts us out one by one, which is effortful and very time-consuming. Tonight, before the arrival of the emergency services, she was berating us for our pride and our materialism. I KNOW YOU, she told us. You think you have HOUSES. In Notting Hill they have HOUSES. I have seen them with my own eyes. In such a house is my friend. A young man, not old and worn out at all. Ten, twelve bathrooms at a time in such houses. Enough bathrooms.

On nights such as tonight, Magda likes to sing. She particularly likes an audience in uniform. You're my best friend, she sings. I love you but you don't love me. This song is freely adapted from her CD of country music hymns, the one she plays to get into a church-going mood on Sunday mornings. Magda has built her own semi-professional singing career around such material. She's appeared in Cape Town and Tottenham and Dalston, she says. Musically speaking, Magda's congregation must be more avant-garde than most: although her voice is an extraordinary phenomenon, it's not tonal, at least not as we usually understand tonality.

Sometimes when Magda comes out onto the steps and speaks, I sit bolt upright in bed. Sometimes it is as if she is in the room with me. My girlfriend has the same experience. Magda's voice is not simply loud. Loud, yes, but not just loud. It has the penetrative force of a piece of heavy industrial equipment, something with a diamond bit or tempered-steel blades. Often it seems disconnected from her body, as if emerging from the bathroom or under the floorboards or the far end of Westerbury Road. When you look at Magda, who is quite short and (when dressed) usually looks neat and smart and more or less conventionally contained inside herself, you'd never guess she possessed such a voice. And, in a way, she doesn't, or at least that's what I believe. I think she's merely the voice's host, its point of entry into the continuum of Westerbury Road.

Magda's Voice Theory #1: Dimensionality. She is the portal through which the voice emerges. There must be some other world, unimaginably fraught and violent, contiguous to ours but not normally permeable.

Magda's Voice Theory #2: Concerning the Nature of Higher-Order Spaces. Its eerie ability to project into my thickly curtained bedroom is evidence of some force as yet unknown to science. Corollary: perhaps higher-order spaces are denser, more difficult as a medium for conversation.

Whatever the physical cause, Magda is racked by tremendous passions. Wake up, my neighbours, she will often command. Wake up and listen. Tonight I love you. I love you, my neighbours, I am filled with love. But you do not love me, so I say to you this: I DON'T GIVE A FUCK ABOUT YOU. That is the truth. Fuck off now. Go. Magda loves us, but she spurns us just as we spurn her. She spurns us out of the vastness of her love. Sometimes she is unhappy and then she will tell us: I am dying. Yes, I have a pain and I am dying, my neighbours. You don't love me. I am dying and you don't even know. I love you, but I don't give a fuck about you. Go now. Go away. Fuck off. Go. I love you. Go. Once she has delivered her tragic message, she will disappear inside to call an ambulance. When it comes she will be ready on the steps with an overnight case. Having told the paramedics briefly about her pain, she will push past them and sit in the back, waiting to go, fuck off, go.

Magda's Voice Theory #3: Metaphysical Origins. After a recent row with Errol, Magda brought home a young Muslim to sit on the steps. He wore a dishdash and a white skullcap. He had a wispy beard and a cardboard suitcase and a bemused expression. I think she'd found him at the station. He looked about twenty-one. Magda waved her rum bottle and told him about the thieves who sometimes steal her parking space. She demonstrated her concern for parking security on Westerbury Road by making a few minor alterations to the construction of wooden planks and road cones she uses to protect the space outside Errol's house. I wasn't sure the boy spoke English. From the suitcase, I'd say he had just arrived in London. Still, he listened intently, ignoring the bottle in her hand.

Even if he didn't understand the words, he seemed to recognize something, something worth listening to. Could he have heard divinity in Magda's voice? At one point that afternoon I passed the steps on my way to the shops. She called out to me: Don't worry, he's my brother. He has very dirty ears. I'm just checking his ears.

It's gradually dawning on the policemen that they will have to effect an arrest. It will be a slippery business. I wonder if they train for this. Are there special holds? Written protocols? Magda can see the way their devious minds are working. She has the element of surprise. I KNOW YOU, she warns, sportingly.

Andy the drummer chooses this moment to drive down the road and park outside his house. He has been out late, gigging somewhere. He once told me he gets a lot of work in Leeds. Andy is a favourite of Magda's. All right, boy, she says. You. Yes, you with the red car. I love you. I've seen this car many a time. I've seen this car a lot of times, I tell you. Go away now. I've done with you. Go, OK? Fuck you. You probably have a small cock. Go. Andy waves to her and starts unloading his drum-kit. YOU ARE A YOUNG MAN, she calls out, blowing him a kiss.

Thinking she is distracted, the policemen advance up the steps. Magda emits a long, high-pitched wail, which rattles the windows and pierces deep into the souls of us neighbours, watching from our upstairs windows.

MVT #4: A survival from the ancient world? Primal, atavistic. Greek mourner. Mammoth-feller. She slithers out of their grasp, waddling down the street in the direction of the main road. Though she's slow, she has a chaotic, lumbering motion that makes her hard to catch. At last two of the policemen grab hold of her, one gripping her arms, the other circling her waist in a sort of static rugby tackle, his head pressed into the flesh of her stomach so that he's eyeballing the triangle of acid-green nylon that is all that stands between his nose and her most intimate zones. Magda's fierce resistance reminds me of the time when her need for a young man led her to climb into the basement of Number 18, where a crew of builders were fitting a kitchen. As they cowered behind the sink unit, she wedged herself halfway through the sash window. I LIVE WITH A OLD MAN, she growled, wiggling and straining. I HAVE A CONDOM. LINE UP. I AM READY.

Walkie-talkies crackle. Doors slam. Magda is placed inside the police van and I climb back into bed. For a few minutes, red and blue lights make flashing patterns on my ceiling, then all is quiet and dark on Westerbury Road. Magda will be back tomorrow. They never keep her for long. She'll sulk for a day or two, listening to pirate radio in Errol's back garden, then she'll forgive us and return to her place on the front steps. What we, her thieving-neighbours-so-smug-in-our-houses don't know is the power of love. Love conquers all. One day we'll discover that this is true and then we'll be sorry. Sometimes I wonder what would happen if we returned Magda's love. If we believed in her, she could do great things for us. But our problem is we are faithless, our problem is we are stupid. Our problem is we just don't listen.

The Monster
Toby Litt

(for Ali Smith)

The monster didn't know what it was – what kind of monster or even, now and again, whether a monster at all. It had lived for what felt like a long time without mirrors, which didn't exist, or puddles, which it instinctively avoided. There were other monsters in creation, or the monster assumed they were other monsters (it did not philosophize on the nature of monstrosity – all could be monsters, without a norm from which to deviate), and, had it asked them, these other monsters would probably have described it to itself, using the few words and concepts available to them: monster, creation, sun, tree, fruit, merd, good, bad, up and down. But the monster was for some reason averse to this, just as it was averse to puddles, and had only learnt of the practice by overhearing one monster being described by another. The sentence it overheard was: 'Monster up up good fruit, down down bad merd.' And so the monster had always found out most about itself by touch. There were two soft floppy growths upon each side of its head, and its long curved back felt rough at the bottom, like the skin of a fruit. The monster couldn't see its own feet because its belly, which was huge, got in the way. Every time the monster explored itself, though, its hands (it definitely had hands) seemed to encounter something different. With no written language, it was impossible for the monster to record these changes or the supposed status quo which had preceded them. For example, the monster had a vague sense that, sometime in the distant past, it had either been smaller or had walked upon four legs rather than two. It didn't have a very good memory, but it was disturbed by the thought that once upon a time it had had to look up at things which now it looked down at, yes, and it had had to stretch on tiptoes to reach things which were now at eye level. Most of these things observed and grabbed were fruit, fruit on trees, and of course trees grew, too – as the monster rediscovered countless times. But not everything in creation grew at the same rate, as the monster had rediscovered more rarely. The monster tended to conclude that one of the best explanations for its sense of bigness was that it was growing faster than the rest of creation. Also, the memory of walking upon all fours could be deceptive: if the monster wanted to, it could still do this – just as, when tired, it would lower itself down until its back was flat on the ground. Because of the size of its belly, the monster could lie in no other position but this. Again because of the belly, the monster had only an intimation of what sex it was – and this it gained socially, from the kinds of monster which most commonly approached it with what seemed to be sexual intent, meaning an intent to sexually describe. 'Up up good fruit down down good good sun creation fruit.' Our monster, however, was not interested in pleasure or reproduction – it was put off the latter by its doubt as to its own nature, the former by its misery. At night, it slept – under the stars, there were many stars in creation, and its dreams were frequently of absolute certainty of being. I am this thing. This thing is me. Waking, the fact of waking and the quality of it, was invariably a disappointment. Despite its morning rage, the monster was almost always gentle with the world of creation. It had never killed anything, and if it had harmed anything, that harm had been done accidentally (except, that is, harm the monster had done to itself). It knew of the quality of good and constantly aspired towards it. And it was this sense, rather than a visual image of beauty or handsomeness, that the monster thought of as its true parentage. Someone had taught the monster not to be unnecessarily cruel, and that was mother, someone had warned it never to be unwarrantedly proud, and that was father. Whatever kinds of creation they had been, the monster's memory had finally failed any longer to remember them. Perhaps this was because the monster had lived so many days and nights. Among all the things it monstrously lacked, an accurate sense of time was the most disturbing. It knew there were days and, halfway through the days, it believed there were nights.

Just after waking, it knew that the time of dreaming had passed in a different way to the time it was now in; just before sleeping, it felt joy: something was about to change and for the better. One definite experience was pain. When our monster hit its head against a tree, by accident or at full force, it knew for certain it had done it. The sharp stab at first and the dull ache afterwards helped it locate parts of its body in relation to one another. The monster wondered whether this behaviour, being cruel to itself and proud of its badness, was bad behaviour. For periods, the monster gave it up – but then it came to an indistinguished lump of time, usually during the middle of the day, and its desire for certain knowledge grew into an unbearable anguish. If the monster could have been content with the pain of anguish rather than the pain of pain, perhaps it could have been content in all areas of its life – though this thought was beyond it. The monster wandered around the areas of creation it knew best, aware that certain features were identities: trees were always different or the plural was a lie; in other words, there was only a single tree which was sometimes close to, sometimes far away from, where the monster had slept, or there were multiple trees but placed so far apart that they were not visible, one to the other, and by the time the monster had walked far enough away from one tree to find another, it had forgotten the memorized features of the first, and so was able to make a comparison. On the tree or trees were fruit, which were tastily colourful – the monster reached in the morning to touch their brightness, then found itself with half of one in its mouth. Eating had been reinvented, yet again – and the monster knew it was something that had happened before. It knew this because the action felt, like mother, both comfortable and comforting; the sensation of chewing seemed repetitive and, thus, repeated from before. This was probably, apart from the moments just after a headbash, when our monster came closest to happiness. Excretion, too, unexpectedly occurred. But, being a business of the unseen nether regions, beneath the belly, the monster wasn't all that involved with it. Just as the fruits were bright, off the ground and attractive, so the merds were dull, underfoot and repellent. Whether by instinct or not, the monster only deposited them at some little distance from the tree or the nearest tree. And when the slight straining was done, which took care of itself, the monster would walk away – usually without looking. Again, because of the belly, if the monster did become curious about its merds, it couldn't examine them from close up – not from above, anyway. The monster could have lain down and rolled towards the dull round smelly objects, but, before it ever did this, a feeling overcame it that nothing dull and smelly was worth the effort of rolling towards. Round objects, the monster had no objection to – and in the case of fruit was actively attracted towards. In hope, sometimes, the monster thought of its belly as a big round fruit. But just as often, in despair, the belly's roundness was that of a merd. It, the belly, was where merds came from, after all – though the monster was capable of forgetting this. The trees were also possessed of leaves. If these taught the monster any lesson, it was one of uselessness – and use. By mistake, the monster sometimes ate some leaf along with the fruit. It wasn't a bad taste, not proud or cruel like a monster could be, but it was useless. The monster spat them out, away from the tree, towards the merds. When the leaves became useful was when the sun overhead became too hot. This was when the cool beside the tree-trunk was the only good place. Several monsters would gather. 'Down tree down sun good.' The leaves were also useful when it rained and made puddles. Then, they stopped the monster becoming too cold. One day, the monster set off to – but no, there was to be no quest for true identity, no storing up of fruit for the long journey into the away-from-this-tree self. No. One day, one day of *that* sort, would never come. One day, instead, would continue to be one day – one day very like the day before and almost indistinguishable from the day after. The monster had no story, unless being a monster is story enough.

Nigora
Adam Thirlwell

These were the names of the men who would have slept with Nigora (thought Nigora), if only she had encouraged them:

Komil
Bakhitiyor.

Then there were the names of men whom Nigora had successfully pursued, but who would not sleep with her again, for various reasons (loyalty to their wives; loyalty to her husband):

Shuhrat
Muhammad.

Next there was the list of men whom Nigora had successfully pursued and who, she thought, would still sleep with her if she wanted to: this list, therefore, could be further and more precisely divided into those whom Nigora would also sleep with, for various reasons (pride; vanity; love) –

Aftandil
Aziz

– and those whom Nigora would not sleep with, for various other reasons (boredom; fidelity; love) –

Khayrullah
Jalol
Abdullah.

And yet this list was complicated by the fact that all these men were absent. They were all in another city, in another country, to which Nigora would never return.

In a cake-shop – in this city which was not her city, this city in the west – Nigora was compiling imaginary lists of her life, while watching the sullen assistant stroke sky-blue ribbon into curlicues with the back of a pair of scissors.

And finally (thought Nigora) there were the men with whom Nigora, in this city, had a chance:

Yaha
Taha
Naguib.

This was the list which mattered to Nigora. Or no. To be more precise: Nigora's imagination dwelt on those she had not pursued, and those she could still pursue – whether conquered already or not. She only left alone the list of those whom she had conquered and to whom she would no longer return. She was haunted by the spectre of non-fulfilment.

But one name was more present than the rest.

Yaha.

It would also be possible to describe Nigora's life in a list of all the films which she had seen with her father, on *Kultura* or the more commercial Russian channels, from the age of six to sixteen. Each Saturday afternoon, they would settle down in the living room, thus avoiding the tantrums and depression of her mother, his wife.

On their satellite television, they watched varieties of romantic comedy, both ancient and modern:

The Lady Eve
The Philadelphia Story
Sullivan's Travels
When Harry Met Sally
Roman Holiday.

They watched teen movies:

Pretty in Pink
The Breakfast Club.

They watched weepies (*An Affair to Remember*) and screwball comedies (*Bringing Up Baby*). They admired the *œuvre* of Preston Sturges – the *unacknowledged genius* of the American 1940s. They watched the Russian mini-series of Sherlock Holmes, with the great Vasily Livanov (Holmes) and Vitaly Solomin (Watson). They made forays into the artistic and silver world of Max Ophuls

(*Le Plaisir*
La Ronde
Madame de)

and the artistic and silver world of Jean Renoir

(*La Règle du jeu*
La Grande illusion
Toni).

They treasured André Hunebelle's films of Fantômas, the sadistic master criminal of Paris – who owned a Citroën DS with retractable wings. Nigora's favourite, disputed by her father, was *Fantômas contre Scotland Yard*. Her father preferred the simplicity of *Fantômas*. They watched Truffaut (*Le Dernier métro*) and Godard (*Le Mépris*). But most of all they watched the American 1970s:

Coppola
Scorsese
Peckinpah
Lumet
Kubrick
Polanski.

Like the list of Nigora's love affairs, perhaps this list is also overly comprehensive. For what predominated, from the weekends of her childhood, was not the films. The films were exorbitant; what remained was a sense of sadness and of loss.

Her mother would stop talking to her and her father for two weeks. She would refuse to address her daughter in front of the mothers at her school. She worked two jobs – one as a lecturer in the university, in classical archaeology, the other as a reader for a specialist ancient history publisher. And these jobs, she would remind her daughter, made her tired. They exhausted her, she said.

Nigora, as a girl, always identified with the minor characters. She always sympathised with the rejected, the marginalised, the small.

In the cake-shop, balancing a cake-box on the tripod of her fingers – like a waiter – Nigora made lists of her life. She remembered the sledge on nails above the front door; the dovecote of slippers beside it. She remembered doing piano practice on a Saturday morning, a metronome becoming hysterical beside her.

In the Maison Thomas pizzeria (*Le Caire, fondée en 1922, Open 24 hours*), Yaha began to write a letter to an older woman. It was the fourth of a collection that would eventually comprise seventeen letters. In this letter – which bore an unnoticed tear of chilli sauce – he would write the sentence: 'Whenever I imagine a future I imagine it with you.' And Nigora, reading this, would be touched, and would not believe him.

Simultaneously, Nigora's husband – Laziz – arranged his elbow in a scalene triangle, pleasantly uncomfortable, on the rim of the perpetually open driver's window. His car was imported from the Communist past of Eastern Europe: it was yellow and outdated. Its window-frames contained no glass whatsoever.

Its meter was printed in Cyrillic, with такси.

Laziz sat in the traffic and looked at the smog on the river. Like Nigora, his thoughts were nostalgic. Unlike Nigora's, they were also romantic. *Lazizjon*, he was thinking. *Lazizjon*.

Oh my Laziz.

A dubbed and imported video of *The Philadelphia Story* – a present for their anniversary – lay clipped inside a clouded plastic box, on the passenger seat beside him. The passenger seat and its headrest were shrouded in the costume of a panda.

Laziz believed in two things. He believed in tribulation. The history of the world was a history of pain. But Laziz did not worry about this world. Its pain did not distress him. Neither loss nor death distressed him. For he also believed in God, and His inscrutable gifts.

He picked a cassette, titled in red felt-tip, from a pile beside the gear-stick, and blew into each spoked wheel before slotting it happily into its slit. After several uncertain and anxious seconds, the voice of Natacha Atlas began to be husky in his car.

Laziz (thought Laziz) was happy. He was a married man. Nothing, therefore, could harm him. He was protected by the love of God, and its earthly counterpart, the love of his wife.

He knew that when he died he would hear a voice, and that voice would greet him by his name.

In Namangan, the city where he was born, and where he had assumed that he would die (but he would not), Laziz had begun a bakery business. He started a chain of shops selling cake, flowers – gladioli in translucent plastic, like a wedding dress – and boxes of outdated chocolate. He had started it in 1989, when everyone believed in *perestroika*, for the West and for the East.

In Namangan, Laziz's sexual encounters had been limited to occasional kisses, occasional fumblings. He would listen with careful unconcern to the stories of his colleagues, his employees – about their wives and their affairs. None of Laziz's affairs were *affairs of the heart*.

As he sat each night in his only armchair, with its pornographic rents and tears, as he read business textbooks in Russian, Laziz used to console himself with the theory that this prolonged virginity was not, as some might argue, due to weakness, or fear. It was instead due to a care for the female; it was a superhuman tenderness. He was a superhero of tenderness.

In this way, Laziz accepted the burden of his inexperience. He developed a way of not caring about girls, by saying that he cared about girls.

And so when he was first and finally in bed with a girl, whose name was Nigora, on a business trip to Samarqand, Laziz was unprepared. He was also thirty-two.

Although both of them acknowledged that *intercourse itself* would not take place, there was still a tacit understanding that, since their clothes had been removed, other actions might be performed. There was an air of expectation. In Nigora's mind, there was an idea of hopes to be fulfilled. But when Laziz's fingers first felt the deep wetness of Nigora, its fur and unexpected sensations, he was not able to control himself. He spurted, a little to the left of Nigora, who was lying on her front.

At this point, Laziz felt his sex life *running away from him*.

How far is a person the same as their sex life? This was what Laziz began to think, naked, beside a naked girl. He became ontological, epistemological. Laziz wanted to believe that his sex life could be separate from his life. Like many people who have caused their own distress, he wanted to believe that events were not a sure guide to character – somewhere, inviolate, and far away from this scene, existed a Laziz who was powerful and perfect.

And yet events are a sure guide to character. Nigora, in the cake-shop queue, considering if she could leave Laziz, would have been able to tell him that. Our characters – she would have argued, sadly – are nothing but events. Everything else is only romance.

One proof of her improvised theory is what Laziz did next, in Namangan, many years ago, on that *fateful night* with Nigora.

He did not talk to Nigora; he did not tell the truth, and trust his charm. Instead, Laziz lay on his left side, with one hand propping up his head. A dying gladiator. He gazed at Nigora. He neglected to mention that he was lying on his own emission.

Nigora looked at him. And in this look began the subsequent relationship of Laziz and Nigora. For Laziz was trying to look cool and unconcerned; while Nigora was looking anxious. Laziz was hoping not to be found out; Nigora was fretting – why had her body, now naked, rendered Laziz so nonchalant, so lolling? Where was his fire? His inner spirit? Where was the lust?

The lust, thought Laziz, was simply premature. It was not on time. The lust would therefore return eventually. He was young and healthy, after all. And so he thought that *the crisis would pass*. He trusted to a timetable.

But the crisis did not pass. Leaning on his hand, Laziz continued to observe his new girlfriend in distress. His pose was classical. It was picturesque.

Oh, the picturesque is no substitute for lust! And yet the picturesque was all Laziz could perform; everything else was beyond him.

This image – in which Laziz was picturesque, leaning on his elbow, and Nigora was distressed, lying naked beside him – is the image of their subsequent marriage.

Two years later, succumbing to *the pressure of events*, they left their country (a country to which they would never return).

Some Night-time Dialogue between Nigora and Laziz

L It's a dodgy haircut, isn't it? It's dodgy.
N Well, yes, you could say that. It's dodgy.
L You think so?
N Well.
L Oh, no.
N I'm only teasing you; I'm only tormenting you.
L Tell me you love me.
N Lazizjon.
L Tell me you love me. Am I handsome? Tell me I'm handsome.
N You're handsome. You're more than handsome. You're a looker.
L But you don't mean that.
N Yes, I mean that.
L Well, you shouldn't mean that.
N *Lazizjon.*

Each night, these facts recurred to her: Nigora was thirty-four; Yaha was twenty-three. These numbers were suddenly becoming fraught for Nigora. She remembered them every morning; at her rising up, and at her going to bed. She remembered them when she went out, and on her coming in.

She was a married woman. She did not know if she still loved her husband. She did not know if she, a married woman, whose hands and breasts – whose every opening – had since her marriage known only one man, was now in love with someone else.

Sometimes, Nigora believed that if she only kissed Yaha, then she would be cured. Her pain would be relieved. Cupid's arrow would be removed from her breast. But she was not sure.

Nigora was a housewife and a part-time secretary. Yaha was a reserve footballer for AHLY.

As she spoke to her immortal and all-powerful God – a God she had disconsolately adopted from Laziz – she reasoned in this way. That she was not to blame. That so long as no sexual acts occurred she was not guilty of any sin. That the definition of a sexual act was problematic. That it necessarily included introduction of the penis into her body; and necessarily included ejaculation of semen, whether inside or outside a female body; and also, necessarily, any touch of a man's hand or mouth on the bareness between her legs. But at this point Nigora grew perplexed. She felt the need for guidance, and could not find it.

Her problem was the kiss. She could not define the moral status of the kiss. If she kissed him, thought Nigora, then maybe she would not want to venture into the unambiguously immoral; she would no longer be tempted by the temptations of his flesh.

Since she thought that the kiss might be her cure, she tended to believe that a kiss was innocent. It was just on the right side of morality.

Nigora was not convinced of the soul's immortality. Laziz was convinced; but she was not. And since she was not convinced, she was also unsure of his belief in crime and punishment. Without the threat of punishment or the promise of reward, her actions were oddly depleted. They existed only for her.

In this way, Nigora was a libertine.

All Nigora's temptations were now refracted through the immortal. Her body's immortal longings were her anxiety, her worry. They seemed more important than the possibility of her soul's immortal life.

And yet, and yet. How much pleasure could her body procure, she wondered? If they slept together, she would not give Yaha pleasure; when he remembered her, she worried, he would remember her only with amusement, with pity. Her memory of passion would be his memory of the laughable.

At what point, she wondered, could she act out of character? When would she have the courage?

Her life was all Laziz: they could not contemplate themselves without each other. It was Laziz / Nigora; Nigora / Laziz; and Laziz bored her.

Laziz wore a baseball cap stitched with a Big Apple badge pinned to its peak. He wore khaki chinos with ironed-in pleating, like a curtain, around the crotch. Below the raised hem of these trousers, which did not reach his shoes, two sports socks were visible. These socks came in trios – three identical roll-mops – tightly in a plastic wrapper. He bought them from a kiosk in Downtown, which arranged its wares neatly outside on an ironing board. He wore a taupe and tucked-in polo neck, which in the language of the fashion magazines unread by Nigora would have been called *unforgiving*. On the fuzzy back-ledge of Laziz's taxi were three miniature rubber dogs, with dislocated and nodding heads. There was a bulldog, a Scotch terrier and a (miniature) miniature Schnauzer.

Nigora had a theory of romantic comedy. It might, perhaps, have helped Laziz to know this theory. It might have helped him in his own thoughts and theories of marriage. But he did not know her theory.

Every plot in the movies (thought Nigora) was the same. She knew the plots. There was the life-changing moment. Then the meet-cute. Then the discovery of an obstruction to happiness. Then the decision to embark on a particular strategy. The test, or tests. The sudden reversal of the obstruction. And finally the happy ending.

These were the plots: but there was another way of describing the plots.

Every plot was about morality: it was the opposition of adultery and marriage; it was saying that there was always a choice to be made between sex and love. Every hero or heroine believed they could not have the two together. And yet this opposition would always be resolved in the coercive paradise of the finale, where sex and love were revealed to be identical.

Nigora was unconvinced by this. For she was not sentimental. However much they tempted her, and moved her, she could not believe in the fantasy of the endings. She still, after all, had some pride.

According to Nigora, romantic comedy was the most morally complex of all the filmic genres. It dramatised the essential moral problem of everybody's life. It represented the gap between desire and fulfilment.

This was the theory she developed as she lay beside her husband; as he caressed the curve of her forehead; as his hands went up and down the floral print of her acrylic night-gown. The flora were daisies, they were cornflowers. *Nigorajonim*, he said. *Nigorajonim*. He told his wife that he loved her. And she told him that she loved him; and she was lying, thought Nigora. She was lying to her Lazizjon.

And yet: Nigora was not lying, not quite.

There was a secret to Laziz's moustache. It was a private joke between him and Nigora. The joke was that Laziz's moustache was not real. From time to time, Laziz applied this drooping line of glutinous plastic to his upper lip. Before he went out, Nigora would take polaroids of him: as he saluted, glaring at the camera; as he leered and pouted like a matinée idol. They loved these photographs. They showed them to their closest friends, as they drank a coffee, with jagged squares of milk chocolate. And no one else found Laziz's moustache funny. It was not, perhaps, that they found it positively unfunny; it was just that they could not see its humour. This humour was reserved for the privacy of Laziz and his Nigora.

The night before they left Uzbekistan, in 2002, Nigora met her friend Faizullo in the park. There was a man selling candyfloss, and a man selling bananas. They held hands and kissed as if they were in love. In this way, Nigora hoped she might not be endangering her friend. They would simply resemble an everyday, humdrum affair. It was nothing to do with alliances, or politics. They sat on a climbing-frame printed with blurred reproductions of Daffy Duck, and Bugs Bunny, and talked about the other singers in the opera house, maliciously. Faizullo was an opera singer. This was Nigora's implicit way of talking about their friendship. And then they walked away and Nigora kissed him on the cheek, lightly, absent-mindedly – as though she were about to see him again in the morning.

Yes, Nigora knew about suffering.

That was the last time she saw him. And, unbeknown to Nigora, she had stayed in Faizullo's memory accompanied by a pigeon, which had drifted behind her as she turned to say goodbye.

Three years later, Faizullo had disappeared. It was rumoured that he had been killed; then it was rumoured he had been imprisoned. And Nigora did not know which of these she preferred: for, although her instinct clung to the life of Faizullo, she also could not allow herself the pain of imagining Faizullo with a number stitched on his breast, ragged, like a raffle ticket.

On her last morning in Uzbekistan, Nigora had seen a pregnant dachshund being driven in the front seat of a hatchback, which Nigora first saw through the car-window beside her and then through the rear window behind her, as she twisted round, entranced.

Nigora could not worry about the humans; the humans were too much for her. But she could worry about the dogs instead. For the dogs were innocent. The dogs were the genuine bystanders; they had nothing to do with revolutions, or beliefs.

If Nigora were asked about the suffering in her own marriage, she would not have been able to talk about it. All her suffering was elsewhere – in the realm of remembered facts.

There was a snobbishness in her suffering, a reserve. It would not countenance comparison.

And yet, and yet: Laziz would go down underneath the covers, in the nights. And he would say to her, 'Never leave me, never leave me.' And how could she? she would reply. Everything she loved was Laziz. And he would say to her, 'Never leave me, never leave me.' Or he would say, 'Tell me I'm not ugly.' For Laziz believed that he was ugly; he believed that he was the ugliest and weakest child. And Nigora, sadly, continued to reassure him; she kissed the galumph of his nose, the crooked line of his mouth, and she said to him, 'You're not ugly. Of course you're not. I love you, you're beautiful,' until Laziz managed to calm down.

The coverlet had been given to her by her grandmother. And underneath the coverlet she felt safe.

She did not believe in her own suffering, Nigora. All her ideas of suffering were reserved for the gone, the missing, the dead.

Somewhere, everywhere, a girl is taking her clothes off. This much was true. Nigora could agree with this. But something else, she thought, was also true. Somewhere, everywhere, a girl was being raped. And the question was: how far away? How far away did something have to happen before it stopped being your responsibility? How far away did a rape need to be? Two streets? A country? A separate universe?

In this rational hysteria lived Nigora, who loved her husband, Laziz – a taxi driver and former businessman. She loved him, and wanted to leave him.

Some Day-time Dialogue between Nigora and Laziz

L   When you're young you can go anywhere but when you're old you can't go everywhere. It's true.
N   It's true.
L   It's true? It's true. Yes. Did I tell you this joke about the rake?
N   The rake, no.
L   Two men are walking down a road.
N   OK.
L   And there's a rake in between them.

N   That's it? It isn't funny.

L   No, it isn't funny, is it? This guy told me it and he
laughed so I thought it must be funny.

N   It isn't funny.

On the sofa which they had bought after a year in their new country, Nigora and Laziz watched *The Philadelphia Story*. Or: Nigora watched, and Laziz slept beside her, his head back, his mouth open. This film was dubbed into Russian, with one male and bass actor doing all the voices. And this made her sad; it created a gap between Nigora and the storyline.

As Nigora watched this film again, she considered that its plot was all about timing: everything had got out of kilter, and yet somehow things would restore themselves. Timing would be restored. Because the couple who move apart are still the same couple. The beauty (thought Nigora) of *The Philadelphia Story* is the fact that the film is about Cary Grant and Katherine Hepburn, and yet all along it looks like it is about Katherine Hepburn and Jimmy Stewart. But Jimmy Stewart is just there to prove a sad truth of timing: that the affair one is having is never the affair one is having. There is always someone else.

The cake she had bought lay crumbling on its paper box in front of them.

She stroked Laziz under his rough chin. She gently extricated his moustache from its precarious angle on his upper lip. *Happy anniversary*, she said, gently, to herself.

Laziz would be picturesque, and she would be distressed. That was the image of their marriage.

She was not sure if the vocabulary for everything really existed. She was not convinced by everyone's assumption of linguistic comprehensiveness. The feeling she got, for instance, when watching *The Philadelphia Story*, was not quite sadness; it was not quite melancholy. It was more to do with a sensation of size, of overwhelming size.

More and more, she was beginning to believe that feelings were not complicated. They were not split into infinite constituent elements. Instead, often, the words were not all there. For Nigora was pragmatic. She had no time for souls with *soul*. No, Nigora did not believe in the indefinable. She believed that everything had a definition, if only the words could be found.

She remembered her father coming into the empty kitchen, letting his keys splay on the table. She remembered him biting the cap off a biro, as he made notes on a pile of manuscript. She remembered the first boy she ever slept with, Shuhrat, who used to swim while she lay and read on the grass by the river. He got out and lay beside her. She remembered his arms, the hair springing awry as it dried. But now she could not quite remember his face. She remembered his eyes were brown, but she could not remember his eyes. She only remembered that she knew they were brown.

And she missed her mother. In this new city, where Laziz was her one companion, she wanted to be home again. She wanted to be there in the kitchen, with her mother talking. And her father, as she talked, would pluck a stray hair from the base of her neck. There was a bowl of sweets on the kitchen table, underneath a tablecloth.

Nigora was a minor character.

She remembered writing her initials on the condensation in the car window, as her father drove her to piano lessons. She remembered the letters leaking downwards, obeying the line of gravity.

In the Gardens of Sunderland Café – renamed from its original Gardens of Allah, after Sunderland had been victorious in the 1973 FA Cup Final – Yaha made notes. For Yaha was not just a footballer. He had also received a university education. According to Yaha, in this world there were three ordinary systems of government: and he had invented a fourth, in which 'virtue was always rewarded'. This was his ideal republic; its constitution formed his constant study, his refuge, his repose.

Nigora considered Yaha, and gave up. She stroked the hairs on the back of Laziz's hands. Where could she go? Everywhere she went, there was her marriage.

The thing about you, her mother used to say, is that you never act out of character. You have no originality.

But Nigora knew this was not true. Because she was going to act out of character. She was going (thought Nigora) to *be herself*. And yet: how could she? How could she?

Judge Gladys Parks-Schultz

Heidi Julavits

On the final dusk of her life, Judge Gladys Parks-Schultz sits in a green velvet armchair reading – or rather not reading – a dull nautical mystery called *Trouble Astern*. Her chair faces a large window overlooking a long driveway lined with oaks. Beyond the furthest oak she can see the ocean and, riding the horizon, a house-lit island.

Behind her is a closed door.

From this vantage point, we cannot see Glad Parks-Schultz. She is blocked from view by her throne-like chair. Glad Parks-Schultz's name suggests she is as dull as her mystery, an insincerely cheery woman compactly assembled, her bland orb face stacked directly atop her middle like a snowman's. Her name suggests a curt and stilted manner. We see her barking monotone pleasantries, scaring children unintentionally. There is no sense arguing with this perception, even if there is only a little truth to it. We cannot see Glad Parks-Schultz, we can only hear her name in our heads, and her name has carved a lumpen shape for her there.

Glad Parks-Schultz tries repeatedly to lose herself in her mystery – a love affair, a sailing trip, a cabin, a knife – but cannot. Following the spat over the Christmas ham ('How can you serve *ham*?' her daughter had asked, a fair question; Sylvia was a vegetarian, something her mother had willfully forgotten), Glad Parks-Schultz finds herself in a familiarly pinched humor, her Holidays Gone Wrong mood. To go with this mood she plays in her head images from another Christmas, images from *Fanny and Alexander*, the only Bergman movie Glad has ever seen, and then only because Sylvia, a film major minoring in psychology and thus a self-appointed Bergman connoisseur, gave it to her as a Christmas present last year ('This is more your speed,' Sylvia had said, not uncritically).

Fine if it was. Glad preferred her cultural enrichment free of anguish.

Outside her window (in which only she can see her faint reflection), the tree-lined drive extends to a distant point. It is the trick of perspective, thinks Glad Parks-Schultz, whose face, in the half-reflection in this dying-light time of day, appears longer and thinner than it might to anyone actually seeing her. Glad Parks-Schultz splays her book over her lap (only twenty more pages to go), giving up on the cowardly pair of lovers who have sailed and anchored in a cove, who have rowed their dinghy to the secluded beach, who are sneaking through the woods to a cabin to kill the woman's husband with a knife. Why the husband is alone in the cabin is itself a bunch of self-reflexive foolery – he is a writer putting the final touches on a mystery book. She wants to ask the husband about this book – not the book he's writing, but the book he's in. What kind of mystery, she would ask him, makes you wait until the very end for a dead person? She is a district judge. She is not interested in crimes before they happen. She detests the *why* of most novels, which is the reason she sticks to mysteries. There is no emotional worrying of the *why* in mysteries – she cheated on him; he wanted her money – there is only the outcome, and the intricately explained *how*.

Meanwhile, Glad waits impatiently for Sylvia and her college boyfriend, her son Rod and his college girlfriend, all of whom she has banished from her house in a fit of ham pique, to return from the beach.

But once these people (her children and their temporary beloveds) are out of her sight she feels unseen, and not terribly easy as a result of it. Better to be loathed on a major holiday. Better to feel hated and alive. She is a stern district judge despised for her imperviousness to human context, to bad-luck stories. ('No Glad-Handing Parks-Schultz'.)

The first snowflake of the season tumbles past the window. Glad huffs. She brushes the spine of *Trouble Astern* and prays for an escape from her tedious self. She'll take any old diversion from this green velvet armchair – her mother's favorite armchair, the upholstery warted with burn marks during her mother's final days smoking in this very chair, *dying* in this very chair. She wants to be free of this Holiday Gone Wrong mood, this overheated pair of woolly mukluks.

This is where, Glad thinks, if I were, say, a less cooperative character in the relentlessly trouble-free *Trouble Astern*, I would set the writer-husband's peg-leg afire (were he to possess a peg-leg), I would crush the whiny lover's head with a winch handle. If impulsive violence isn't part of my character, I could instead (as is the annoying tendency of the characters in *Trouble Astern*) flash backward to some baldly moral exemplar from my childhood. I could allow myself to be sucked backward and molecularly reassembled as a younger, sweeter person, available to be efficiently known by others via some traumatic event involving – preferably – my mother. This is the way of the world, Glad knows. She hears it from the lawyers every week. Mothers are, in some soupy way, to blame for every act of criminality.

Glad rubs at the spine as if it were some tinny magic lamp, promising instantaneous transport to an enthralling past. For the purposes of heightening the intrigue at this particular moment she thinks of this enthralling past as Her Secret Life. Everything has a secret life these days – birds, bees, alphabets, armoires, the characters in *Trouble Astern* – and Glad feels quite comfortable in claiming one for herself as well, even if she's not entirely clear on what constitutes a secret exactly. If she's never spoken of it, is it a secret, even if the content isn't particularly combustible? After all, it's not that she failed to tell this 'secret' on purpose (to deceive, protect, gain financial or emotional advantage, whatever); really it existed as a part of her past-person that was inextricable from her current person, and so to know her was to know this about her.

Or so she'd assumed. During the ham incident, when Sylvia had unfairly accused Glad of *not knowing her* (didn't Sylvia know that Glad's way of knowing was what looked like not knowing?), she had then gone on to say something that was, perhaps, true. She had claimed that Glad *refused to be known*. I don't know anything about you, Sylvia said, and I've known you for twenty years. I don't know why you are the way you are.

A person needs a reason to be herself? thought Glad. But instead she said – *fair enough*. This is her measured, judicially minded parry to every little trauma Sylvia kicks her way. *Fair enough*.

Glad looks at the falling snowflakes, thicker now, ghosting the branches of the oaks. The green velvet prickles the backs of her arms. She squirms uncomfortably, then settles down to concentrate, closing her eyes and straining her face muscles. Pushing her brain backward is like trying to nag a boulder uphill with a feather. She begins with something easy. Where was she when she heard the explosion? She was hiding from her mother behind one of the oaks lining the drive, fingering the bark as she is now fingering her book. The scientist's house next door, unseen behind a wall of arbor vitae, emitted a cloud of white smoke. The slate tiles from the garage roof scattered through the air like shot from a rifle, growing larger and larger as they spun towards her. A late-blooming sense of self-preservation drove her behind a tree trunk, into the front of which, a second later, two tiles thunked themselves with the sickening sound of axe-heads. Her mother emerged from the house. She noted her sunflowers, decapitated by a low-flying tile. She spied a speck of Glad's dress, protruding from behind the impaled oak.

Get in here and finish your chowder, she said angrily. Or did she? Glad honestly couldn't remember. She was only sure that her mother treated her as if she were to blame for the accident, as if Glad's availability to be freakishly killed had caused the neighbor's house to explode.

(She can imagine Sylvia asking at this point: why *really* did the house explode? And was anybody killed? But this is not the secret. Or rather these questions, the inevitability of Sylvia's literal-minded questions, discourage her from sharing this secret past of hers. Not to blame Sylvia and her pointless redirects. But to moderately blame Sylvia. Yes, indeed. If Sylvia's searching for the *why*, the why Glad is the way she is, why Sylvia has never been permitted to know her in a way that feels satisfactory to her, Sylvia must in part take responsibility.)

But returning to the flashback. Her own mother, Glad remembers, steered her into the house. Glad felt invigorated by proximity to annihilation, her head lighter for having nearly been detached, airborne – and then her mother's total inability to accurately read Glad's emotional state made her remember (she actually remembered remembering) an incident with her piano teacher who had quit the previous year.

(*Your piano teacher*, Sylvia would say skeptically, implying that, after a near-death experience and an explosion, some actual lesson might be extracted.) But soon she was remembering inside of a reminiscence (this was another reason why she'd never revealed her secret life to anyone, such an aimless tributary it was), feeling quite viscerally beneath the hands of her mother the touch of her old piano teacher, Mr Phillips. Something about Mr Phillips's sleazy availability, especially as he hovered over the keyboard with his chin practically brushing her sort-of breasts as she clunked her way through 'Greensleeves', appealed to her. Or not his availability – his stupidity. He was so certain that she was a hapless, naive girl of what – twelve? eleven? – that he could nearly brush her breasts and she wouldn't notice. That he could caress her elbow as she mutilated 'Good King Wenceslas' and she would read his attentions as teacherly.

It was a sweetly vile arrangement, everyone more or less content to behave dishonestly, until Mr Phillips came late one day, so late that Glad convinced herself that he was not coming. And thus she allowed Harold Blunt to kiss her by her back door, the door Mr Phillips used because he was a back-door sort of man. She often kissed Harold Blunt because Harold Blunt was such a far-flung outcast that no one would ever believe him if he claimed to be kissing Glad Parks practically daily. On this day that she was kissing Harold Blunt, Harold Blunt had been chasing her with a water balloon. He cornered her by her back door and, balloon held threateningly over her head, clamped his lips over hers. When Mr

Phillips found her kissing Harold Blunt, he stared at her as an adulterer might stare at his cuckolding mistress. She averted her eyes, but even so it was as if every belittling, superior thought she'd ever had about the man was broadcast over the neighborhood loudspeaker. He knew he'd been had. Harold Blunt responded by smashing the water balloon on Glad's head and running away. Glad stared at Mr Phillips through her raining-down bangs. He hardened to her in a matter of mere seconds; she was no innocent, she was just another 'Greensleeves'-mangling trollop who'd made a fool of him.

As the balloon water dripped into her eyes, she was reminded (a reminiscence inside a reminiscence inside a reminiscence) of another moment in her life, although in fact this moment was in her then-future, so how could she have 'remembered' forward from the past? Confusing, and yet this was how it happened, or rather this was how this past of hers *existed*. As an ever-shifting matrix of falsely interconnected selves. Somehow as a twelve- or eleven-year-old she remembered being sixteen, she remembered riding in the back of a rental car driven by her parents, rain sheeting down the windshield, too much for the the hairpin wipers. Their Bermuda vacation had 'turned', as her father phrased it – a hurricane loomed, the three of them had colds, her mother, an incessant liar who lied about things that shouldn't be lied about, was 'in her element', i.e. raucously miserable. When miserable she told stories that Glad herself knew to be untrue because they had happened, or rather *hadn't* happened, to her. At this moment she was telling Glad about the time she and Glad had taken the ferry to the Vineyard and Glad had tried to jump overboard. 'You loved to self-destruct in a crowd,' her mother said, forgetting that Glad had climbed atop the railing in an attempt to rescue an old lady's escaped parakeet, clinging to a porthole bolt. She'd lost her footing and slipped safely back to the deck, but not before knocking the parakeet from its perch and sending it hurtling to its death in the wake below. When the old lady approached them worriedly for a report, her mother patted the old lady's forearm and said, 'He flew away, dear.'

From that moment on the boat (which was, technically, an

anecdote inside a reminiscence inside a reminiscence inside a reminiscence), she recalled a time when, at nine, her mother calmly watched her fall out of an apple tree; at ten, when she ran over a baby vole with her bicycle, and her mother, who was poisoning voles by the thousands in her vegetable garden, called her a murderer; at twelve, when she meticulously sliced her own thumb open with a penknife and bled over her mother's silk party dress, hanging on the bedroom hook. The pattern was unrepeatable, and thus more dangerously ineffable than a single memory. The sensation felt like spinning too fast on a merry-go-round. Each fraction of a second her eyes focused on a new face in a crowd. Within seconds the face was gone, whisked to a blur, replaced by another face that would just as soon be lost.

Glad clutches her book, feeling rather sick. She finds herself recalling incidents that are technically impossible to recall, looking up from her changing table as a weeks-old infant, a miserable ball of heat and squirm observing the haggard look on her mother's face, then gradually moving forward again, each memory chain-linked only by this: all involved her mother. This is why she doesn't put much stock in so-called secrets, or the meaningfulness of untold recollections that become, in their airtight echo chambers, the supposed stuff of secrets. They are only a way to become retrospectively enraged at somebody else so that your own adult weaknesses can be tidily excused.

But even more alarming is this: the woman who appears as her mother in these memories begins to morph into a woman resembling Sylvia – thinner and more likeably imperious, but Sylvia nonetheless. And she, Glad, is nowhere to be found. Yes, a corner of the red dress she was wearing the day of the explosion protrudes from behind the tree; possibly she can even see her transparent reflection in the rainy Bermuda car window. But she is not an active participant in these recalled scenarios with the unnerving mother / Sylvia composite, she is not a person at all. She is just a psychic recorder, an eye attached to a woundable spirit.

The lights between the oaks snap on, illuminating the drive like a smuggler's runway, startling her. She is alone, isn't she? Who turned on the lights? Then Glad remembers the timer she'd had the caretaker install after her brother – a drunk – drove into a tree after dinner and blamed the dark rather than the umpteen glasses of wine he'd consumed. When inebriated, her brother took to confessing amped-up, profanity- and sex-laced versions of his childhood to a painting of their mother. The painting featured their mother as a gimlet-eyed sixteen-year-old girl, one finger encased by a bulky signet ring, both hands resting over a prop book splayed in her lap.

This painting stares at Glad from the wall to her left. The prop book's spine features a single rectangle of black; the title, though indicated by a line of white-painted switchbacks, remains maddeningly indiscernible. At just the right distance, she'd always believed, the letters would coalesce and she would be able to read the title. As a child she'd stood in front of the painting and stepped forward and backward, forward and backward, adjusting her position by fractions of inches, but no matter – the switchbacks failed to signify. What was this book her mother held for eternity? Why did it matter? Why did she need to know?

Her old frustration disentangles itself from the painting and redirects itself full-forcedly at the absent Sylvia – Sylvia whose shadow she thinks she's spotted skittering between the oaks. She wishes Sylvia would come back, if only to tell her that her 'need to know' was as pointless as Glad's need to know the title of the book in the painting. It would reveal nothing. And, what's worse, Glad's memories are not only opaque and meaningless, they are ultimately more boring than *Trouble Astern*, in which (Glad flips skimmingly ahead) people are *still* failing to die. Glad is half tempted to kill someone herself.

Why not? The sky has purpled behind the oak trees, the island indicated only by the faraway blinking of disembodied lights. The kids are still not home, and when they do return, Glad expects they will be drunk or high. It is the perfect time for a murder. She recalls the time when she'd been grounded for half the summer for dropping one of her mother's diamond studs down a heater vent.

She decided to run away with her best friend, and the two had canoed to a nearby island, pitched a tent, tried to build a campfire, and settled down to sleep before realizing that they were cut out for neither campfire-building nor tent-sleeping. At 3 am Glad's friend deposited her on the beach across from her driveway. Glad expected to be met by her angry parents, but instead the beach was spookily quiet. She walked down the drive, growing increasingly panicked by the property's creaking emptiness. She picked up a rock and cocked it overhead, planning to strike whatever bear / moose / murderer might try to attack her on the way to the house. Lamplight from the study spread like a white carpet over the lawn. Someone was awake. Her mother, no doubt.

Still terrified, she cocked the rock overhead as she opened the front door, blood thudding in her ears. She couldn't pinpoint her nervousness; was she still in danger? Or was she the source of danger? She walked through a blue room, then a hall, then to the closed door of the study. She put her hand on the knob. Once she opened the door, there was no going back. She knew this.

She turned the knob. The door opened soundlessly. From above the high back of the armchair covered in green velvet, she could see the graying head of a woman. Glad tiptoed closer, the shadow of her arm extending across the face of her mother in the painting, then rounding the corner like a snake. The woman in the chair did not move. Glad thought she could hear the sound of snoring. How pitiful, she thought. What kind of sad old woman falls asleep at night in her reading chair? What kind of person would so willingly lose control of herself like that? Angrily, Glad raised the rock higher above her head; a sense that she is acting nobly energizes her arm, causing the muscles to tingle. She is saving this person from her own pitiful dreamy tendencies. This is not an act of murder. This is a mercy killing. Just before the rock strikes the woman's temple, she looks into the window. The last thing Judge Gladys Parks-Schultz sees before she dies is the translucent reflection of her own sleeping face, her hands folded peacefully on top of a book whose title is inscrutable.

Puppy
George Saunders

Twice already Marie had pointed out the brilliance of the autumnal sun on the perfect field of corn, because the brilliance of the autumnal sun on the perfect field of corn put her in mind of a haunted house – not a haunted house she had ever actually seen but the mythical one that sometimes appeared in her mind (with adjacent graveyard and cat on a fence) whenever she saw the brilliance of the autumnal sun on the perfect etc., etc., and she wanted to make sure that, if the kids had a corresponding mythical haunted house that appeared in their minds whenever they saw the brilliance of the etc., etc., it would come up now, so that they could all experience it together, like friends, like college friends on a road trip, sans pot, ha ha ha!

But no. When she, a third time, said, 'Wow, guys, check that out,' Abbie said, 'OK, Mom, we get it, it's corn,' and Josh said, 'Not now, Mom, I'm Leavening my Loaves,' which was fine with her; she had no problem with that, Noble Baker being preferable to Bra Stuffer, the game he'd asked for.

Well, who could say? Maybe they didn't even have any mythical vignettes in their heads. Or maybe the mythical vignettes they had in their heads were totally different from the ones she had in her head. Which was the beauty of it, because, after all, they were their own little people! You were just a caretaker. They didn't have to feel what *you* felt; they just had to be supported in feeling what *they* felt.

Still, wow, that cornfield was such a classic.

'Whenever I see a field like that, guys?' she said. 'I somehow think of a haunted house!'

'Slicing Knife! Slicing Knife!' Josh shouted. 'You nimrod machine! I chose that!'

Speaking of Halloween, she remembered last year, when their cornstalk column had tipped their shopping cart over. Gosh, how they'd laughed at that! Oh, family laughter was golden; she'd had none of that in her childhood, Dad being so dour and Mom so ashamed. If Mom and Dad's cart had tipped, Dad would have given the cart a despairing kick and Mom would have stridden purposefully away to reapply her lipstick, distancing herself from Dad, while she, Marie, would have nervously taken that horrid plastic Army man she'd named Brady into her mouth.

Well, in this family laughter was encouraged! Last night, when Josh had goosed her with his Game Boy, she'd shot a spray of toothpaste across the mirror and they'd all cracked up, rolling around on the floor with Goochie, and Josh had said, such nostalgia in his voice, 'Mom, remember when Goochie was a puppy?' Which was when Abbie had burst into tears, because, being only five, she had no memory of Goochie as a puppy.

Hence this Family Mission. And as far as Robert? Oh, God bless Robert! There was a man. He would have no problem whatsoever with this Family Mission. She loved the way he had of saying 'Ho HO!' whenever she brought home something new and unexpected.

'Ho HO!' Robert had said, coming home to find the iguana. 'Ho HO!' he had said, coming home to find the ferret trying to get into the iguana cage. 'We appear to be the happy operators of a menagerie!'

She loved him for his playfulness – you could bring home a hippo you'd put on a credit card (both the ferret and the iguana had gone on credit cards) and he'd just say 'Ho HO!' and ask what the creature ate and what hours it slept and what the heck they were going to name the little bugger.

In the back seat, Josh made the *git-git-git* sound he always made when his Baker was in Baking Mode, trying to get his Loaves into the oven while fighting off various Hungry Denizens, such as a Fox with a distended stomach; such as a fey Robin that would improbably carry the Loaf away, speared on its beak, whenever it had succeeded in dropping a Clonking Rock on your Baker – all of which Marie had learned over the summer by studying the Noble Baker manual while Josh was asleep.

And it had helped, it really had. Josh was less withdrawn lately, and when she came up behind him now while he was playing and said, like, 'Wow, honey, I didn't know you could do Pumpernickel,' or 'Sweetie, try Serrated Blade, it cuts quicker. Try it while doing Latch the Window,' he would reach back with his non-controlling hand and swat at her affectionately, and yesterday they'd shared a good laugh when he'd accidentally knocked off her glasses.

So her mother could go right ahead and claim that she was spoiling the kids. These were not spoiled kids. These were *well-loved* kids. At least she'd never left one of them standing in a blizzard for two hours after a junior-high dance. At least she'd never drunkenly snapped at one of them, 'I hardly consider you college material.' At least she'd never locked one of them in a closet (a closet!) while entertaining a literal ditchdigger in the parlor.

Oh, God, what a beautiful world! The autumn colors, that glinting river, that lead-colored cloud pointing down like a rounded arrow at that half-remodeled McDonald's standing above I-90 like a castle.

This time would be different, she was sure of it. The kids would care for this pet themselves, since a puppy wasn't scaly and didn't bite. ('Ho HO!' Robert had said the first time the iguana bit him. 'I see you have an opinion on the matter!')

Thank you, Lord, she thought, as the Lexus flew through the cornfield. You have given me so much: struggles and the strength to overcome them; grace, and new chances every day to spread that grace around. And in her mind she sang out, as she sometimes did when feeling that the world was good and she had at last found her place in it, 'Ho HO, ho HO!'

Callie pulled back the blind.

Yes. Awesome. It was still solved so *perfect.*

There was plenty for him to do back there. A yard could be a whole world, like her yard when she was a kid had been a whole world. From the three holes in her wood fence she'd been able to

see Exxon (Hole One) and Accident Corner (Hole Two), and Hole
Three was actually two holes that if you lined them up right your
eyes would do this weird crossing thing and you could play Oh My
God I Am So High by staggering away with your eyes crossed,
going, 'Peace, man, peace.'

When Bo got older, it would be different. Then he'd need his
freedom. But now he just needed not to get killed. Once they found
him way over on Testament. And that was across I-90. How had
he crossed I-90? She knew how. Darted. That's how he crossed
streets. Once a total stranger called them from Hightown Plaza.
Even Dr Brile had said it: 'Callie, this boy is going to end up dead
if you don't get this under control. Is he taking the medication?'

Well, sometimes he was and sometimes he wasn't. The meds
made him grind his teeth and his fist would suddenly pound down.
He'd broken plates that way, and once a glass tabletop and got four
stitches in his wrist.

Today he didn't need the medication because he was safe in the
yard, because she'd fixed it so *perfect*.

He was out there practicing pitching by filling his Yankees helmet
with pebbles and winging them at the tree.

He looked up and saw her and did the thing where he blew a kiss.

Sweet little man.

Now all she had to worry about was the pup. She hoped the lady
who'd called would actually show up. It was a nice pup. White,
with brown around one eye. Cute. If the lady showed up, she'd
definitely want it. And if she took it, Jimmy was off the hook. He'd
hated doing it that time with the kittens. But if no one took the
pup he'd do it. He'd have to. Because his feeling was, when you
said you were going to do a thing and didn't do it, that was how
kids got into drugs. Plus, he'd been raised on a farm, or near a farm
anyways, and anybody raised on a farm knew that you had to do
what you had to do in terms of sick animals or extra animals – the
pup being not sick, just extra.

That time with the kittens, Jessi and Mollie had called him a
murderer, getting Bo all worked up, and Jimmy had yelled, 'Look,

you kids, I was raised on a farm and you got to do what you got to do!' Then he'd cried in bed, saying how the kittens had mewed in the bag all the way to the pond, and how he wished he'd never been raised on a farm, and she'd almost said, 'You mean near a farm' (his dad had run a car wash outside Cortland), but sometimes when she got too smart-assed he would do this hard pinching thing on her arm while waltzing her around the bedroom, as if the place where he was pinching was like her handle, going, 'I'm not sure I totally heard what you just said to me.'

So, that time after the kittens, she'd only said, 'Oh, honey, you did what you had to do.'

And he'd said, 'I guess I did, but it's sure not easy raising kids the right way.'

And then, because she hadn't made his life harder by being a smart-ass, they had lain there making plans, like why not sell this place and move to Arizona and buy a car wash, why not buy the kids 'Hooked on Phonics', why not plant tomatoes, and then they'd got to wrestling around and (she had no idea why she remembered this) he had done this thing of, while holding her close, bursting this sudden laugh / despair snort into her hair, like a sneeze, or like he was about to start crying.

Which had made her feel special, him trusting her with that.

So what she would love, for tonight? Was getting the pup sold, putting the kids to bed early, and then, Jimmy seeing her as all organized in terms of the pup, they could mess around and afterward lie there making plans, and he could do that laugh / snort thing in her hair again.

Why that laugh / snort meant so much to her she had no freaking idea. It was just one of the weird things about the Wonder That Was Her, ha ha ha.

Outside, Bo hopped to his feet, suddenly curious, because (here we go) the lady who'd called had just pulled up?

Yep, and in a nice car, too, which meant too bad she'd put 'Cheap' in the ad.

★

Abbie squealed, 'I love it, Mommy, I want it!', as the puppy looked up dimly from its shoebox and the lady of the house went trudging away and one-two-three-four plucked up four *dog turds* from the rug.

Well, wow, what a super field trip for the kids, Marie thought, ha ha (the filth, the mildew smell, the dry aquarium holding the single encyclopedia volume, the pasta pot on the bookshelf with an inflatable candy cane inexplicably sticking out of it), and although some might have been disgusted (by the spare tire *on the dining-room table*, by the way the glum mother dog, the presumed in-house pooper, was dragging its rear over the pile of clothing in the corner, in a sitting position, splay-legged, a moronic look of pleasure on her face), Marie realized (resisting the urge to rush to the sink and wash her hands, in part because the sink had *a basketball in it*) that what this really was was deeply sad.

Please do not touch anything, please do not touch, she said to Josh and Abbie, but just in her head, wanting to give the children a chance to observe her being democratic and accepting, and afterward they could all wash up at the half-remodeled McDonald's, as long as they just please please kept their hands out of their mouths, and God forbid they should rub their eyes.

The phone rang, and the lady of the house plodded into the kitchen, placing the daintily held, paper-towel-wrapped turds *on the counter.*

'Mommy, I want it,' Abbie said.

'I will definitely walk him like twice a day,' Josh said.

'Don't say "like",' Marie said.

'I will definitely walk him twice a day,' Josh said.

OK, then, all right, they would adopt a white-trash dog. Ha ha. They could name it Zeke, buy it a little corncob pipe and a straw hat. She imagined the puppy, having crapped on the rug, looking up at her, going, *Cain't hep it*. But no. Had she come from a perfect place? Everything was transmutable. She imagined the puppy grown up, entertaining some friends, speaking to them in a British accent: *My family of origin was, um, rather not, shall we say, of the most respectable . . .*

Ha ha, wow, the mind was amazing, always cranking out these –

Marie stepped to the window and, anthropologically pulling the blind aside, was shocked, so shocked that she dropped the blind and shook her head, as if trying to wake herself, shocked to see a young boy, just a few years younger than Josh, harnessed and chained to a tree, via some sort of doohickey by which – she pulled the blind back again, sure she could not have seen what she thought she had –

When the boy ran, the chain spooled out. He was running now, looking back at her, showing off. When he reached the end of the chain, it jerked and he dropped as if shot.

He rose to a sitting position, railed against the chain, whipped it back and forth, crawled to a bowl of water, and, lifting it to his lips, took a drink: a drink *from a dog's bowl.*

Josh joined her at the window. She let him look. He should know that the world was not all lessons and iguanas and Nintendo. It was also this muddy simple boy tethered like an animal.

She remembered coming out of the closet to find her mother's scattered lingerie and the ditchdigger's metal hanger full of orange flags. She remembered waiting outside the junior high in the bitter cold, the snow falling harder, as she counted over and over to two hundred, promising herself each time that when she reached two hundred she would begin the long walk back –

God, she would have killed for just one righteous adult to confront her mother, shake her, and say, 'You idiot, this is your child, your child you're –'

'So what were you guys thinking of naming him?' the woman said, coming out of the kitchen.

The cruelty and ignorance just radiated from her fat face, with its little smear of lipstick.

'I'm afraid we won't be taking him after all,' Marie said coldly.

Such an uproar from Abbie! But Josh – she would have to praise him later, maybe buy him the Italian Loaves Expansion Pak – hissed something to Abbie, and then they were moving out through the trashed kitchen (past some kind of *crankshaft* on a cookie sheet, past a partial red pepper afloat *in a can of green paint*) while the lady of the house scuttled after them, saying, wait, wait, they could have it for free, please take it – she really wanted them to have it.

No, Marie said, it would not be possible for them to take it at this time, her feeling being that one really shouldn't possess something if one wasn't up to properly caring for it.

'Oh,' the woman said, slumping in the doorway, the scrambling pup on one shoulder.

Out in the Lexus, Abbie began to cry softly, saying, 'Really, that was the perfect pup for me.'

And it was a nice pup, but Marie was not going to contribute to a situation like this in even the smallest way.

Simply was not going to do it.

The boy came to the fence. If only she could have said to him, with a single look, *Life will not necessarily always be like this. Your life could suddenly blossom into something wonderful. It can happen. It happened to me.*

But secret looks, looks that conveyed a world of meaning with their subtle blah blah blah – that was all bullshit. What was not bullshit was a call to Child Welfare, where she knew Linda Berling, a very no-nonsense lady who would snatch this poor kid away so fast it would make that fat mother's thick head spin.

Callie shouted, 'Bo, back in a sec!', and, swiping the corn out of the way with her non-pup arm, walked until there was nothing but corn and sky.

It was so small it didn't move when she set it down, just sniffed and tumped over.

Well, what did it matter, drowned in a bag or starved in the corn? This way Jimmy wouldn't have to do it. He had enough to worry about. The boy she'd first met with hair to his waist was now this old man shrunk with worry. As far as the money, she had sixty hidden away. She'd give him twenty of that and go, 'The people who bought the pup were super-nice.'

Don't look back, don't look back, she said in her head as she raced away through the corn.

Then she was walking along Teallback Road like a sportwalker, like some lady who walked every night to get slim, except that she was nowhere near slim, she knew that, and she also knew that when sportwalking you did not wear jeans and unlaced hiking boots. Ha ha! She wasn't stupid. She just made bad choices. She remembered Sister Carol saying, 'Callie, you are bright enough but you incline toward that which does not benefit you.' *Yep, well, Sister, you got that right*, she said to the nun in her mind. But what the hell. What the heck. When things got easier moneywise, she'd get some decent tennis shoes and start walking and get slim. And start night school. Slimmer. Maybe medical technology. She was never going to be really slim. But Jimmy liked her the way she was, and she liked him the way he was, which maybe that's what love was, liking someone how he was and doing things to help him get even better.

Like right now she was helping Jimmy by making his life easier by killing something so he – no. All she was doing was walking, walking away from –

Pushing the words *killing puppy* out of her head, she put in her head the words *beautiful sunny day wow I'm loving this beautiful sunny day so much –*

What had she just said? That had been good. *Love was liking someone how he was and doing things to help him get better.*

Like Bo wasn't perfect, but she loved him how he was and tried to help him get better. If they could keep him safe, maybe he'd mellow out as he got older. If he mellowed out, maybe he could someday have a family. Like there he was now in the yard, sitting quietly, looking at flowers. Tapping with his bat, happy enough. He looked up, waved the bat at her, gave her that smile. Yesterday he'd been stuck in the house, all miserable. He'd ended the day screaming in bed, so frustrated. Today he was looking at flowers. Who was it that thought up that idea, the idea that had made today better than yesterday? Who loved him enough to think that up? Who loved him more than anyone else in the world loved him?

Her.

She did.

Rhoda

Jonathan Safran Foer

Have a cookie. It's good for you. You know what your problem is? The problem with you is that your wife is a little too, let me put it this way, she's intelligent. I hope you don't mind me saying that. I'm not telling you you should be married to someone ignorant, which has been my experience. I'm only telling you it's better to have a life partner who is somewhat unintelligent. I know things. She doesn't feed you because she's too intelligent. It's none of my business.

It's good to see you, from what my eyes can make out. You could be a super-model! It brings a smile to my heart. Your brother is growing a bosom, but you still have all of your hair. Lemme touch it. That beautiful, thick hair. You're so handsome! So gorgeous! My joy! It doesn't matter. You should be healthy. That beautiful, Kennedy hair. Enjoy your hair in good health.

Have a drink. Lemme get you a soda from the basement. Go get a soda from the basement. Drink something. Please. For me. I have some orange juice in the freezer. I could warm it up for you. A slice of bread? What would make you happy? You're gorgeous, I'm telling you. Gorgeous! Just looking at you, I'm forgetting every-thing. I got a tea bag I used last night that's still good.

I don't want to take your time, but I'll tell you about my heart scan, and then we'll do your business. I'll tell you about your cousin Daniel. The machine is recording? Your cousin Daniel called from Brown University last night. The machine heard that? He's making A's in all of his classes, and two B's, and he's going with a girl, not a schwartze. She's studying – how do you call it? I can't remember the American word. Anyway, I don't know what are her grades, but her family lives in Philadelphia and belongs to Congregation Beth David, which is Reform, but that's none of my business. Her father is a lawyer, and I don't know what is her mother. This girl,

183

she's a little overweight, but otherwise very nice. They've been on four dates. Over there there's a picture of her on the refrigerator.

I'll tell you about the first schwartze I ever saw. Because I was thinking about Daniel, I was thinking about schwartzes, from the one he went with briefly. Remember that one? It was his life, and that's why I didn't say anything, but it was my death. I told him, You can fall in love with anyone if you have to, so why mix blood?

When we came over, in 1950, I didn't even know there was such a thing as a schwartze. Nobody told me. Nobody sat me down and said, By the way, there's schwartzes. I got off the boat, and I'm holding your mother, and your grandfather, your real grandfather, was looking for our bags, and the first person I saw was a schwartze. I thought maybe he had a disease. What did I know from schwartzes? And then I saw another schwartze, and then another schwartze. It was like seeing green people to me, only with longer arms and bigger lips and, you know, the schwartze-hair. Then, when we opened the grocery store on K Street, that was in a neighborhood that was full of schwartzes. Only schwartzes, I'm telling you, because that was all we could afford at the time. If there had been coins smaller than pennies we would have saved those, too. Money can't buy you happiness, but happiness isn't everything. My only point is I don't have any problem with schwartzes, but I'm happy for Daniel that he found a nice girl, even Reform. Lemme give you a piece of free advice: if you have to wash your hands after going to the bathroom, you did something wrong. I'm talking about number one only.

We knew all the schwartzes that robbed us, and this will be the last thing that I say about schwartzes. They would come in with masks on, and once I said, 'Jimmy, if you need money, just ask. You don't have to make a scene.' And so he asked, 'Can I have some money, Rhoda?' I told him not over my dead body. He made to put the gun at my head. I told him I had to refrigerate some cold items, so if he was gonna shoot me he should do it already. He said, 'I'm not messing around, Rhoda.' I said, 'Who's messing around?' The schwartzes loved us, to tell you the truth.

I'll tell you about my heart scan. Have a cookie. I'm not gonna take your time. I got a popsicle in the basement. Your father told me they didn't find anything. I'm begging you, drink a little Coke for me. I'm not gonna push. I didn't ask him to double-check. Not even a sip for your grandmother? When the news is that your heart scan is OK, you believe it. I hope you don't mind me saying that. You're perfect, but I know things. I told Dr Horowitz that I've had the kind of life that Spielberg could make a pretty good movie about. He said he was honored to know me. I'm gonna make to send him a card. I wonder when he'll be fifty, 'cause I got one of those cards around. Can you drive me to the bank when we're done with this? And then to the supermarket? And then to the other supermarket? And then to the bakery? There's a nice Oriental girl there who gives me a discount. She has an ugly face, but that's her business. Your father would put me in a taxi. He thinks I'm cheap, but he's the cheap one, because he won't come out here to get me. It's good to hold your money in a fist. If you don't believe me, no one will.

And anyway – you wanna fresh sliced tomato? – some mornings I don't feel any pain. I'm not complaining. There are worse things than pain. How could I be unhappy with that hair of yours! You probably didn't appreciate this, but when you were a baby I used to sing you to sleep with the American alphabet. By the time you were two you could speak better than me. That was my Nobel Prize! You were my diamonds and pearls! My revenge!

But then I have pains, I gotta tell you. They start at the ends of my fingernails, almost like little animals biting me. Eventually they spread somewhat. And in the chest. The scan said nothing is wrong, but you think that makes any difference to my chest? Who do you trust? My body isn't good anymore. What did I expect? With my hemorrhoids it's OK to be sitting or standing. But even sitting is difficult when I'm making a number two. Can I ask you a personal question? Do you have a list of the serial numbers of your savings bonds? I know it's none of my business.

How's your brother? He's doing great. I think he's great. I think he's somewhat lonely. He calls me every day. He thinks I'm lonely. When's he gonna get married? He needs to meet a nice girl. Such a brain! There's nothing he can't do. He's losing his hair, but that doesn't matter. Everyone gets older. Whenever I think about you I go crazy. You're so gorgeous! I'm somewhat lonely in this house. I've taken your time. The machine's working? You think I'm dying. It's OK. You don't have to say anything. I know. I know you all have been lying to me. When they bring out the tape recorder, it's either because of a school project or because you're dying. And you graduated from Princeton University nine years ago.

So I need you to promise me something. Come close. Somewhat closer. You know that your grandmother never asks anything of you, but this is one thing. I beg you, no matter what happens, no matter where you go in life or how many millions you make, no matter anything, I *beg* you: never buy a German car.

So wha'd'ya wanna talk about?

Soleil
Vendela Vida

'Well, looks like Soleil is coming to visit,' Gabrielle's mother announced, hanging up the phone. Gabrielle was setting the kitchen table while her father concocted a dressing for the salad.

'You mean S-s-s-soleil,' Gabrielle's father said.

'Stop it,' her mother said, but laughed. The orange lipstick she'd worn all day at the bank had faded, leaving only a few vertical stripes in the dry creases of her lips.

'S-s-s-s-stop it,' her father said.

Gabrielle's mother turned to her. 'Soleil stutters.'

The name Soleil began to collect random anecdotes and attributes from the corners of Gabrielle's memory. Wasn't Soleil her mother's college roommate in Hawaii? Gabrielle had seen a photo of this woman waterskiing while wearing a top hat – it made her look six feet tall and, Gabrielle thought, like a magician.

'Is she still a hand model?' Gabrielle's father asked.

Gabrielle suddenly remembered something else. 'Didn't she used to go through your garbage?'

'No, she's not a hand model. And it was just one time with the garbage,' her mother said dismissively. 'She said it was work-related.' Gabrielle's mom shared a smile with her husband. 'I think, if anything, she had a little crush on your dad.'

Gabrielle didn't look at her father – his reaction, she was sure, would embarrass or upset her, though she couldn't say why. She hoped he wouldn't stutter again; Gabrielle felt sorry for Soleil, and for anyone with any sort of impediment. Her best friend at school, Melanie, had only four toes on her right foot, and Gabrielle had recently been successful at convincing her she could wear sandals.

'Where's Soleil living now?' Gabrielle's father asked.

'You know, I don't know,' her mother said slowly. 'Maybe Texas? A part of me thinks she's still going from friend to friend, man to man.'

'Huh,' her father said, sounding impressed.

Soleil arrived at the house on a Tuesday evening in July. Gabrielle's parents were both at work, but they had instructed her to let Soleil in and to give her fresh towels and a snack.

'Hi, beauty,' Soleil said when she stepped inside the door. 'You look just like Jack.'

Jack was Gabrielle's father. She didn't know how Soleil had reached such a verdict so quickly.

'Thank you,' Gabrielle said, and studied Soleil's face. Her eyes were the color of nutmeg, and her wide cheeks were so flat they seemed pressed up against glass. Her hair was brown and straight, except at the bangs, where it hung in a series of 'S's.

'Wow, there are more mirrors here than at Versailles,' Soleil said, looking around her. 'Your parents are rich.'

It felt like a judgment. 'Not really,' Gabrielle said.

'What do you mean, not really?'

'I don't know,' Gabrielle said. 'I've never really thought about it.'

'Well, the fact that you've never thought about it means you're rich.'

Gabrielle knew they weren't rich and she knew they weren't poor. She wanted her parents to come home so Soleil wouldn't talk about money. 'The only place it's appropriate to talk about money is at the bank,' Gabrielle's mother often said. Maybe that's why she worked at one; she was senior teller.

'There's food in the kitchen,' Gabrielle offered. 'My parents won't be home for another couple hours.'

'Are you kidding?' Soleil said.

Gabrielle didn't know what she would be kidding about.

'I'm not going to waste a night in Santa Cruz waiting in a

kitchen. Let's go and get a drink. Is there an Italian restaurant nearby?'

They sat at the bar. Gabrielle had never been so aware of her posture and her age. She was eleven. She wore a lavender corduroy dress with a long-ribboned bow at the collar. Soleil wore a camisole under a burgundy velvet blazer, a small electronic heart pinned to her left lapel. The heart blinked its red light twice in rapid succession, and then paused before blinking twice again.

Within minutes, two men were standing near their bar stools. Gabrielle went to the bathroom and returned to find one of them had taken her seat. She tapped Soleil on the shoulder. 'The hostess said because I'm underage we have to sit at a table,' she lied. She pointed to one by the window with room for only two.

'Nice meeting you gentlemen,' Soleil said, and inexplicably saluted them before following Gabrielle to the table. Soleil ordered appetizers as main courses, and over dinner she talked to Gabrielle about marriage (she had been married at twenty-four, for three months), the merits of reading Ayn Rand (just by pronouncing her first name correctly you could intimidate people, Soleil claimed), and the serious decision as to whether or not a woman should ever start using deodorant.

'I never use it and smell me,' Soleil instructed.

'Now?'

'No,' she said, rolling her eyes, 'ten years from now.'

Gabrielle leaned in toward her.

'What do I smell like?'

'Sweet, like strawberries,' Gabrielle said. It was true, she did smell like strawberries, but she also smelled like sweat. Not in a bad way, and not in a French way – there was just a trace of something fermenting.

'You're sweet, too, Bree,' Soleil said. Over dinner, Soleil had started calling her Bree without ever asking if she liked it. She did like it.

'Thank you, you're too kind,' Gabrielle said, sounding like some-one else.

'That took longer than I thought it would,' Soleil said, as they walked hurriedly back to Gabrielle's house. 'How mad will your parents be?'

'Beats me,' Gabrielle said. 'We don't have guests that often.'

Gabrielle's parents were sitting in the kitchen, facing each other. Her mother's foot was propped on her father's lap. He was massaging it.

'Oh, there you are,' Gabrielle's mother said, as though she was addressing a pair of misplaced sunglasses that had turned up.

'Long day on her feet,' Gabrielle's father explained, replacing the shoe on his wife's foot.

'Look at you,' Soleil said. 'Cinderella.'

Gabrielle's mother smiled and stood and Soleil hugged her. Then Soleil hugged Gabrielle's father for several seconds longer, until he broke away.

'Welcome,' her father rasped.

Gabrielle's mother looked Soleil up and down. 'You look great,' she said.

'Thank you, Dorothy,' Soleil said. Everyone waited a moment for Soleil to return the compliment. She didn't.

In the living room, Gabrielle's father and mother sat in the loveseat, like they always did, side by side and facing the same direction, as though riding in a bus. Gabrielle and Soleil sat in arm-less chairs. Gabrielle's father was wearing a blazer, and Gabrielle could not understand why; he owned a furniture store and never dressed up for work. He poured each of the women a large glass of wine.

Gabrielle's father called the Thai restaurant and announced his order so loudly no one else could talk. Soleil adjusted her rings so their stones were centered on her long fingers.

Gabrielle's father hung up the phone and looked at Gabrielle: 'I got the rice you like.'

'I heard,' Gabrielle wanted to say, but didn't. Things already seemed tense.

'Can I ask you a favor?' Gabrielle's mother said to Soleil.

'Anything,' Soleil said, discouragingly.

'Can you turn off that pin?'

'This? It's my heartlight.'

There was a pulsating silence.

'Turn off your heartlight,' Gabrielle's father sang. He was prone to quick bouts of song.

'I just get panic attacks sometimes from blinking lights,' Gabrielle's mother said.

'It happened last week,' Gabrielle added. 'With an ambulance.'

Soleil didn't turn off the light. Instead she removed her blazer. Her camisole was thin, the pattern of her lace bra easy to see. Her oddly triangular breasts were medium sized, and her arms, Gabrielle noticed, were hairless, waxed. Gabrielle's father's eyes stayed fixed on Soleil's forehead.

The adults talked about Hawaii but they didn't talk about what everyone had been doing in the years after they left Hawaii. When Gabrielle's father disappeared into the kitchen to get more wine, Gabrielle's mother leaned forward. 'I don't want to embarrass you, Sol, but how did you get rid of your stutter?'

The edges of Soleil's wide lips trembled for a second, and then were still. 'What stutter?' she said.

'You used to complain about it. You used to say you were going to go to an institute in Minnesota where they worked with people with your –'

'I think you're confusing me with someone else,' Soleil said.

Gabrielle's father returned to the room with a bottle of wine in each hand. 'Red or white?' he asked, holding them up like trophy fish.

'Red,' said both women simultaneously, and then laughed.

'See, Gabrielle,' Soleil said. 'Your mother and I aren't *that* different.'

Gabrielle's mother looked as though she was about to disagree, but instead she took a final sip of her wine, and held her glass up to her husband for a refill.

'Do you think they're natural around each other?' Soleil asked, later that night. Soleil was staying in Gabrielle's room, in her bed, while Gabrielle slept on the trundle below. There was no guest bedroom in Gabrielle's house – further proof, she thought, that they weren't rich.

'What do you mean?' Gabrielle asked.

'I mean, do you think they're putting on a show?'

'For who?' Gabrielle asked. Then corrected herself. 'For whom?'

'For me. Trying to show how *in love* they are.' Soleil said 'in love' like a boy in Gabrielle's class did, with a guttural emphasis on 'love'.

'No,' Gabrielle said truthfully. 'They're acting the way they always do.'

Soleil fell asleep a few seconds later, as if only the whiff of scandal or deception could keep her awake. Gabrielle sat up watching her, the light of the moon sliding through the blinds, striping their bodies. Soleil slept on her stomach with one leg falling off the side of the bed, like she had been poisoned.

By Thursday it was clear Soleil was bored. She walked around the house balancing water glasses on her head and turning the flowers in vases upside down. 'I learned this from a florist in Denmark,' she said. She had learned everything – candle-making, Tai Chi, Portuguese – somewhere else.

That afternoon, Soleil decided she and Gabrielle and Gabrielle's mother should go to Lake Tahoe for the weekend, for what she called a 'girls' getaway.' She had a friend there, a woman named Katy, who owned a café on the water.

'You'll like Katy,' Soleil said, now sunning herself in the back yard. 'She's a free spirit. Very sexy.'

Gabrielle was sitting on the grass next to her. 'So all your friends are pretty then? My mom, Katy . . .' Gabrielle was testing. She knew her mother was attractive. 'Your mother's a good-looking woman,' her father was fond of saying. Then he would break into song.

But Soleil hesitated. Gabrielle immediately regretted saying anything. 'Your mother's cute,' she said, wrinkling her nose, 'but she's not *sexy*. She just doesn't have that vibe about her.'

'I can't leave Jack alone for the weekend,' Gabrielle's mother said flatly that evening. They were sitting in the living room and Soleil had laid out her Lake Tahoe plan.

'Well, he can come too,' Soleil said.

'I don't think he can,' Gabrielle's mother said, without offering an explanation. She appeared beleaguered by Soleil's visit, and had gone to bed early every night since Soleil had arrived.

The plan seemed dead to both Soleil and Gabrielle's mother, but Gabrielle found herself desperate to save it.

'Can I go with Soleil even if you don't come?' she said.

'Let me think about it,' said her mother.

Her father entered the room, waltzing with an imaginary partner. 'What's going on?' he said, looking at their faces. He stopped waltzing. 'A summit meeting?'

Gabrielle told him about the trip, and appealed to him to let her go. 'I want to see how self-sufficient a single woman has to be,' Gabrielle said. She had picked this up from Mrs Terwilliger, her history teacher, who was newly divorced.

'Sounds like a good plan,' her father said.

Gabrielle smiled at him, and forced herself not to look at her mother. She stared at her father even as she heard her mother stand up and walk out of the room, the sound of her practical heels heavy on the hardwood floor.

'Dorothy?' Gabrielle's father called after her.

'I'm just checking the fridge to see what I'm going to make us for dinner,' her mother replied, but Gabrielle could tell by her footsteps that she was in the study, not the kitchen.

★

On Friday, Soleil dressed in a snug white shirt and white pants, no panty lines visible. Or maybe, Gabrielle thought, she wasn't wearing any. Soleil was big-boned and tall, and the whiteness of her outfit highlighted her size. She looked like a small ship.

Soleil's van was also white. 'I hate this car,' Soleil said, as they pulled out onto the road. 'But I need it for my job.'

Gabrielle realized she didn't know what Soleil did for a living. She didn't seem like someone with a job.

'What is your profession?' Gabrielle asked.

Soleil laughed. 'Why so formal? Do you work at passport control?'

Gabrielle shook her head. Soleil laughed again.

'I'm an antique collector,' Soleil said. 'I specialize in Coca-Cola merchandise.'

'Oh, like old bottles,' Gabrielle said, too quickly.

'Not *bottles*,' said Soleil, and Gabrielle saw the skin around her eyes tighten. 'I collect beautiful mirrors and old vending machines from the twenties and sell them at Coca-Cola conventions. You wouldn't believe how many people are into that stuff. When I lived in Minnesota I made a really good living.'

'You lived in Minnesota?' Gabrielle asked.

'Yes,' Soleil said, and Gabrielle detected a slight stutter, a repetitive 'Y'.

A billboard advertised an upcoming refreshment center called the Nut House. 'I think I have a few ex-lovers who live there,' Soleil said. Then she turned to Gabrielle and grew very serious. 'If anyone ever invites you to Belgium, please promise me you won't go.'

'Did something bad happen there?' Gabrielle asked.

'No, nothing happens there. That's the point. It's Belgium.'

'Oh shit,' Soleil called out, waking Gabrielle.

'What?'

'We're almost at Katy's house, and we didn't go grocery shopping. That's what you do when you stay with someone – you stock their fridge.'

'Oh,' Gabrielle said, though Soleil hadn't brought anything into her mother's kitchen.

They stopped at a grocery store designed to look like a log cabin. Soleil pulled out a shopping cart.

'Do we need a cart?' Gabrielle said.

'We're buying for the whole weekend,' Soleil said. 'The wine alone would break your arm.'

In the far corner of the cart, Gabrielle saw something brown. Square. A wallet. She gave it to Soleil, who quickly flipped through it. 'Henry Sam Stewart,' she read. 'Blue eyes, overweight. Lives on the Nevada side of Lake Tahoe.' She looked at Gabrielle. 'You know what that means?'

'He's a gambler.'

'No,' Soleil said. 'It means you'll get a big reward.'

'Because he's a gambler.'

'No, stop with that. Because, Bree, he lives far away. He'll be really grateful we made the effort.'

Soleil bought a map along with the groceries, and they climbed back into the van and set out to find Henry Sam Stewart. The wallet sat between them in the cup-holder.

'How much do you think we'll get?'

'*You*'ll get it. You found the wallet,' Soleil said. 'And I would say fifty dollars would be a fair reward.'

'Fifty!' Gabrielle didn't know what she'd spend it on. Maybe a present for Soleil.

It took over an hour to get to the house of Henry Sam Stewart.

'We're getting close,' Soleil said as they turned off onto his street. 'Hand me my lipstick.'

Soleil could apply lipstick – she was partial to a dark plum shade – to her wide, thin lips without looking. Gabrielle tucked her hair behind her ears.

'Hmm,' Soleil said, as they pulled up to the house.

'What?' said Gabrielle, but she saw what Soleil was seeing. The house was falling apart. They got out of the car. The wooden stairs leading up to the front door creaked like they might collapse beneath their feet.

Henry Sam Stewart answered the door. He looked remarkably like the picture on his driver's license. He was wearing shiny blue jogging shorts and a white turtleneck. 'What can I do you for?' he said.

'Hi,' Soleil said. 'We have something we think you might want.'

'I can see that,' he said, staring at Soleil's chest.

'Your wallet,' Soleil said. She held out her hand toward Gabrielle. Gabrielle placed the wallet in Soleil's hand, and she put it in Henry's.

'Jeez. Where'd you find this?' he said. 'I didn't know it was gone.'

'At the grocery store,' Soleil said.

'On the other side of the lake,' Gabrielle added.

'Well, thank you, ladies,' he said. He tipped an imaginary hat toward them.

'That's it?' Soleil said.

'You want to come in?' he said, his eyes on Soleil's mouth.

'No, thank you. I'm just wondering where this young woman's reward money is.'

'Reward?'

'Yes, that's customary when someone returns a wallet.'

'I don't like beggars,' Henry Sam Stewart said. 'I might have given you a reward if you hadn't been so pushy.'

'The reward's not for me. It's for Bree here. An eleven-year-old girl who's too honest to take the money from your cheap wallet.'

'Well, thank you, Bree,' he said to Gabrielle. 'Sometimes kindness is its own reward. Maybe your mother hasn't learned that yet?'

Gabrielle looked at Soleil. Her hair was wild, her eyes glazed over. She looked beautiful.

'Do you know what kind of lesson you're teaching this child?' Soleil said. 'I can't stand people who think they don't owe people anything. What kind of world is that? I'm going to write down her

198

address here and when you become a decent person, I want you to send her the reward money.'

Soleil took a piece of paper from her purse. 'What's your address again, Bree?' she asked.

Henry Sam Stewart shut the door on them.

Soleil clenched her fists, tilted her head to the sky and mimed screaming. Then, composing herself, she wrote down Gabrielle's address and pushed the paper under the door.

'Moron!' she yelled.

Gabrielle first saw Katy through the window of her living room. She was bent over, brushing the underside of her blonde hair furiously, as if beating a rug.

Soleil knocked on the door and walked in. Katy turned upright, her face pink, her hair enormous.

Soleil and Katy kissed each other on both cheeks, and then Katy kissed Gabrielle on both cheeks. Katy had the air of being pretty, with a small nose and a golden tan.

'We brought groceries,' Soleil said.

'You're always the best guest,' Katy said.

'I'm always a guest.'

'Not settled down yet?'

'Catch me if you can.'

'Gin and tonic?'

Soleil answered by clapping her hands together.

'Bree?' Soleil said. 'You want a Coke?'

An hour later Soleil and Katy were drunk. Rod Stewart sang from the record player, and Katy and Soleil were trying on clothes and dancing around the green-carpeted living room. Gabrielle sat on an itchy plaid couch. Her job, the women said, was to rate their outfits. They were taking a dinner-boat cruise on the lake that night.

'We want to look like a million bucks,' Soleil said.

'It's a fine line,' Katy added, 'between looking like a million and looking like you cost a million.'

Soleil laughed. If this was a joke, Gabrielle didn't get it. Soleil and Katy modeled outfits that would have been right for an opera; they modeled outfits that would have looked appropriate on the moon. Finally, they settled on dresses that required them to adjust their bra straps with safety pins. Katy's hemline was high; Soleil's neckline was low; watching them standing side by side, Gabrielle thought they looked like they'd gone crazy with a pair of scissors.

'Now it's time for us to dress *you* up,' Katy said.

'It sure is,' said Soleil and pulled Gabrielle into Katy's bedroom with a force that scared her.

Katy followed them, and she and Soleil stood looking at Gabrielle's reflection in the closet mirror.

'You would look so good in ivory,' Katy said. 'Your skin is so olive-y.'

'It's her dad's skin,' Soleil said.

'Jack?' Katy said to Soleil in a hushed tone.

Soleil nodded, and closed her lips tight. Gabrielle watched the women's faces, and saw the stern look that passed between their inebriated eyes. She felt as though she'd swallowed a stone and it was making its way to her stomach.

'If I were you, I'd show off those legs,' Katy said, turning her attention back to Gabrielle. 'I have just the thing.'

Katy pulled an ivory slip out of her dresser drawer and draped it over Gabrielle's head.

Soleil examined her with one eye closed. 'I think you need a piece of jewelry so it's clear you're wearing it as a dress. Hold on a second.' She left the room.

'You look like a picture of a girl I saw in a French painting!' Katy said. 'It was a painting of a girl who dropped her pail . . .'

'Here,' Soleil said, returning with something in her hand. The electronic heart pin. Soleil pinned it onto the slip, right above Gabrielle's real heart, and turned it on.

'What do you think?' Katy said.

Gabrielle stared at the mirror. She couldn't focus on anything she was seeing – she saw a ghostly shape and a flashing light. She didn't look anything like herself, and, at the moment, this was an enormous relief. The stone in her throat was gone.

'Look at her,' Soleil said. 'She's fucking gorgeous.'

'I wish,' Katy said, 'I wish I had a pail for her to carry.'

They arrived at the boat late.

'We were about to leave without you,' said the man taking their tickets. He was wearing jeans with suspenders. Gabrielle looked around: all of the passengers appeared to have come straight from a game of tennis or a hike. Was anyone else wearing lingerie as a dress?

A horn blew and the boat started moving. Soleil and Katy waved at the two or three people on the shore as though they were setting out on a two week cruise.

At the dinner buffet, Gabrielle moved quickly, passing over food she liked, anything to expedite getting to a chair and not bringing attention to her clothing. She spotted an empty table at the back of the dining room and suggested they sit there.

'What? No, this one's better,' Katy said, pointing to a table near the dance floor. Two men wearing patterned shirts were already there.

'It's your lucky night,' Katy said to them, as she and Soleil and Gabrielle sat down. Their names were Keith and Peter, and both had firm handshakes and deep tans. As the sun set and the cold came over the lake, Gabrielle wished she had brought a jacket. Her mother would have packed one for her.

A man with a sombrero came by each table with roses. Keith bought one and gave it to Gabrielle.

'Really?' she said. Keith's eyes, she noticed, were like her dad's – green and feline.

'Yes, a rose for a budding rose,' Keith said.

'It smells amazing,' she said, though it didn't.

Soleil looked at Keith intently, as if he were a full glass of wine she didn't want to spill.

After dinner Keith danced with Soleil, and Peter danced with Katy. Gabrielle moved to the edge of the boat and stared out at the water, at the moon. Everything looked the way it was supposed to look; nothing looked spectacular. She held the rose upright, twisting the stem in her fingers.

'You're too young for flowers,' a voice said. Gabrielle turned to find two elderly women dressed in rain gear.

'You should be at least fifteen before you get flowers,' the other woman said. 'Especially a rose.'

Gabrielle wanted to look at the sky and mime screaming, the way Soleil had done. But she couldn't fake a scream. She couldn't say a word. Instead, she walked away from the women and sat down at the table, watching the dance floor, and for the first time in her life she believed she understood the word *regret*. She regretted not saying anything to the women, she regretted the prickling of pride she'd felt when Henry Sam Stewart had mistaken Soleil for her mother.

The song ended, and Peter had his hands on Katy's shoulders, steering her in the direction of their table. Soleil was pulling Keith by the hand, and he mockingly resisted. 'Moon River' began playing and he tried to twirl her. She twirled twice and Keith dipped her. It was the wrong sort of dance for the music, but Soleil looked thrilled. For a moment Gabrielle had an image of Soleil at age eight, riding a bike down a hill, her hands in the air.

Peter and Katy sat down clumsily at the table, and Peter slid a glass of water toward Katy and removed the glass of wine that sat in front of her.

'What'd the grandmas want?' Soleil asked, as she and Keith joined them. Gabrielle recounted what they had said.

'Some people . . .' Soleil said. Everyone waited for her to finish her sentence, but instead she refolded her napkin.

'Hags!' said Keith. 'People get so jealous when they're not getting any.'

'Well, Bree's not exactly getting any,' Katy said. 'And they're still jealous.'

Everyone laughed, and Gabrielle made herself laugh too. If she didn't, the joke would be on her.

By the time the boat docked, it was clear alcohol had affected Katy and Soleil in different ways: Soleil was loud and Katy was quiet. Peter and Keith drove them all back to Katy's house. Gabrielle was anxious for the night to be over, for Katy and Soleil to wake up the next day, sober and casually dressed.

'Goodnight, thank you,' Gabrielle said, when Keith's car pulled up to Katy's house.

Everyone laughed again.

'They're coming in for a night-cap,' Soleil explained, as Keith circled around the car, opening each of the doors.

They all spilled into Katy's living room, which, Gabrielle thought, suddenly seemed too small to accommodate their limbs, their smells, their shrieks. The adults must have felt the same way: within a minute Keith and Soleil pretended to race each other into the guest room; Peter and Katy stumbled into the master bedroom.

Gabrielle slept on the itchy living room couch. Or tried to – noises filled the house. Doors closed and toilets flushed and a bed squeaked like a child's toy.

In the morning Gabrielle woke to Soleil's voice coming from the porch: 'Are you sure I can't make you waffles?'

Gabrielle sat up and looked out of the open window.

'That's okay, doll,' Keith said. 'I gotta skedaddle.'

At the edge of the porch, Keith kissed Soleil hard and then walked toward his car. Without turning around, he lifted his hand and waved goodbye.

Soleil came back into the house. Her eyes met Gabrielle's. 'W-w-w-what are you l-l-l-looking at?' she said.

Gabrielle ran out the door and followed Keith to his car. 'Excuse me,' she called out.

'Well, look who's awake,' Keith said, putting on his seatbelt. The top button on his shirt was hanging from a long thread. 'Good morning, camper.'

'Do you have a piece of paper and a pen?'

He opened his glove compartment and handed her a pad of paper and a pen. At the top of the pad was a cartoon drawing of a man skiing. The caption said: 'Life is good.'

'Here's where I live,' Gabrielle said, as she wrote down her address. 'Soleil will be home with my family after the weekend.'

'Okay, partner,' Keith said, taking the paper from her like it was a receipt. 'I thank you kindly.'

Gabrielle had no idea why he was talking the way he was. She walked back to the house, where Soleil was standing in the living room. It was clear she'd been watching through the window. 'What were you doing?' she said, accusingly.

'Giving him my address.'

'What?' Soleil said.

'So he knows where to find you this week.'

'W-w-why would he need to find me?'

'To apologize,' Gabrielle said.

Soleil tightened her fingers into fists. She mimed screaming at the ceiling, she mimed screaming at the wall. Finally, she turned to Gabrielle with eyes that were strangely dull, dark as wet soil. 'Oh, grow up,' she said.

Roy Spivey
Miranda July

Twice I have sat next to a famous man on an airplane. The first man was Jason Kidd of the New Jersey Nets. I asked him why he didn't fly first class, and he said that it was because his cousin worked for United.

'Wouldn't that be all the more reason to get first class?'

'It's cool,' he said, unfurling his legs into the aisle.

I let it go, because what do I know about the ins and outs of being a sports celebrity? We didn't talk for the rest of the flight.

I can't say the name of the second famous person, but I will tell you that he is a Hollywood heart-throb who is married to a starlet. Also, he has the letter V in his first name. That's all – I can't say anything more than that. Think espionage. OK, the end – that really is all. I'll call him Roy Spivey, which is almost an anagram of his name.

If I were a more self-assured person I would not have volunteered to give up my seat on an overcrowded flight, would not have been upgraded to first class, would not have been seated beside him. This was my reward for being a pushover. He slept for the first hour, and it was startling to see such a famous face look so vulnerable and empty. He had the window seat and I had the aisle, and I felt as though I were watching over him, protecting him from the bright lights and the paparazzi. Sleep, little spy, sleep. He's actually not little, but we're all children when we sleep. For this reason, I always let men see me asleep early on in a relationship. It makes them realize that, even though I am five feet eleven, I am fragile and need to be taken care of. A man who can see the weakness of a giant knows that he is a man indeed. Soon small women make him feel almost fey – and, lo, he now has a thing for tall women.

Roy Spivey shifted in his seat, waking. I quickly shut my own eyes, and then slowly opened them, as if I, too, had been sleeping. Oh, but he hadn't quite opened his yet. I shut mine again and right away opened them, slowly, and he opened his, slowly, and our eyes met, and it seemed as if we had woken from a single sleep, from the dream of our entire lives. Me, a tall but otherwise undistinguished woman; he a distinguished spy, but not really, just an actor, but not really, just a man, maybe even just a boy. That's the other way that my height can work on men, the more common way: I become their mother.

We talked ceaselessly for the next two hours, having the conversation that is specifically about everything. He told me intimate details about his wife, the beautiful Ms M. Who would have guessed that she was so troubled?

'Oh, yeah, everything in the tabloids is true.'

'It is?'

'Yeah, especially about her eating disorder.'

'But the affairs?'

'No, not the affairs, of course not. You can't believe the 'bloids.'

''Bloids?'

'We call them 'bloids. Or tabs.'

When the meals were served it felt as if we were eating breakfast in bed together, and when I got up to use the bathroom he joked, 'You're leaving me!'

And I said, 'I'll be back!'

As I walked up the aisle, many of the passengers stared at me, especially the women. Word had traveled fast in this tiny flying village. Perhaps there were even some 'bloid writers on the flight. There were definitely some 'bloid readers. Had we been talking loudly? It seemed to me that we were whispering. I looked in the mirror while I was peeing and wondered if I was the plainest person he had ever talked to. I took off my blouse and tried to wash under my arms, which isn't really possible in such a small bathroom. I tossed handfuls of water toward my armpits and they landed on my skirt. It was made from the kind of fabric that turns much darker when it is wet. This was a real situation I had got myself into. I acted quickly, taking off my skirt and soaking the whole thing in the sink, then wringing it out and putting it back on. I smoothed it out with my hands. There. It was all a shade darker now. I walked back down the aisle, being careful not to touch anyone with my dark skirt.

When Roy Spivey saw me he shouted, 'You came back!'

And I laughed and he said, 'What happened to your skirt?'

I sat down and explained the whole thing, starting with the armpits. He listened quietly until I was done.

'So were you able to wash your armpits in the end?'

'No.'

'Are they smelly?'

'I think so.'

'I can smell them and tell you.'

'No.'

'It's OK. It's part of showbiz.'

'Really?'

'Yeah. Here.'

He leaned over and pressed his nose against my shirt.

'It's smelly.'

'Oh. Well, I tried to wash it.'

But he was standing up now, climbing past me to the aisle and rummaging around in the overhead bin. He fell back into his seat dramatically, holding a pump bottle.

'It's Febreze.'

'Oh, I've heard about that.'

'It dries in seconds, taking odor with it. Lift up your arms.'

I lifted my arms and with great focus he pumped three hard sprays under each sleeve.

'It's best if you keep your arms out until it dries.'

I held them out. One arm extended into the aisle and the other arm crossed his chest, my hand pressing against the window. It was suddenly obvious how tall I was. Only a very tall woman could shoulder such a wingspan. He stared at my arm in front of his chest for a moment, then he growled and bit it. Then he laughed. I laughed, too, but I did not know what this was, this biting of my arm.

'What was that?'

'That means I like you!'

'OK.'

'Do you want to bite me?'

'No.'

'You don't like me?'

'No, I do.'

'Is it because I'm famous?'

'No.'

'Just because I'm famous doesn't mean I don't need what everyone else needs. Here, bite me anywhere. Bite my shoulder.'

He slid back his jacket, unbuttoned the first four buttons on his shirt and pulled it back, exposing a large, tanned shoulder. I leaned over and very quickly bit it lightly, and then picked up my *SkyMall* catalogue and began reading. After a minute he re-buttoned himself and slowly picked up his copy of *SkyMall*. We read like this for a good half-hour.

During this time I was careful not to think about my life. My life was far below us, in an orangey-pink stucco apartment building. It seemed as though I might never have to return to it now. The salt of his shoulder buzzed on the tip of my tongue. I might never stand in the middle of the living room and wonder what to do next. I sometimes stood there for up to two hours, unable to generate enough momentum to eat, to go out, to clean, to sleep. It seemed unlikely that someone who had just bitten and been bitten by a celebrity would have this kind of problem.

I read about vacuum cleaners designed to suck insects out of the air. I studied self-heating towel racks and fake rocks that could hide a key. We were beginning our descent. We adjusted our seat backs and tray-tables. Roy Spivey suddenly turned to me and said, 'Hey.'

'Hey,' I said.

'Hey, I had an amazing time with you.'

'I did, too.'

'I'm going to write down a number and I want you to guard it with your life.'

'OK.'

'This phone number falls into the wrong hands and I'll have to get someone to change the number and that is a big headache.'

'OK.'

He wrote the number on a page from the *SkyMall* catalogue and ripped it out and pressed it into my palm.

'This is my kid's nanny's personal line. The only people who call her on this line are her boyfriend and her son. So she'll always answer it. You'll always get through. And she'll know where I am.'

I looked at the number.

'It's missing a digit.'

'I know, I want you to just memorize the last number, OK?'

'OK.'

'It's four.'

We turned our faces to the front of the plane and Roy Spivey gently took my hand. I was still holding the paper with the number, so he held it with me. I felt warm and simple. Nothing bad could ever happen to me while I was holding hands with him, and when he let go I would have the number that ended in four. I'd wanted a number like this my whole life. The plane landed gracefully, like an easily drawn line. He helped me pull my carry-on bag down from the bin; it looked obscenely familiar.

'My people are going to be waiting for me out there, so I won't be able to say goodbye properly.'

'I know. That's all right.'

'No, it really isn't. It's a travesty.'

'But I understand.'

'OK, here's what I'm going to do. Just before I leave the airport I'm going to come up to you and say, "Do you work here?"'

'It's OK. I really do understand.'

'No, this is important to me. I'll say, "Do you work here?" And then you say your part.'

'What's my part?'

'You say, "No."'

'OK.'

'And I'll know what you mean. We'll know the secret meaning.'

'OK.'

We looked into each other's eyes in a way that said that nothing else mattered as much as us. I asked myself if I would kill my parents to save his life, a question I had been posing since I was fifteen. The answer always used to be yes. But in time all those boys had faded away and my parents were still there. I was now less and less willing to kill them for anyone; in fact, I worried for their health. In this case, however, I had to say yes. Yes, I would.

We walked down the tunnel between the plane and real life, and then, without so much as a look in my direction, he glided away from me.

I tried not to look for him in the baggage-claim area. He would find me before he left. I went to the bathroom. I claimed my bag. I drank from the water fountain. I watched children hit each other. Finally, I let my eyes crawl over everyone. They were all not him, every single one of them. But they all knew his name. Those who were talented at drawing could have drawn him from memory, and everyone else could certainly have described him, if they'd had to, say, to a blind person – the blind being the only people who wouldn't know what he looked like. And even the blind would have known his wife's name, and a few of them would have known the name of the boutique where his wife had bought a lavender tank top and matching boy-shorts. Roy Spivey was both nowhere to be found, and everywhere. Someone tapped me on the shoulder.

'Excuse me, do you work here?'

It was him. Except that it wasn't him, because there was no voice in his eyes; his eyes were mute. He was acting. I said my line.

'No.'

A pretty young airport attendant appeared beside me.

'*I* work here. *I* can help you,' she said enthusiastically.

He paused for a fraction of a second and then said, 'Great.' I waited to see what he would come up with, but the attendant glared at me, as if I were rubbernecking, and then rolled her eyes at him, as if she were protecting him from people like me. I wanted to yell, 'It was a code! It had a secret meaning!' But I knew how this would look, so I moved along.

That evening I found myself standing in the middle of my living-room floor. I had made dinner and eaten it, and then I had an idea that I might clean the house. But halfway to the broom I stopped on a whim, flirting with the emptiness in the center of the room. I wanted to see if I could start again. But, of course, I knew what the answer would be. The longer I stood there, the longer I had to stand there. It was intricate and exponential. I looked like I was doing nothing, but really I was as busy as a physicist or a politician. I was strategizing my next move. That my next move was always not to move didn't make it any easier.

I let go of the idea of cleaning and just hoped that I would get to bed at a reasonable hour. I thought of Roy Spivey in bed with Ms M. And then I remembered the number. I took it out of my pocket. He had written it across a picture of pink curtains. They were made out of a fabric that was originally designed for the space shuttle; they changed density in reaction to fluctuations of light and heat. I mouthed all the numbers and then said the missing one out loud. 'Four.' It felt risky and illicit. I yelled, 'FOUR!' And moved easily into the bedroom. I put on my nightgown, brushed my teeth, and went to bed.

Over the course of my life I've used the number many times. Not the telephone number, just the four. When I first met my husband, I used to whisper 'four' while we had intercourse, because it was so painful. Then I learned about a tiny operation that I could have to enlarge myself. I whispered 'four' when my dad died of lung cancer. When my daughter got into trouble doing God knows what in Mexico City, I said 'four' to myself as I gave her my credit-card number over the phone. Which was confusing – thinking one number and saying another. My husband jokes about my lucky number, but I've never told him about Roy. You shouldn't underestimate a man's capacity for feeling threatened. You don't have to be a great beauty for men to come to blows over you. At my high-school reunion I pointed out a teacher I'd once had a crush on, and by the end of the night this teacher and my husband were wrestling in a hotel parking garage. My husband said that it was about issues of race, but I knew. Some things are best left unsaid.

This morning, I was cleaning out my jewelry box when I came upon a little slip of paper with pink curtains on it. I thought I had lost it long ago, but, no, there it was, folded underneath a dried-up carnation and some impractically heavy bracelets. I hadn't whispered 'four' in years. The idea of luck made me feel a little weary now, like Christmas when you're not in the mood.

I stood by the window and studied Roy Spivey's handwriting in the light. He was older now – we all were – but he was still working. He had his own TV show. He wasn't a spy anymore; he played the father of twelve rascally kids. It occurred to me now that I had missed the point entirely. He had wanted me to call him. I looked out the window; my husband was in the driveway, vacuuming out the car. I sat on the bed with the number in my lap and the phone in my hands. I dialed all the digits, including the invisible one that had shepherded me through my adult life. It was no longer in service. Of course it wasn't. It was actually preposterous for me to have thought that it would still be his nanny's private line. Roy Spivey's children had long since grown. The nanny was probably working for someone else, or maybe she had done well for herself – put herself through nursing school or business school. Good for her. I looked down at the number and felt a tidal swell of loss. It was too late. I had waited too long.

I listened to the sound of my husband beating the car mats on the sidewalk. Our ancient cat pressed itself against my legs, wanting food. But I couldn't seem to stand up. Minutes passed, almost an hour. Now it was starting to get dark. My husband was downstairs making a drink and I was about to stand up. Crickets were chirping in the yard and I was about to stand up.

Cindy Stubenstock

A. M. Homes

Cindy Stubenstock is trading up – at a recent auction, she flipped two Gurskys, an early Yuskavage and her husband's bonus, and was on the phone later live from London topping the bidding on a rare Picasso etching that looked 'beautiful over the fireplace'.

'Gives whole new meaning to up in smoke,' the cryptic British auctioneer mumbled under his breath.

Now Cindy and her Scarsdale sisterhood – aka the ladies who linger at lunch – are on the tarmac at Teterboro, wandering from plane to plane.

'There never used to be so many,' one says.

'Do we really need to take two planes?'

'Well, there are six of us and I just hate being crowded, and besides, what if I want to leave early?' They all nod, knowing the feeling.

'Just the thought of being trapped somewhere makes me nervous – does anyone have anything – a little blue, a little yellow?'

'I've got Ativan.'

'I'll take it.'

'We're going to Miami, it's not the rain forest, not the darkest Peru, you can get a commercial flight out any time you want – just call JetBlue,' one of the women says.

And the others look at her horrified, aghast, shocked that she can even say the words 'commerical flight' so easily, without pause. Flying private is one of the perks of being who they are; it's why they put up with so much. NO airport security.

'Soon that will change, they're going to have scented dogs everywhere.'

'It's not scented dogs, it's sniffing dogs. Scented dogs would be like soaps, verbena, vanilla, Macchu Picchu.'

'Why do you always correct me? I'm an old woman – leave me alone.'

'You're forty-eight, you're not old.'

And then there is silence.

'Which plane is it? He keeps trading them in. I never know which one is ours.'

'She calls it trading them in – he calls it fractional ownership,' one of the women whispers.

'G4, Falcon, Citation, Hawker, Learjet – remember when they were all "Learjets"? Remember when the word "Learjet" used to mean something?'

'Who is that bald man in the wheelchair? He looks familiar – do I know him from somewhere?'

'Is it Philip Johnson?'

'Philip Johnson died two years ago.'

'Really?'

'Yes.'

'That's so sad.'

'Is that Yul Brynner?'

'It's someone with cancer.'

'What's he doing here?'

'He's getting an Angel Flight back to where he lives,' one of the ground crew says. 'People donate flights – for those who are basically too sick to travel.'

'Oh, I don't think I could ever do that – I couldn't have a sick person on the plane – I mean, what about the germs?'

'I don't normally think of cancer as contagious.'

'You never know.' She runs her hand through her hair – which she gels in the morning with Purell – prophylactically.

The group divides; Sally Stubenstock, the society sister of Cindy, and her 'friend' Tasha, the yoga instructor, go on their own plane. 'We want alone time,' Tasha says.

'She wants to downward dog me at 10,000 feet,' Sally says.

'It's gross,' someone whispers.

'What do you care – they're not asking you to do it.'

'Women kiss better than men – it's a fact.'

'How would you know?'

'Because one night Wallis (the weird woman who has a man's last name for her first name) Wallingford planted one right on me.'

'Was she drunk?'

'I don't think so. It felt very good.'

'Better than a man?'

She nods. 'Softer, more thoughtful.'

Cindy Stubenstock puts her fingers in her ears and hums loudly and sings, 'This is something I don't want to know. I don't want to know-oh-o.'

The conversation stops. They climb aboard. The pilot pulls the door closed and locks it. The women take their seats and then take other seats. They move around the cabin until they are comfortable. They put all their fur coats together on one seat.

'Where are you staying? The Raleigh, the Delano, the Biltmore?'

'I'm staying at Pinkie and Paulie's.'

'Really?' Cindy asks.

Her friend nods.

'I've never stayed at someone's house,' Cindy Stubenstock confesses. 'How do you do it? When you get there – what do you do – how do you check in?'

'It's like going for dinner or cocktails – you knock on the door and hopefully someone answers.'

'Does someone take your bag? Do you tip them? And what if you can't sleep – what if you need to get up and walk around? Do you have your own bathroom – I can't stay anywhere without my own bathroom even with my husband. If you pee, do you flush? What if someone hears you? It just seems so stressful.'

'When you were growing up, did you ever go on a sleepover?'

'Just once – I got homesick and my father came and got me – it seemed like the middle of the night but my parents always used to tease me – it was really only about 11 pm.'

'When I go to someone's house – I bring a clean sheet,' another woman chimes in.

'And remake the bed?'

'No, I wrap myself in it – do you know how infrequently most blankets are laundered – including hotel blankets – think of the hundreds of people who have used the same blanket.'

'What's for dinner tonight?' someone asks.

'A big corned-beef sandwich. That's what I go to Miami for – Wolfie's. I get sick every time – but I can't resist. It reminds me of my grandparents – and of my childhood.'

'I thought you were a vegetarian?'

'I am.'

'By the way, whatever happened with that Brice Marden painting you were trying to buy?'

'It's still pending – we haven't completed our interview.'

'Some of the galleries now have a vetting process – there is a company that will interview potential buyers, about everything from their assets, hobbies and intentions for their collections – and once that's done – they schedule a home visit.'

'Exactly, we still need the home visit, but CeeCee has been so busy with the re-do that she won't let anyone from the gallery into the house.'

'What are you doing?'

'We're going from day to night – swapping all the black paintings for white, we sold the Motherwells and the Stills and now she's bringing in Ryman, Richter and a Whiteread bookcase.'

'Sounds great – very relaxing – no color at all.'

'I heard you bought a Renoir in London.'

'We had a good year. I like it so much I want to fuck it.'

'When we got our Rothko – we had sex on the floor in front of it.'

'Those were the days . . .'

'And when we got the Pollock.'

'Well, you got that really big one.'

'Fairly big.'

'The room is so large that it's all relative.'

'Do you remember that time we were all on that art tour and they let us touch a few things – Stanley stroked the *Birth of Venus* and got excited?'

'Stanley, the seeing-eye horse – or Stanley your husband?'

'Stanley, the human. He was mortified.'

'I thought it was cute.'

'Where is Stanley this weekend?'

'Stan, the man, is playing golf and Stanley the seeing-eye horse is having his teeth cleaned this weekend and so the society gave me a stick.' She holds up a white cane. 'Like this is going to do me any good. I've got a docent meeting me for the fair – a young curator.'

'God, I remember when Stanley, the horse, tried to mount the stuffed pony that your parents sent your son . . .'

'We were all there – the Hanukah party.'

'It plagued my son – the sight of Stanley trying to "hop" the pony. He said hop – instead of hump – it was soo sweet.'

'There are people who are into that – stuffed animals. "Plushies" they call them.'

'I have no idea what you're talking about.'

'Sex parties!'

'And they invite stuffed animals?'

'Speaking of animal behaviour – are we preparing for takeoff yet?'

'I'm sorry, Mrs Stubenstock,' the pilot says. 'There's military aircraft in the area – and the airspace has been closed down.'

'Oh now, is the President coming to town again? Thank God we're leaving – he always blocks traffic.'

'We're third in line for takeoff as soon as the air opens.'

'We usually fly on Larry's plane, he redecorates it for every flight. Different art work depending on where we're going. Something for LA, something for Basel, something for Venice.'

'That's because he's trying to sell you something.'

'No, I don't think so. We always ask, and he tells us that whatever it is we want – it's not for sale.'

'That's how he does it – that's how he gets you.'

'Did you hear about Sarah and Steve's Warhol worries?'

'No, what?'

'Turns out their Warhols aren't Warhols – they're knockoffs like cheap Louis Vuittons on Canal Street.'

'But they have Polaroids of Andy signing the pictures. Andy and Steve standing together while Andy signed them.'

'Apparently he would sign anything, but that didn't mean that he made it.'

'They were banking on those pictures – literally.'

'Well, you know what they say – you should never be dependent on your art collection to do anything for you that you can't do for yourself.'

'Are you invited to the VIP party?'

'The VIP parties aren't the good parties – there are no invites for the real parties, you just have to know where they are.'

'I told Susie that I would go to the dinner but only as long as I didn't have to sit next to an artist – I never know what to say to them.'

'I always ask them if they're starving – and they never get it,' Cindy says. 'I've noticed that most of the younger artists are carnivores. Remember when artists only ate things like sprouts and bags of "greens" that they carried with them? Now they all eat meat – it's all post-Damien.'

'Like how?'

'Don't you remember – Damien Hirst's first big piece was really very small . . . It was a piece of steak that his father had choken on. Young Damien gave his father the Heimlich maneuver and the steak came flying out of his mouth and he could breathe again. Damien saved the piece of steak and put it in a jar of formaldehyde that he got from the school and called it *I Saved My Father's Life – Now What Will Become of Us.*'

'I never heard that story.'

Cindy Stubenstock shrugs. 'It's famous. I think the piece is in the Saatchi collection in London.'

Theo
Dave Eggers

Long had the poets pointed to the steep green hills around the village, noting in prose and song that with their irrational curves, their ridges rising and falling just so, the low mountains resembled the shapes of sleeping men and women. Most practical people thought the poets were pushing it a bit too far, poets being poets, but then something new happened one morning, just after most of the humans, about five or so hundred in that village at that time, were finishing their breakfast and dressing their children.

The land shook. Homes, all of them built with stone and barley, trembled and soon collapsed. Animals stampeded, birds dropped from the sky, and in the midst of the chaos, the first giant emerged. The soft green rolls of the hillside gave way to a pale shoulder, an arm of twisted muscle, a waist, a hip. In minutes the hill had become a man, a colossal man everywhere striped with dirt and grass, rubbing his eyes. He sat up, his legs akimbo before him, and he began chuckling. He wiped the grass from his bald head and his shoulders, swept the dirt from his stomach, and, while he did so, he laughed softly, nodding to himself as if something long mysterious was finally clear.

His name was Soren.

Soon after, a mile or so away, the ground rattled again. The villagers looked south and saw another hillside rise. It was a range that the poet Eythor had called The Woman, and all the humans who watched the giant emerge from it thought, Too bad Eythor is dead, he would have loved to see this. This hill became a woman, as tall as Soren, and she rose from the earth covered in oil and soot, hair long and wild. Like Soren, she was greatly amused and only somewhat surprised by her awakening. She wiped her eyes clean and picked stones from between her aristocratic toes.

This was Magdelena.

By the time Theo, the last giant, arose from the hill closest to the human settlements, his arrival caused little notice. He was shorter than the other two giants, with a ruddy complexion and wide-set eyes. While Soren and Magdelena were tall, of noble and sinewy form, Theo had long arms but short legs, a flat face and narrow shoulders. But no one noticed the differences between them, at least not on that day. Already four people were dead, crushed under falling debris. There were tears, prayers, wails of men and women. Already the landscape had been broken, recast. Already the sky was brown with dust, and it was into this day, full of misery and regret and rebirth, that Theo awakened.

In those first days, Theo could only sit, dazed from thousands of years of sleep, and watch Magdelena. Yes, Magdelena. At first she was nothing much to see. Her hair gray with ash, her body covered in mica and sandstone, she barely looked female. But then, after some hours sitting, blinking and grinning, she rose and walked to the ocean, dove from the chalky cliffs into the surf below, and emerged a woman. A woman of many enticements.

Theo was not the only one who noticed. The tinies below seemed endlessly fascinated by her. Groups of young men gathered on the mountain called Toto-Hesker, at the level of her chest, and watched her wash herself in the waterfall; they were willing to watch her do anything. Most important to them was that a 200-foot woman had 35-foot breasts, ten-foot-tall lips, legs eighty feet high.

Where had she come from? Theo wondered. She was not awake the last time he was conscious. Or perhaps she had been. He knew that his memory was not good. His memory of this land bore little resemblance to what lay around him now. Hadn't it been colder before? Had there not been a glacier between those peaks? He had no great faith in his memory, and yet he was almost certain that this region had changed. The villagers called it Northland now, and the name seemed apt enough. They were not far from the top of the earth, and during the summer, the days stretched elliptically, morning meeting morning. That much had not changed.

But certain variations were beyond debate. When he last roamed this land, there had not been the tiny people – built like himself but so very small. They had almost certainly appeared in the intervening epochs. Once they knew that the giants meant them no harm, as he lay down to sleep and his ears were close to earth, they asked Theo about other nearby mountains, foothills. Are they all like you? Will they awaken? Theo tried to reassure them, but he could not lie. He didn't know who was a mountain and who was not a mountain. So much was unfamiliar to him. There had not been so many deer, so many moose and bears. He remembered being very hungry when he last walked these hills; he had been forced to eat trees, turtles, whales. Now there was plenty of delicious food, easily caught. Soren and Magdelena could eat whole forests of animals at any meal, carelessly tossing the bones on rooftops. Theo could get by on a few deer, maybe a few dozen rabbits, eating everything whole, leaving no mess. Afterward he would enjoy a long drink from the white-cold runoff of the snow-capped peak to the west.

Magdelena could be mine, Theo thought, foolishly, in the first hours and days. After all, the three of them spoke together, ate together. There was equanimity, he thought. Those first days were good days. Theo and Soren and Magdelena chased herds of buffalo off the cliffs, ate what they needed and stored the rest in nets they hung from the tallest trees. They made fires and slept well in the valley where the bobcats chased the antelope.

Because it was he who made Magdelena laugh, Theo presumed she would be his. There were so many things that only he and Magdelena shared. Only he knew how to swim and so swam with Magdelena for hours while Soren dug massive holes for no apparent reason. Only he had a sense of rhythm, so when the villagers played their mandolin jigs he danced with Magdelena. She did so while looking at her feet and placing the fallen strands of her hair behind her ears. Theo moved with light feet, trying not to upset the buildings below, but Magdelena had no such control. She jumped, she shuffled, and stood on her hands. And though the church's roof caved when she did, no one minded. The music continued and the men above and below watched, unbreathing.

Soren did not mind. He watched Magdelena dance with Theo, and watched her swim with Theo, and never did he appear jealous. Theo almost felt bad for him. When there are two men and one woman, the math was cruel. What was the third to do? Theo did not want to think about the plight of poor Soren.

It was on the ninth day of consciousness that Theo saw them, Soren and Magdelena, standing shin-deep in a fjord where the villagers lured whales and sea lions. They were standing, talking quietly, facing each other. There was a low rolling fog that day, woolen and colorless, and it eclipsed their bodies below the waist. Still, Theo could see that below the waves of white rolling through them, their hands were touching. Her knee was bent slightly, leaning in to kiss his.

Theo was not a confrontational man. He simply took this information and walked away. While Soren and Magdelena roared and laughed and sang tuneless songs, Theo sat silently near the chalky cliffs of Toto-Mootn, eating bears, lost in thought. There he spent most of his days, alone, talking to the sea, watching the whales, waiting for the days when the moon was visible across the sky from the sun.

Soren and Magdelena came to him often, asking if he was alright, if he wanted to swim, if he wanted to dig or run or eat buffalo. He smiled to them politely and declined. I'm trying to remember this land when we were last awake, he told them, and they accepted this explanation. They wanted to know his findings when he found them, they said. They considered him a serious man and respected his privacy.

Still, there was pleasure in certain parts of a day. The first break of sun through the oval-shaped stand of pines in the flatlands to the east. A swim in the cold ocean in the afternoon. Laying on the bald peak, letting the warm rock dry his front while the sun dried his back. And yet, he did not know why he should live, why he should keep his eyes open. After a few days of near-joy, he had settled into something between life and sleep. He had seen so much. He was tired. He remained, weeks after awakening, in that period of early-morning consciousness that allows easy re-entry to dreaming. His limbs still tingled with the residue of sleep, and most days he wanted badly to allow it to overtake him again.

He decided he would leave. He thought it best to go north, to another place, to see if there were others like him, others like Magdelena. And so he rose early one morning and left, walking as quietly as he could. After all the weeks with the giants, the tinies below had learned to live with the rumbling of the earth caused when any of them moved about. He rose and woke no one, certainly not Soren and Magdelena, who by then slept side by side, unmoveable, their bodies connected in a dozen ruthless ways.

He walked north, the sun a rising friend at his side, and found that the trees dwindled as he strode. The further north he walked, the more the grass shrank away, the earth paled. Soon there was only ice, and he was cold, and he missed being near Magdelena, taken or not. After some time, each step away from her caused him ache. First a cramp in his abdomen, then a stiffness in his legs, then a headache that radiated with fervor and rhythm.

So he returned, and for a few weeks he tried to find a balance. Soren and Magdelena were happy to see him, and he enjoyed his time with her, with Soren, together and alone. Magdelena still swam with him, and they laughed as they had before, and they danced, Magdelena smiling at her shuffling feet. Making her laugh gave him something like pleasure, though in the moments of quiet he felt he was on the moon, frozen and dark. Soren, so confident, allowed it all, was sincere in his friendship with Theo, who to him posed no threat.

So this is how they lived. For some time Theo, like a tree living in the shadow of taller trees, found a way to live off reflected light.

He had found a sort of equilibrium, but equilibrium is temporary and fickle. One day he discovered that he was not satisfied. He wanted the full attention of love.

So again he walked. He knew that to walk too far would cause him more pain than he could bear, so he limned the perimeter within which he could journey each day – far enough to be alone but not so far that he was lonely. He walked over glaciers and through unknown craters, he bathed in cold black lakes, and he caught flocks of birds from the sky and ate them with something like hunger.

One day, while traveling west, through an ocher-colored canyon, he saw something ahead, something odd. There was a low mountain range rising from a flat tundra. It was a solitary thing, without foothills, without reason. All around was plain flat earth and so he felt himself drawn to it. He jogged through the canyon, his eyes set upon it. He crawled up from the canyon and ran to this exceptional mountain laying in the middle of the level dusty land.

He walked around the range, examining it from every angle. This was something very strange. He knew enough about his own kind to know that a giant hibernating here in the middle of nowhere was unlikely, but not impossible. He lay next to it, and it was about as long as he was. There was a rise that could be a shoulder, a dip where a waist might be, a bundle at the end that could be ankles crossed. His pulse raced, his breath shortened. He stood up, walking around the outcropping, guessing at legs, toes, a head.

It could be, he thought.

He sat with the mountain for a day and a night, examining it closely, to be sure that the form of a giant – a woman – could be waiting below its rough surface of rock and snow.

Feeling foolish at first, he began to talk to her. When did you go to sleep? he asked. There was no answer. He asked more questions, thinking that she might awaken if the right query struck her as demanding an answer. He asked her name, and began to guess. Marketa? Dora? Siobhan? He settled on Amaranth, and began his sentences with Oh, Amaranth! and he surprised himself by growing comfortable hearing his own voice. He talked to her in verse, in song. He wondered, he speculated, he named clouds for her. He confided in her, telling her the best ways to eat bears, and about Magdelena and Soren, referring to them only as friends, a couple that he knew some other place, some other time.

After a few weeks or months he wondered if he should return to them, to tell them where he had gone, whom he had met. But when he stood to do so, he found it harder, so much harder than before, when leaving Magdelena's perimeter. To be more than a few steps away from Amaranth caused him vertigo. His legs were not what they once were, and leaving her seemed a foolish act. There was doubt here, yes, for he could not be certain that Amaranth was a woman and not a mountain. But he would gladly trade this uncertainty – small, he thought, for he was sure she was she – for what he had left with Magdelena and Soren – the certainty of pain.

He sat again and decided that he would perhaps visit the others another day.

Sleep came like the lightest rain. He felt it on his skin, something like a mist, numbing his legs, his arms. He could not recall how the last long sleep had begun, but what was happening now to him seemed familiar and right. A sigh escaped him as he lay next to Amaranth, Amaranth so warm, the contour of his side echoing hers, a valley forming between them. His eyes grew heavy and could no longer stay open to the world. When he closed them, though, he still saw her shape. Her constancy kept him strong and allowed him rest.

Perkus Tooth
Jonathan Lethem

I first met Perkus Tooth in an office. Not an office where he worked, though I was confused about this at the time. (Which is itself hardly an uncommon situation, for me.)

This was in the headquarters of the Criterion Collection, on 52nd Street and Third Avenue, on a weekday afternoon. I'd gone there to record a series of voiceovers for one of Criterion's high-end DVD reissues, a 'lost' 1950s *film noir* called *The City is a Maze*. My role was to play the voice of that film's director, the late émigré auteur Von Leopold Dresden. I would read a series of statements culled from Dresden's interviews and articles, as part of a supplemental documentary being prepared by the curatorial geniuses at Criterion, a couple of whom I'd met at a dinner party. In drawing me into the project they'd supplied me with a batch of research materials, which I'd browsed unsystematically, and a working version of their reconstruction of the film, in order for me to glean what the excitement was about. It was the first I'd heard of Dresden, so this was hardly a labor of passion. But the enthusiasm of buffs is infectious, and I liked the movie. I no longer considered myself a working actor. This was the only sort of stuff I did anymore, riding the exhaust of my former and vanishing celebrity, the smoky half-life of a child star. An eccentric favor, really. Anyway, I was curious to see the inside of Criterion's operation. In those days, with Janice far away, I lived too much on the surface of things, parties, gossip, assignations in which I was the go-between or vicarious friend. Workplaces fascinated me, the places where Manhattan's veneer gave way to what I liked to think of as the practical world.

I recorded Dresden's words in a sound chamber in the technical wing of Criterion's crowded, ramshackle offices. In the room outside the chamber, where the sound man sat giving me cues through a headset, a restorer also sat peering at a screen and guiding a cursor with a mouse, diligently erasing celluloid scratches and blots, frame by digital frame, from the bare bodies of hippies cavorting in a mud puddle. I was told he was restoring *I Am Curious (Yellow)*. Afterwards I was retrieved by the producer who'd enlisted me, Susan Eldred. It had been Susan and another colleague I'd met at the dinner party – unguarded, embracing people with a passion for a world of cinematic minutiae, for whom I'd felt an instantaneous homely affection. Susan led me to her office, a cavern with one paltry window and shelves stacked with VHS tapes, more lost films petitioning for Criterion's rescue. Susan shared her office, it appeared. Not with the colleague from the party, but another person. He sat beneath the straining shelves, notebook in hand, gaze distant. It seemed too small an office to share. The glamour of Criterion's brand wasn't matched by these scenes of thrift and improvisation I'd gathered from my behind-the-scenes glimpse, but why should it have been? No sooner had Susan introduced me to Perkus Tooth and given me an invoice to sign than she was called away for some consultation elsewhere.

He was, that first time, in what I would soon learn to call one of his 'ellipsistic' moods. Perkus Tooth himself later supplied that descriptive word: ellipsistic, derived from *ellipsis*. A species of blank interval, a nod or fugue in which he was neither depressed nor undepressed, not struggling to finish a thought or begin one. Merely between. Pause button pushed. I certainly stared. With Tooth's turtle posture and the utter slackness of his being, his receding hairline and antique manner of dress – trim-tapered suit, ferociously wrinkled silk with the shine worn off, over moldering tennis shoes – I could have taken him for elderly. When he stirred, his hand brushing the open notebook page as if taking dictation with an invisible pen, and I read his pale, adolescent features, I guessed he was in his forties – still ten or fifteen years wrong, though Perkus Tooth had been out of the sunlight for a little while. He was in his thirties, no older than me. I'd mistaken him for old because I'd taken him for important. He now looked up and I saw one undisciplined hazel eye wander, under its calf-lid, toward his nose. That eye wanted to cross, to discredit Perkus Tooth's whole sober aura with a comic jape. His other eye ignored the gambit, trained on me.

'You're the actor.'

'Yes.'

'So, I'm doing the liner notes. For *The City is a Maze*, I mean.'

'Oh, good.'

'I do a lot of them. *Prelude to a Certain Midnight* . . . *Recalcitrant Women* . . . *The Unholy City* . . . *Echolalia* . . .'

'All *film noir*?'

'Oh, gosh, no. You've never seen Herzog's *Echolalia*?'

'No.'

'Well, I wrote the liner note, but it isn't exactly released yet. I'm still trying to convince Eldred –'

Perkus Tooth, I'd learn, called everyone by their last name. As though famous, or arrested. His mind's landscape was epic, dotted with towering figures like Easter Island heads. At that moment Susan Eldred returned.

'So,' he said to her, 'have you got that tape of *Echolalia* around here somewhere?' He cast his eyes, the good left and the meandering right, at her shelves, the cacophony of titles scribbled on labels there. 'I want him to see it.'

Susan raised her eyebrows and he shrank. 'I don't know where it is,' she said.

'Never mind.'

'Have you been harassing my guest, Perkus?'

'What do you mean?'

Susan Eldred turned to me and collected the signed release, and we made our farewell. Then, as I got to the elevator, Perkus Tooth hurried through the sliding door to join me, crushing his antique felt hat onto his crown as he did. The elevator, like so many others behind midtown façades, was tiny and rattletrap, little more than a glorified dumb-waiter – there was no margin for pretending we hadn't just been in that office together. Bad eye migrating slightly, Perkus Tooth gave me a lunar look, neither unfriendly nor apologetic. Despite the vintage costume, he wasn't some dapper retrofetishist. His shirt's collar was grubby and crumpled; the green-gray sneakers like mummified sponges glimpsed within a janitor's bucket.

'So,' he said again. This 'so' of Perkus's – his habit of introducing any subject as if in resumption of earlier talk – wasn't in any sense coercive. Rather, it was as if Perkus had startled himself from a daydream, heard an egging voice in his head and mistaken it for yours. 'So, I'll lend you my own copy of *Echolalia*, even though I never lend anything. Because I think you ought to see it.'

'Sure.'

'It's a sort of essay film. Herzog shot it on the set of Morrison Roog's *Nowhere Near*. Roog's movie was never finished, you know. *Echolalia* documents Herzog's attempts to interview Marlon Brando on Roog's set. Brando doesn't want to give the interview, and whenever Herzog corners him Brando just parrots whatever Herzog's said . . . you know, echolalia . . .'

'Yes,' I said, flummoxed, as I would so often later find myself, by Tooth's torrential specifics.

'But it's also the only way you can see any of *Nowhere Near*. Morrison Roog destroyed the footage, so the scenes reproduced in *Echolalia* are, ironically, all that remains of the film –'

Why 'ironically'? I doubted my hopes of inserting the question. 'It sounds incredible,' I said.

'Of course you know Roog's suicide was probably faked.'

My nod was a lie. The doors opened, and we stumbled together out to the pavement, tangling at every threshold: 'You first –' 'Oops –' 'After you –' 'Sorry.' We faced one another, October mid-Wednesday Manhattan throngs islanding us in their stream. Perkus grew formally clipped, perhaps belatedly eager to show he wasn't harassing me.

'So, I'm off.'

'Very good to see you.' I'd quit using the word 'meet' long

ago, replacing it with this foggy equivocation, chastened after the thousandth time someone explained to me that we'd actually met before.

'So –' He ground to a halt, expectant.

'Yes?'

'If you want to come by for the tape . . .'

I might have been failing some test, I wasn't sure. Perkus Tooth dealt in occult knowledge, and measured with secret callipers. I'd never know when I'd crossed an invisible frontier, visible to Perkus in the air between us.

'Do you want to give me a card?'

He scowled. 'Eldred knows where to find me.' His pride intervened, and he was gone.

For a call so life-altering as mine to Susan Eldred's, I ought to have had some fine reason. Yet here I was, dialing Criterion's receptionist later that afternoon, asking first for Perkus Tooth and then, when she claimed no familiarity with that name, for Susan Eldred, spurred by nothing better than a cocktail of two parts whim and one part guilt. Manhattan's volunteer, that's me, I may as well admit it. Was I curious about *Echolalia*, or Morrison Roog's faked suicide, or Perkus Tooth's curious intensities and lulls, or the slippage in his right eye's gaze? All of it and none of it, that's the only answer. Perhaps I already adored Perkus Tooth, and already sensed that it was his friendship I required to usher me into the strange next phase of my being. To unmoor me from the curious eddy into which I'd drifted. How very soon after our first encounter I'd come to adore and need Perkus makes it awfully hard to know to what extent such feelings were inexplicably under way in Susan Eldred's office or that elevator.

'Your office mate,' I said. 'They didn't recognize his name at the front desk. Maybe I heard it wrong –'

'Perkus?' Susan laughed. 'He doesn't work here.'

'He said he wrote your liner notes.'

'He's written a couple, sure. But he doesn't *work* here. He just comes up and occupies space sometimes. I'm sort of Perkus's babysitter. I don't even always notice him anymore – you saw how he can be. I hope he wasn't bothering you.'

'No . . . no. I was hoping to get in touch with him, actually.'

Susan Eldred gave me Perkus Tooth's number, then paused. 'I guess you must have recognized his name . . .'

'No.'

'Well, in fact he's really quite an amazing critic. When I was at NYU my friends and I all used to idolize him. When I first got the chance to hire him to do a liner note I was quite in awe. It was shocking how young he was, it seemed like I'd grown up seeing his posters and stuff.'

'Posters?'

'He used to do this thing where he'd write these rants on posters and put them up all around Manhattan, these sort of brilliant critiques of things, current events, media rumours, public art. They *were* a kind of public art, I guess. Everyone thought it was very mysterious and important. Then he got hired by *Rolling Stone*. They gave him this big column, he was sort of, I don't know, Hunter Thompson meets Pauline Kael, for about five minutes. If that makes any sense.'

'Sure.'

'Anyway, the point is, he sort of used up a lot of people's patience with a certain kind of . . . paranoid stuff. I didn't really get it until I started working with him. I mean, I *like* Perkus a lot. I just don't want you to feel I wasted your time, or got you enmeshed in any . . . schemes.'

People could be absurdly protective, as if a retired actor's hours were so precious. This was, of course, a second-hand affect, a leakage from Janice's other-worldly agendas. I was famously in love with a woman who had no time to spare, not even a breath, for she dwelled in a place beyond time or the reach of any-one's Rolodex, her every breath measured out of pressurized tanks. If an astronaut made room for me on her schedule, my own prerogatives must be as crucial as an astronaut's. The opposite was true.

'Thank you,' I said. 'I'll be sure not to get enmeshed.'

Perkus Tooth was my neighbor, it turned out. His apartment was six blocks from mine, on East 84th Street, in one of those anonymous warrens tucked behind innocuous storefronts, buildings without lobbies, let alone doormen. The shop down-stairs, Brandy's Piano Bar, was a corny-looking nightspot I could have passed a thousand times without once noticing. BRANDY'S CUSTOMERS, PLEASE RESPECT OUR NEIGHBORS! pleaded a small sign at the doorway, suggesting a whole tale of complaint calls to the police about noise and fumes. To live in Manhattan is to be persistently amazed at the worlds squirreled inside one another, like those lines of television cable and fresh water and steam heat and outgoing sewage and telephone wire and whatever else which cohabit in the same intestinal holes that pavement-demolishing workmen periodically wrench open to the daylight and to our passing, disturbed glances. We only pretend to live on something as orderly as a grid. Waiting for Perkus Tooth's door's buzzer to sound and finding my way upstairs, I felt my interior map expand to allow for the reality of this place, the corridor floor's lumpy checkerboard mosaic, the cloying citrus of some superintendent's disinfectant oil, the bank of dented brass mailboxes and the keening of a dog from behind an upstairs door, alerted to the buzzer and my scuffling boot heels. I have trouble believing anything exists until I know it bodily.

Perkus Tooth widened his door just enough for me to slip inside, directly into his kitchen. Perkus, though barefoot, wore another antique-looking suit, green corduroy this time, the only formal thing my entry revealed. The place was a bohemian grotto, the kitchen a kitchen only in the sense of having a sink and stove built in, and a sticker-laden refrigerator wedged into an alcove beside the bathroom door. Books filled the open cabinet spaces above the sink. The countertop was occupied by a CD player and hundreds of disks, in and out of jewel cases, many hand-labeled with a permanent marker. A hot-water pipe whined. Beyond, the other rooms of the apartment were dim at midday, the windows draped.

They likely only looked onto ventilation shafts or a paved alley anyway.

And then there were the broadsides Susan Eldred had described. Unframed, thumb-tacked to every wall bare of bookshelves, in the kitchen and in the darkened rooms, were Perkus Tooth's famous posters, their paper yellowing, the lettering veering from a stylish cartoonist's or grafittist's hand-made font to the obsessive scrawl of an outsider artist, or a schizophrenic patient's pages reproduced in his doctor's monograph. I recognized them. Remembered them. They'd been ubiquitous downtown a decade before, on construction-site boards, over subway advertisements, another element in the graphic cacophony of the city one gleans helplessly at the edges of vision.

Perkus retreated to give me clearance to shut the door. Stranded in the room's center in his suit and bare feet, palms defensively wide as if expecting something unsavory to be tossed his way, Perkus reminded me of an Edvard Munch painting I'd once seen, a self-portrait showing the painter wide-eyed and whiskered, shrunken within his clothes. Which is to say, again, that Perkus Tooth seemed older than his age. (I'd never once see Perkus without some part of a suit, even if it was only the pants, topped with a filthy white t-shirt. He never wore jeans.)

'I'll get you the videotape,' he said, as if I'd challenged him.

'Great.'

'Let me find it. You can sit down –' He pulled out a chair at a small, linoleum-topped table, like something you'd see in a diner. The chair matched the table – a dinette set, a collector's item. Perkus Tooth was nothing if not a collector. 'Here.' He took a perfect finished joint from where it waited in the lip of an ashtray, clamped it in his mouth and ignited the tip, then handed it to me unquestioningly. It takes one, I suppose, to know one. I drew on it while he went into the other room. When he returned – with a VHS cassette and his sneakers and a balled-up pair of white socks – he accepted the joint from me and smoked an inch of it himself, intently.

'Do you want to get something to eat? I haven't been out all day.' He laced his hi-tops.

'Sure,' I said.

Out, for Perkus Tooth, I'd now begun to learn, wasn't usually far. He liked to feed at a glossy hamburger palace around the corner on Second Avenue, called Jackson Hole, a den of gleaming chrome and newer, faker versions of the linoleum table in his kitchen, lodged in chubby red-vinyl booths. At four in the afternoon we were pretty well alone there, the jukebox blaring hits to cover our bemused, befogged talk. It had been a while since I'd smoked pot; everything was dawning strange, signals received through an atmosphere murky with hesitations, the whole universe drifting untethered like Perkus Tooth's vagrant eyeball. The waitress seemed to know Perkus, but he didn't greet her or touch his menu. He asked for a cheeseburger deluxe and a Coca-Cola. Helpless, I dittoed his order. Perkus seemed to dwell in this place as he had at Criterion's offices, indifferently, obliquely, as if he'd been born there yet still hadn't taken notice of it.

In the middle of our meal Perkus halted some rant about Werner Herzog or Marlon Brando or Morrison Roog to announce what he'd made of me so far. 'So, you've gotten by to this point by being cute, haven't you, Chase?' His spidery fingers, elbow-propped on the linoleum, kept the oozing, gory, Jackson Hole burger aloft to mask his expression, and cantilevered far enough from his lap to protect those dapper threads. One eye fixed me while the other crawled, now seeming a scalpel in operation on my own face. 'You haven't changed, you're like a dreamy child, that's the secret of your appeal. But they love you. They watch you like you're still on television.'

'Who?'

'The rich people. The Manhattanites – you know who I mean.'

'Yes,' I said.

'You're supposed to be the saddest man in Manhattan,' he said. 'Because of the astronaut who can't come home.'

'Yes.'

'That's what they adore.'

'I guess so.'

'So, just keep your eyes and ears open,' he said. 'You're in a position to learn things.'

What things? Before I could ask, we were off again. Perkus's spiel encompassed Monte Hellman, eBay, Greil Marcus's *Lipstick Traces*, the Mafia's blackmailing of J. Edgar Hoover over erotic secrets (resulting in the bogus amplification of Cold War fear and therefore the whole of our contemporary landscape), Vladimir Mayakovsky and the Futurists, Chet Baker, Nothingism, the ruination Giuliani's administration had brought to the sacred squalor of Times Square, the genius of *The Gnuppet Show*, Frederick Exley, Jacques Rivette's impossible-to-see thirteen-hour movie *Out 1*, corruption of the arts by commerce generally, Slavoj Zizek on Hitchcock, Franz Marplot's biography of G. K. Chesterton, Norman Mailer on Muhammad Ali, Norman Mailer on graffiti and the space program, Brando as dissident icon, Brando as sexual saint, Brando as Napoleon in exile. Names I knew and didn't. Others I'd heard once and never troubled to wonder about. Mailer, again and again, and Brando even more often – Perkus Tooth's primary idols seemed to be this robust and treacherous pair, which only made Perkus seem frailer and more harmless by contrast, without ballast in his pencil-legged suit. Maybe he ate Jackson Hole burgers in an attempt to burgeon himself, seeking girth in hopes of attracting the attention of Norman and Marlon, his chosen peers.

He had the waitress refill his gallon-sized Coke, then, as our afternoon turned to evening, washed it all down with black coffee. In our talk, marijuana confusion now gave way to caffeinated jags, like a cloudbank penetrated by buzzing Fokker airplanes. Did I read the *New Yorker*? This question had a dangerous urgency. It wasn't any one writer or article he was worried about, but the *font*. The meaning embedded, at a preconscious level, by the look of the magazine; the seal, as he described it, that the typography and layout put on dialectical thought. According to Perkus, to read the *New Yorker* was to find that you always already agreed, not with the *New Yorker* but, much more dismayingly, with *yourself*. I tried hard to understand. Apparently here was the paranoia Susan Eldred had warned me of: the *New Yorker*'s font was controlling, perhaps attacking, Perkus Tooth's mind. To defend himself he frequently retyped their articles and printed them out in simple Courier, an attempt to dissolve the magazine's oppressive context. Once, I'd entered his apartment to find him on his carpet with a pair of scissors, furiously slicing up and rearranging an issue of the magazine, trying to shatter its spell on his brain. 'So, how', he asked me another time, apropos of nothing, 'does a *New Yorker* writer become a *New Yorker* writer?' The falsely casual 'so' masking a pure anxiety. It wasn't a question with an answer.

But I'm confused in this account, surely. Can we have discussed so much the very first time? The *New Yorker*, at least. Giuliani's auctioning 42nd Street to Disney. Mailer on NASA as a bureaucracy stifling dreams. J. Edgar Hoover in the Mafia's thrall, hyping Reds, instilling self-patrolling fear in the American Mind. In the midst of these variations the theme was always ingeniously and excitingly retrieved. In short, some human freedom had been leveraged from view at the level of consciousness itself.

Liberty had been narrowed, winnowed, *amnesiacked*. Perkus Tooth used this word without explaining, and in the way that the Mafia itself would: to mean a whack, a rub-out. Everything that mattered most was a victim in this perceptual murder plot. Further: always to blame was everyone; when rounding up the suspects, begin with yourself. Complicity, including his own, was Perkus Tooth's only doubtless conviction. The worst thing was to be sure you knew what you knew, the mistake the *New Yorker*'s font induced. The horizon of everyday life was a mass daydream – below it lay the crucial material, the crux. By now we'd paid for our burgers and returned to his apartment. At his dinette table we sat and he strained some pot for seeds, then rolled another joint. The dope came out of a little plastic box marked with a laser-printed label reading CHRONIC in rainbow colors, a kind of brand name. We smoked the new joint relentlessly to a nub and went on talking,

Perkus now free to gesticulate as he hadn't at Jackson Hole. Yet he never grew florid, never, in all his ferment, hyperventilated or, like some epileptic, bit his tongue. The feverish words were delivered with a merciless cool. Like the cut of his suit, wrinkled though it might be. And the obsessively neat lettering on the VHS tape and on his CDs. Perkus Tooth might have one crazy eye, but it served almost as a warning not to underestimate his scruples, how attentively he measured his listener's skepticism, making those minute adjustments that were the signature of his or anyone's sanity – the interpersonal realpolitik of persuasion. The eye was mad and the rest of him was almost steely.

Perkus rifled through his CDs to find a record he wished to play for me, a record I didn't know – Peter Blegvad's '(Something Else) Is Working Harder'. The song was an angry and incoherent blues, it sounded to me, gnarled with disgruntlement at those who 'get away with murder'. Then, as if riled by the music, he turned and said, almost savagely, 'So, I'm not a *rock critic*, you know.'

'Okay.' This was a point I found easy enough to grant.

'People will say I am, because I wrote for *Rolling Stone* – but I hardly ever write about music.' In fact, the broadsides hung in his rooms seemed to be full of references to pop songs, but I hesitated to point out the contradiction.

He seemed to read my mind. 'Even when I do, I don't use that *language*.'

'Oh.'

'Those people, the rock critics, I mean – do you want to know what they really are?'

'Oh, sure – what are they?'

'Super-high-functioning autistics. Oh, I don't mean they're diagnosed or anything. But *I* diagnose them that way. They've got Asperger's Syndrome. I mean, in the same sense that, say, David Byrne or Al Gore has it. They're brilliant, but they're *social misfits*.'

'Uh, how do you know?' As far as I knew, I'd never met anyone with Asperger's Syndrome, or, for that matter, a rock critic. (Although I had once seen David Byrne at a party.) Yet I knew enough already to find it odd hearing Perkus Tooth denouncing misfits.

'It's the way they talk.' He leaned in close to me, and demonstrated his point as he spoke. *'They aspirate their vowels nearer to the front of their mouths.'*

'Wow.'

'And when you see them talking in groups they do it even more. It's self-reinforcing. Rock critics gather for purposes of mutual consolation, though they'd never call it that. They believe they're *experts.'* Perkus, whether he knew it or not, continued to aspirate his vowels at the front of his mouth as he made his case. 'They can't see the forest for the trees.'

'Thelf-reinforthing exthperts,' I said, trying it on for size. 'Can't thee the foretht for the threes.' I am by deepest instinct a mimic. Anyway, a VHS tape labeled ECHOLALIA lay on the table between us.

'That's right,' said Perkus seriously. 'Some of them even whistle when they speak.'

'Whisthle?'

'Exactly.'

'Thank God we're not rock critics.'

'You can say that again.' He tongued the gum on another joint he'd been assembling, then inspected it for smoke-worthiness, running it under his odd eye as if scanning for a barcode. Satisfied, he ignited it. 'So, I'm self-medicating,' he explained. 'I smoke grass because of the headaches.'

'Migraine headaches?'

'Cluster headaches. It's a variant of migraine. One side of the head.' With two fingers he tapped his skull – of course it was his right side, the headaches gravitating toward the deviant eye. 'They're called cluster headaches because they come in runs, every day for a week or two at exactly the same time. Like a clock, like a rooster crowing.'

'That's crazy.'

'I know. Also, there's this visual effect . . . a blindspot on one side . . .' Again, his right hand waved. 'Like a blot in the center of my visual field.'

A riddle: what do you get when you cross a blindspot with a wandering eye? But we'd never once mentioned his eye, so I hung fire. 'The pot helps?' I asked instead.

'The thing about a migraine-type experience is that it's like being only half alive. You find yourself walking through this tomb-like world, everything gets far away and kind of dull and dead. Smoking pulls me back into the world, it restores my appetites for food and sex and conversation.'

Well, I had evidence of food and conversation – Perkus Tooth's appetites in sex were to remain mysterious to me for the time being. This was still the first of the innumerable afternoons and evenings I surrendered to Perkus's kitchen table, to his smoldering ashtray and pot of scorched coffee, to his ancient CD boombox, which audibly whined as it spun in the silent gap between tracks, to our booth around the corner at Jackson Hole when a fierce craving for burgers and cola came over us, as it often did. Soon enough those days all blurred happily together, for in the disconsolate year of Janice's broken orbit Perkus Tooth was probably my best friend. I suppose Perkus was the curiosity, I the curiosity-seeker, but he surely added me to his collection as much as the reverse.

I did watch *Echolalia*. The way Brando tormented his would-be interviewer was funny, but the profundity of the whole thing was lost on me. I suppose I was unfamiliar with the required context. When I returned it I said so, and Perkus frowned.

'Have you seen *The Nascent*?'

'Nope.'

'Have you seen *Anything That Hides*?'

'Not that one either.'

'Have you seen *any* of Morrison Roog's films, Chase?'

'Not knowingly.'

'How do you survive?' he said, not unkindly. 'How do you even get along in the world, not understanding what goes on around you?'

'That's what I have you for. You're my brain.'

'Ah, with your looks and my brain, we could go far,' he joked in a Bogart voice.

'Exactly.'

Something lit up inside him, then, and he climbed on his chair in his bare feet and performed a small monkey-like dance, singing impromptu, 'If I'm your brain you're in a whole lot of trouble . . . you picked the wrong brain!' Perkus had a kind of beauty in his tiny, wiry body and his almost feral, ax-blade skull, with its gracefully tapered widow's peak and delicate features. 'Your brain's on drugs, your brain's on fire . . .'

Despite this lunatic warning, Perkus took charge of what he considered my education, loading me up with tapes and DVDs, sitting me down for essential viewings. Perkus's apartment was a place for consuming archival wonders, whether at his kitchen table or in the sagging chairs before his flatscreen television: bootlegged unreleased recordings by those in Tooth's musical pantheon, like Chet Baker, Nina Simone or Neil Young, and grainy tapes of scarce *film noir* taped off late-night television broadcasts. Among these treasures was a videotape of a ninety-minute episode of the detective show *Columbo*, from 1981, directed by Paul Mazursky and starring John Cassavetes as a wife-murdering orchestra conductor, the foil to Peter Falk's famously rumpled detective. It also featured, in roles as Cassavetes's two spoiled children, Molly Ringwald and myself. The TV-movie was something Mazursky had tossed off around the time of the making of *Tempest*, a theatrical release featuring Cassavetes and Ringwald, though not, alas, me. That pretty well summed up my luck as an actor, the ceiling I'd always bumped against – television but never the big screen.

Cassavetes was among Perkus's holy heroes, so he'd captured this broadcast, recorded it off some twilight-hour rerun. The tape was complete with vintage commercials from the middle eighties, O. J. Simpson sprinting through airports and so forth, all intact. I hadn't seen the *Columbo* episode since it was first aired, and it gave me a feeling of seasick familiarity. Not that Mazursky, Falk,

Cassevetes and Ringwald had been family to me – I'd barely known them – yet still it felt like watching a home movie. And it led to the odd sense that in some fashion I'd already been here in Perkus's apartment for twenty-odd years before I'd met him. His knowledge of culture, and the weirdly synesthetic connections he traced inside it, made it seem as though this moment of our viewing the tape together was fated. Indeed, as if at twelve years old I'd acted in this forgettable and forgotten television show alongside John Cassevetes as a form of private communion with my future friend Perkus Tooth.

Of course Perkus paid scant attention to the sulky children tugging at Cassevetes's sleeves – his interest was in the scenes between the great director and Peter Falk, as he scoured the TV-movie for any whiff of genius that recalled their great work together in Cassevetes's own films, or in Elaine May's *Mikey and Nicky*. He intoned reverently at the sort of details I never bothered to observe, either then, as a child actor on the set, or as a viewer now. Of course he also catalogued speculative connections among the galaxy of cultural things that interested him.

For instance: 'This sorry little TV movie is one of Myrna Loy's last-ever appearances. You know, Myrna Loy, *The Thin Man*? She was in dozens of silent movies in the twenties, too.' My silence permitted him to assume I grasped these depth soundings. 'Also in *Lonelyhearts*, in 1958, with Montgomery Clift and Robert Ryan.'

'Ah.'

'Based on the Nathanael West novel.'

'Ah.'

'Of course it isn't really any good.'

'Mmm.' I gazed at the old lady in the scene with Falk, waiting to feel what Perkus felt.

'Montgomery Clift is buried in the Quaker cemetery in Prospect Park, in Brooklyn. Very few people realize he's there, or that there even *is* a cemetery in Prospect Park. When I was a teenager a girlfriend and I snuck in there at night, scaled the fence and looked around, but we couldn't find his grave, just a whole bunch of voodoo chicken heads and other burnt offerings.'

'Wow.'

Only half listening to Perkus, I went on staring at my childhood self, a ghost disguised as a twelve-year-old, haunting the corridors of the mansion owned by Cassavetes's character, the villainous conductor. It seemed Perkus's collection was a place where one might turn a corner and unexpectedly find oneself, a conspiracy that was also a mirror.

Perkus went on connecting dots: 'Peter Falk was in *The Gnuppet Movie*, too, right around this time.'

'Really.'

'Yeah. So was Marlon Brando.'

Marijuana might have been constant, but coffee was Perkus Tooth's muse. With his discombobulated eye Perkus seemed to be watching his precious cup always while he watched you. It might not be a defect so much as a security system, an evolutionary defense against having his java stolen. Once, left alone briefly in his place, among his scattered papers I found a shred of lyric, the only writing I ever saw from Perkus that wasn't some type of critical exegesis. An incomplete, second-guessed ode, it read: 'Oh caffeine! / you contemporary ~~fiend~~ screen / ~~into your face I've seen / into my face~~ / through my face –' And yes, the sheet of paper was multiply imprinted with rings by his coffee mug.

It was impossible for me not to picture the fugue that eventually produced this writing being interrupted by a seizure of migraine, the pen dropping from Perkus's hand as he succumbed to one of his cluster headaches. Impossible not to picture it this way because of the day I walked in on him in the grip of a fresh one. He'd e-mailed earlier to invite me to drop by, then fell victim. The door was unlocked and he called me inside from where he lay on his couch, in his suit-pants and a yellowed t-shirt, with a cool cloth draped over his eyes. He told me to sit down, and not to worry, but his voice was withered, drawn down inside his skinny chest. I was persuaded at once that he spoke to me from within that half-life, that land of the dead he'd so precisely evoked with his first descriptions of cluster headache.

'It's a bad one,' he said. 'The first day is always the worst. I can't look at the light.'

'You never know when it's coming?'

'There's a kind of warning aura an hour or two before,' he croaked out. 'The world begins shrinking . . .'

I moved for his bathroom, and he said: 'Don't go in there. I puked.'

What I did I will admit is unlike me: I went in and cleaned up Perkus's vomit. Further, seeking out a sponge in his kitchen sink, I ran into a mess there, a cereal bowl half filled with floating Cheerios, cups with coffee evaporating to filmy stain-rings. While Perkus lay on the couch breathing heavily through a washcloth, I quietly tinkered at his kitchen, putting things in a decent order, not wanting him to slip into derangement and squalor on what it had suddenly occurred to me was *my watch* – he appeared so disabled I could imagine him not budging from that couch for days. And I'd still never seen another soul in Perkus's apartment, though he claimed to have other visitors. The dinette table was scattered with marijuana, half of it pushed through a metal strainer, the rest still bunchy with seeds. I swept it all back into a plastic box labeled FUNKY MONKEY – another of his dealer's brand names – and scooped the joints Perkus had completed into the Altoids tin he kept for that purpose. Then, growing compulsive (I do keep my own apartment neat, though I'd before never felt any anxiety at Perkus's squalor), I started reorganizing his scattered CDs, matching the disks to their dislocated jewel cases. This kind of puttering may be how I set myself at ease, another type of self-medication. It was certainly the case that blundering in on Perkus's headache had made me self-conscious and pensive, but I felt I couldn't go. I made no attempt to conceal my actions, and Perkus offered no comment, apart from the slightest moan. But after I'd been clattering at his compact disks for a while he said: 'Find Sandy Bull.'

'What?'

'Sandy Bull . . . he's a guitarist . . . the songs are very long . . . I can tolerate them in this state . . . it gives me something to listen to besides this throbbing . . .'

I found the disk and put it in his player. The music seemed to me insufferably droning, psychedelic in a minor key, more suitable for a harem than a sickroom. But then I really know nothing about music or headaches.

'You can go . . .' said Perkus. 'I'll be fine . . .'

'Do you need food?'

'No . . . when it's like this I can't eat . . .'

Well, Perkus couldn't eat one of Jackson Hole's fist-sized burgers, I'd grant that. I wondered if a plate of some vegetable or a bowl of soup might be called for, but I wasn't going to mother him. So I did go, after lowering the lights but leaving the creepy music loud, as Perkus wished. I found myself strangely bereft, discharged into the vacant hours. I'd come to rely on my Perkus afternoons, and how they turned into evenings. The light outside was all wrong. I realized I couldn't recall a time I'd not gone back through his lobby, brain pleasantly hazy, into a throng of Brandy's Piano Bar patrons ignoring the sign and smoking and babbling outside on the pavement, while piano tinkling and erratic choruses of sing-along drifted from within the bar to the street. Now all was quiet, the stools upturned on the tables. And all I could think of was Perkus, stilled on the couch, his lids swollen beneath the washcloth.

The next time I saw Perkus I made the mistake of asking if his tendency to veer into ellipsis was in any way connected to the cluster migraines. He'd been bragging the week before about his capacity for shifting into the satori-like state he called 'ellipsistic'; how, when he ventured there, he glimpsed bonus dimensions, worlds inside the world. Most of his proudest writing, he'd explained, emanated from some glimpse of this variety of *ellipsistic knowledge*.

'There's no connection,' he said now, where we sat in our Jackson Hole booth, his distaff eye bulging. 'Cluster's a death state, where all possibilities shut down . . . I'm not myself there . . . I'm not anyone. Ellipsis is *mine*, Chase.'

'I only wondered if they might somehow be two sides of the same coin . . .' Or two ways of peering out of the same skull, I thought but didn't say.

'I can't even begin to explain. It's totally different.'

'I'm sorry,' I said spontaneously, wanting to calm him.

'Sorry for what?' He'd spat out a gobbet of burger in his fury at refuting me.

'I . . . didn't mean . . . anything.'

'Ellipsis is like a window opening, Chase. Or like – art. It stops time.'

'Yes, you've said.' The clot of chewed beef sat beside his napkin, unnoticed except by me.

'Cluster, on the other hand – they're enemies.'

'Yes.' He'd persuaded me. It hadn't taken much. I wanted to persuade *him*, now, to see an Eastern healer I knew, a master of Chinese medicine who, operating out of offices in Chelsea, and with a waiting list of six months or more, ministered to Manhattan's wealthy and famous, charming and acupuncturing away their ornate stresses and decadent ills. I promised myself I'd try, later, when Perkus's anger cooled. I wanted so badly for him to have his ellipsis, have it wholly and unreservedly, wanted him to have it without cluster – however terribly much I suspected that one might be the price of the other. I wanted this selfishly, for, it dawned on me then, Perkus Tooth – his talk, his apartment, the space that had opened from the time I'd run into him at Criterion, then called him on the telephone – *was my ellipsis*. It might not be inborn in me, but I'd discovered it nonetheless in him. Where Perkus took me, in his ranting, in his enthusiasms, in his abrupt, improbable asides, was the world inside the world. And I didn't want him smothered in the tomb-world of migraine.

Donal Webster
Colm Tóibín

The moon hangs low over Texas. The moon is my mother. She is full tonight, and brighter than the brightest neon; there are folds of red in her vast amber. Maybe she is a harvest moon, a Comanche moon, I do not know. I have never seen a moon so low and so full of her own deep brightness. My mother is six years dead tonight, and Ireland is six hours away and you are asleep.

I am walking. No one else is walking. It is hard to cross Guadalupe; the cars come fast. In the Community Whole Food Store, where all are welcome, the girl at the checkout asks me if I would like to join the store's club. If I pay seventy dollars, my membership, she says, will never expire, and I will get a seven per-cent discount on all purchases.

Six years. Six hours. Seventy dollars. Seven per cent. I tell her I am here for a few months only, and she smiles and says that I am welcome. I smile back. I can still smile. If I called you now, it would be half two in the morning; you could easily be awake.

If I called, I could go over everything that happened six years ago. Because that is what is on my mind tonight, as though no time had elapsed, as though the strength of the moonlight had by some fierce magic chosen tonight to carry me back to the last real thing that happened to me. On the phone to you across the Atlantic, I could go over the days surrounding my mother's funeral. I could go over all the details as though I were in danger of forgetting them. I could remind you, for example, that you wore a white shirt at the funeral. It must have been warm enough not to wear a jacket. I remember that I could see you when I spoke about her from the altar, that you were over in the side aisle, on the left. I remember that you, or someone, said that you had parked your car almost in front of the cathedral because you had come late from Dublin and could not find parking anywhere else. I know that you moved your car before the hearse came after Mass to take my mother's coffin to the graveyard, with all of us walking behind. You came to the hotel once she was in the ground, and you stayed for a meal with me and Suzie, my sister. Jim, her husband, must have been near, and Cathal, my brother, but I don't remember what they did when the meal was over and the crowd had dispersed. I know that as the meal came to an end a friend of my mother's, who noticed everything, came over and looked at you and whispered to me that it was nice that my friend had come. She used the word 'friend' with a sweet, insinuating emphasis. I did not tell her that what she had noticed was no longer there, was part of the past. I simply said, yes, it was nice that you had come.

You know that you are the only person who shakes his head in exasperation when I insist on making jokes and small talk, when I refuse to be direct. No one else has ever minded this as you do. You are alone in wanting me always to say something that is true. I know now, as I walk towards the house I have rented here, that if I called and told you that the bitter past has come back to me tonight in these alien streets with a force that feels like violence, you would say that you are not surprised. You would wonder only why it has taken six years.

I was living in New York then, the city about to enter its last year of innocence. I had a new apartment there, just as I had a new apartment everywhere I went. It was on 90th and Columbus. You never saw it. It was a mistake. I think it was a mistake. I didn't stay there long – six or seven months – but it was the longest I stayed anywhere in those years or the years that followed. The apartment needed to be furnished, and I spent two or three days taking pleasure in the sharp bite of buying things: two easy chairs that I later sent back to Ireland; a leather sofa from Bloomingdale's, which I eventually gave to one of my students; a big bed from 1-800-Mattress; a table and some chairs from a place downtown; a cheap desk from the thrift shop.

And all those days – a Friday, a Saturday, and a Sunday, at the beginning of September – as I was busy with delivery times, credit cards, and the whiz of taxis from store to store, my mother was dying and no one could find me. I had no cell phone, and the phone line in the apartment had not been connected. I used the pay phone on the corner if I needed to make calls. I gave the delivery companies a friend's phone number, in case they had to let me know when they would come with my furniture. I phoned my friend a few times a day, and she came shopping with me sometimes and she was fun and I enjoyed those days. The days when no one in Ireland could find me to tell me that my mother was dying.

Eventually, late on the Sunday night, I slipped into a Kinko's and went online and found that Suzie had left me message after message, starting three days before, marked 'Urgent' or 'Are you there' or 'Please reply' or 'Please acknowledge receipt' and then just 'Please!!!' I read one of them, and I replied to say that I would call as soon as I could find a phone, and then I read the rest of them one by one. My mother was in the hospital. She might have to have an operation. Suzie wanted to talk to me. She was staying at my mother's house. There was nothing more in any of them, the urgency being not so much in their tone as in their frequency and the different titles she gave to each e-mail that she sent.

I woke her in the night in Ireland. I imagined her standing in the hall at the bottom of the stairs. I would love to say that Suzie told me my mother was asking for me, but she said nothing like that. She spoke instead about the medical details and how she herself had been told the news that our mother was in the hospital and how she had despaired of ever finding me. I told her that I would call again in the morning, and she said that she would know more then. My mother was not in pain now, she said, although she had been. I did not tell her that my classes would begin in three days, because I did not need to. That night, it sounded as though she wanted just to talk to me, to tell me. Nothing more.

But in the morning when I called I realized that she had put quick thought into it as soon as she heard my voice on the phone, that she had known I could not make arrangements to leave for

Dublin late on a Sunday night, that there would be no flights until the next evening; she had decided to say nothing until the morning. She had wanted me to have an easy night's sleep. And I did, and in the morning when I phoned she said simply that there would come a moment very soon when the family would have to decide. She spoke about the family as though it were as distant as the urban district council or the government or the United Nations, but she knew and I knew that there were just the three of us. We were the family, and there is only one thing that a family is ever asked to decide in a hospital. I told her that I would come home; I would get the next flight. I would not be in my new apartment for some of the furniture deliverers, and I would not be at the university for my first classes. Instead, I would find a flight to Dublin, and I would see her as soon as I could. My friend phoned Aer Lingus and discovered that a few seats were kept free for eventualities like this. I could fly out that evening.

You know that I do not believe in God. I do not care much about the mysteries of the universe, unless they come to me in words, or in music maybe, or in a set of colours, and then I entertain them merely for their beauty and only briefly. I do not even believe in Ireland. But you know, too, that in these years of being away there are times when Ireland comes to me in a sudden guise, when I see a hint of something familiar that I want and need. I see someone coming towards me, with a soft way of smiling, or a stubborn, uneasy face, or a way of moving warily through a public place, or a raw, almost resentful stare into the middle distance. In any case, I went to JFK that evening, and I saw them as soon as I got out of the taxi: a middle-aged couple pushing a trolley that had too much luggage on it, the man looking fearful and mild, as though he might be questioned by someone at any moment and not know how to defend himself, and the woman harassed and weary, her clothes too colourful, her heels too high, her mouth set in pure, blind determination, but her eyes humbly watchful, undefiant.

I could easily have spoken to them and told them why I was

going home and they both would have stopped and asked me where I was from, and they would have nodded with understanding when I spoke. Even the young men in the queue to check in, going home for a quick respite – just looking at their tentative stance and standing in their company saying nothing, that brought ease with it. I could breathe for a while without worry, without having to think. I, too, could look like them, as though I owned nothing, or nothing much, and were ready to smile softly or keep my distance without any arrogance if someone said, 'Excuse me', or if an official approached.

When I picked up my ticket, and went to the check-in desk, I was told to go to the other desk, which looked after business class. It occurred to me, as I took my bag over, that it might be airline policy to comfort those who were going home for reasons such as mine with an upgrade, to cosset them through the night with quiet sympathy and an extra blanket or something. But when I got to the desk I knew why I had been sent there, and I wondered about God and Ireland, because the woman at the desk had seen my name being added to the list and had told the others that she knew me and would like to help me now that I needed help.

Her name was Frances Carey, and she had lived next door to my aunt's house, where we – myself and Cathal – were left when my father got sick. I was eight years old then. Frances must have been ten years older, but I remember her well, as I do her sister and her two brothers, one of whom was close to me in age. Their family owned the house that my aunt lived in, the aunt who took us in. They were grander than she was and much richer, but she had become friendly with them, and there was, since the houses shared a large back garden and some outhouses, a lot of traffic between the two establishments.

Cathal was four then, but in his mind he was older. He was learning to read already, he was clever and had a prodigious memory, and was treated as a young boy in our house rather than as a baby; he could decide which clothes to wear each day and what television he wanted to watch and which room he would sit in and what food he would eat. When his friends called at the house, he could freely ask them in, or go out with them. When relatives or friends of my parents called, they asked for him, too, and spoke to him and listened avidly to what he had to say.

In all the years that followed, Cathal and I never once spoke about our time in this new house with this new family. And my memory, usually so good, is not always clear. I cannot remember, for example, how we got to the house, who drove us there, or what this person said. I know that I was eight years old only because I remember what class I was in at school when I left and who the teacher was. It is possible that this period lasted just two or three months. Maybe it was more. It was not summer, I am sure of that, because Suzie, who remained unscathed by all of this (or so she said, when once, years ago, I asked her if she remembered it), was back at boarding school. I have no memory of cold weather in that house in which we were deposited, although I do think that the evenings were dark early. Maybe it was from September to December. Or the first months after Christmas. I am not sure.

What I remember clearly is the rooms themselves, the parlour and dining room almost never used and the kitchen, larger than ours at home, and the smell and taste of fried bread. I hated the hot thick slices, fresh from the pan, soaked in lard or dripping. I remember that our cousins were younger than we were and had to sleep during the day, or at least one of them did, and we had to be quiet for hours on end, even though we had nothing to do; we had none of our toys or books. I remember that nobody liked us, either of us, not even Cathal, who, before and after this event, was greatly loved by people who came across him.

We slept in my aunt's house and ate her food as best we could, and we must have played or done something, although we never went to school. Nobody did us any harm in that house; nobody came near us in the night, or hit either of us, or threatened us, or made us afraid. The time we were left by our mother in our aunt's house has no drama attached to it. It was all greyness, strangeness.

Our aunt dealt with us in her own distracted way. Her husband was mild, distant, almost good-humoured.

And all I know is that our mother did not get in touch with us once, not once, during this time. There was no letter or phone call or visit. Our father was in the hospital. We did not know how long we were going to be left there. In the years that followed, our mother never explained her absence, and we never asked her if she had ever wondered how we were, or how we felt, during those months.

This should be nothing, because it resembled nothing, just as one minus one resembles zero. It should be barely worth recounting to you as I walk the empty streets of this city in the desert so far away from where I belong. It feels as though Cathal and I had spent that time in the shadow world, as though we had been quietly lowered into the dark, everything familiar missing, and nothing we did or said could change this. Because no one gave any sign of hating us, it did not strike us that we were in a world where no one loved us, or that such a thing might matter. We did not complain. We were emptied of everything, and in the vacuum came something like silence – almost no sound at all, just some sad echoes and dim feelings.

I promise you that I will not call. I have called you enough, and woken you enough times, in the years when we were together and in the years since then. But there are nights now in this strange, flat, and forsaken place when those sad echoes and dim feelings come to me slightly louder than before. They are like whispers, or trapped, whimpering sounds. And I wish that I had you here, and I wish that I had not called you all those other times when I did not need to as much as I do now.

My brother and I learned not to trust anyone. We learned then not to talk about things that mattered to us, and we stuck to this, as much as we could, with a sort of grim, stubborn pride, all our lives, as though it were a skill. But you know that, don't you? I do not need to call you to tell you that.

★

At JFK that night, Frances Carey smiled warmly and asked me how bad things were. When I told her that my mother was dying, she said that she was shocked. She remembered my mother so well, she said. She said she was sorry. She explained that I could use the first-class lounge, making it clear, however, in the most pleasant way, that I would be crossing the Atlantic in coach, which was what I had paid for. If I needed her, she said, she could come up in a while and talk, but she had told the people in the lounge and on the plane that she knew me, and they would look after me.

As we spoke and she tagged my luggage and gave me my boarding pass, I guessed that I had not laid eyes on her for more than thirty years. But in her face I could see the person I had known, as well as traces of her mother and one of her brothers. In her presence – the reminder she offered of that house where Cathal and I had been left all those years ago – I could feel that this going home to my mother's bedside would not be simple, that some of our loves and attachments are elemental and beyond our choosing, and for that very reason they come spiced with pain and regret and need and hollowness and a feeling as close to anger as I will ever be able to manage.

Sometime during the night in that plane, as we crossed part of the Western Hemisphere, quietly and, I hope, unnoticed, I began to cry. I was back then in the simple world before I had seen Frances Carey, a world in which someone whose heartbeat had once been mine, and whose blood became my blood, and inside whose body I once lay curled, herself lay stricken in a hospital bed. The fear of losing her made me desperately sad. And then I tried to sleep. I pushed back my seat as the night wore on and kept my eyes averted from the movie being shown, whatever it was, and let the terrible business of what I was flying towards hit me.

I hired a car at the airport, and I drove across Dublin in the washed light of that early September morning. I drove through Drumcondra, Dorset Street, Mountjoy Square, Gardiner Street, and the streets across the river that led south, as though they were a skin that I had shed. I did not stop for two hours or more, until I reached the house, fearing that if I pulled up somewhere to have breakfast the numbness that the driving with no sleep had brought might lift.

Suzie was just out of bed when I arrived, and Jim was still asleep. Cathal had gone back to Dublin the night before, she said, but would be down later. She sighed and looked at me. The hospital had phoned, she went on, and things were worse. Your mother, she said, had a stroke during the night, on top of everything else. It was an old joke between us: never 'our mother' or 'my mother' or 'Mammy' or 'Mummy,' but 'your mother'.

The doctors did not know how bad the stroke had been, she said, and they were still ready to operate if they thought they could. But they needed to talk to us. It was a pity, she added, that our mother's specialist, the man who looked after her heart, and whom she saw regularly and liked, was away. I realized then why Cathal had gone back to Dublin – he did not want to be a part of the conversation that we would have with the doctors. Two of us would be enough. He had told Suzie to tell me that whatever we decided would be fine with him.

Neither of us blamed him. He was the one who had become close to her. He was the one she loved most. Or maybe he was the only one she loved. In those years, anyway. Or maybe that is unfair. Maybe she loved us all, just as we loved her as she lay dying.

And I moved, in those days – that Tuesday morning to the Friday night when she died – from feeling at times a great remoteness from her to wanting fiercely, almost in the same moment, my mother back where she had always been, in witty command of her world, full of odd dreams and perspectives, difficult, ready for life. She loved, as I did, books and music and hot weather. As she grew older she had managed, with her friends and with us, a pure charm, a lightness of tone and touch. But I knew not to trust it, not to come close, and I never did. I managed, in turn, to exude my own lightness and charm, but you know that, too. You don't need me to tell you that, either, do you?

I regretted nonetheless, as I sat by her bed or left so that others might see her – I regretted how far I had moved away from her, and how far away I had stayed. I regretted how much I had let those months apart from her in the limbo of my aunt's house, and the years afterwards, as my father slowly died, eat away at my soul. I regretted how little she knew about me, as she, too, must have regretted that, although she never complained or mentioned it, except perhaps to Cathal, and he told no one anything. Maybe she regretted nothing. But nights are long in winter, when darkness comes down at four o'clock and people have time to think of everything.

Maybe that is why I am here now, away from Irish darkness, away from the long, deep winter that settles so menacingly on the place where I was born. I am away from the east wind. I am in a place where so much is empty because it was never full, where things are forgotten and swept away, if there ever were things. I am in a place where there is nothing. Flatness, a blue sky, a soft, unhaunted night. A place where no one walks. Maybe I am happier here than I would be anywhere else, and it is only the poisonous innocence of the moon tonight that has made me want to dial your number and see if you are awake.

As we drove to see my mother that morning, I could not ask Suzie a question that was on my mind. My mother had been sick for four days now and was lying there maybe frightened, and I wondered if she had reached out her hand to Cathal and if they had held hands in the hospital, if they had actually grown close enough for that. Or if she had made some gesture to Suzie. And if she might do the same to me. It was a stupid, selfish thing I wondered about, and, like everything else that came into my mind in those days, it allowed me to avoid the fact that there would be no time any more for anything to be explained or said. We had used up all our time. And I wondered if that made any difference to my mother then, as she lay awake in the hospital those last few nights of her life: we had used up all our time.

She was in intensive care. We had to ring the bell and wait to be admitted. There was a hush over the place. We had discussed what

I would say to her so as not to alarm her, how I would explain why I had come back. I told Suzie that I would simply say that I'd heard she was in the hospital and I'd had a few days free before classes began and had decided to come back to make sure that she was OK.

'Are you feeling better?' I asked her.

She could not speak. Slowly and laboriously, she let us know that she was thirsty and they would not allow her to drink anything. She had a drip in her arm. We told the nurses that her mouth was dry, and they said that there was nothing much we could do, except perhaps take tiny drops of cold water and put them on her lips using those special little sticks with cotton-wool tips that women use to put on eye make-up.

I sat by her bed and spent a while wetting her lips. I was at home with her now. I knew how much she hated physical discomfort; her appetite for this water was so overwhelming and so desperate that nothing else mattered.

And then word came that the doctors would see us. When we stood up and told her that we would be back, she hardly responded. We were ushered by a nurse with an English accent down some corridors to a room. There were two doctors there; the nurse stayed in the room. The doctor who seemed to be in charge, who said that he would have been the one to perform the operation, told us that he had just spoken to the anaesthetist, who had insisted that my mother's heart would not survive an operation. The stroke did not really matter, he said, although it did not help.

'I could have a go,' he said, and then immediately apologized for speaking like that. He corrected himself: 'I could operate, but she would die on the operating table.'

There was a blockage somewhere, he said. There was no blood getting to her kidneys and maybe elsewhere as well – the operation would tell us for certain, but it would probably do nothing to solve the problem. It was her circulation, he said. The heart was simply not beating strongly enough to send blood into every part of her body.

He knew to leave silence then, and the other doctor did, too. The nurse looked at the floor.

'There's nothing you can do, then, is there?' I said.

'We can make her comfortable,' he replied.

'How long can she survive like this?' I asked.

'Not long,' he said.

'I mean, hours or days?'

'Days. Some days.'

'We can make her very comfortable,' the nurse said.

There was nothing more to say. Afterwards, I wondered if we should have spoken to the anaesthetist personally, or tried to contact our mother's consultant, or asked that she be moved to a bigger hospital for another opinion. But I don't think any of this would have made a difference. For years, we had been given warnings that this moment would come, as she fainted in public places and lost her balance and declined. It had been clear that her heart was giving out, but not clear enough for me to have come to see her more than once or twice in the summer – and then when I did come I was protected from what might have been said, or not said, by the presence of Suzie and Jim and Cathal. Maybe I should have phoned a few times a week, or written her letters like a good son. But, despite all the warning signals, or perhaps even because of them, I had kept my distance. And as soon as I entertained this thought, with all the regret that it carried, I imagined how coldly or nonchalantly a decision to spend the summer close by, seeing her often, might have been greeted by her, and how difficult and enervating for her, as much as for me, some of those visits or phone calls might have been. And how curtly efficient and brief her letters in reply to mine would have seemed.

And, as we walked back down to see her, the nurse coming with us, there was this double regret – the simple one that I had kept away, and the other one, much harder to fathom, that I had been given no choice, that she had never wanted me very much, and that she was not going to be able to rectify that in the few days that she had left in the world. She would be distracted by her own pain and discomfort, and by the great effort she was making to be dignified and calm. She was wonderful, as she always had been. I touched her hand a few times in case she might open it and seek my hand, but she never did this. She did not respond to being touched.

Some of her friends came. Cathal came and stayed with her. Suzie and I remained close by. On Friday morning, when the nurse asked me if I thought she was in distress, I said that I did. I knew that, if I insisted now, I could get her morphine and a private room. I did not consult the others; I knew that they would agree. I did not mention morphine to the nurse, but I knew that she was wise, and I saw by the way she looked at me as I spoke that she knew that I knew what morphine would do. It would ease my mother into sleep and ease her out of the world. Her breathing would come and go, shallow and deep, her pulse would become faint, her breathing would stop, and then come and go again.

It would come and go until, in that private room late in the evening, it seemed to stop altogether, as, horrified and helpless, we sat and watched her, then sat up straight as the breathing started again, but not for long. Not for long at all. It stopped one last time, and it stayed stopped. It did not start again.

She was gone. She lay still. We sat with her until a nurse came in and quietly checked her pulse and shook her head sadly and left the room.

We stayed with her for a while; then, when they asked us to leave, we touched her on the forehead one by one, and we left the room, closing the door. We walked down the corridor as though for the rest of our lives our own breathing would bear traces of the end of hers, of her final struggle, as though our own way of being in the world had just been halved or quartered by what we had seen.

We buried her beside my father, who had been in the grave waiting for her for thirty-three years. And the next morning I flew back to New York, to my half-furnished apartment on Columbus and 90th, and began my teaching a day later. I understood, just as you might tell me now – if you picked up the phone and found me on the other end of the line, silent at first and then saying that I needed to talk to you – you might tell me that I had over all the years postponed too much. As I settled down to sleep in that new bed in the dark city, I saw that it was too late now, too late for everything. I would not be given a second chance. In the hours when I woke, I have to tell you that this struck me almost with relief.

Newton Wicks
Andrew Sean Greer

Newton's best friend, back when he was New, was chosen for him. First friends often are. Hard to know how it started, though two children, five years old and wary from the world of kindergarten, must have been put in a living room together, as zoo handlers will place two creatures of the same species in the painted setting of their habitat. The young adults – untenured colleagues – sat in some other room and laughed over the clattering ice of their drinks, over the Peter, Paul and Mary album (they will call the kids in when *Puff* comes on), and the boys were left to stare wildly at each other. Who knows if they even recognized their own kind? Who knows if this was even hard for them, a first friendship, when every single thing is thorned with newness? The boy's name was Martin, and, since this was his house, he introduced Newton to his various toys. There was a tense silence as Newton held a small plastic fireman with Felix-the-Cat eyes; he moved the arms and legs, and suddenly he was miniaturized into the deep beige pile of the carpet, shoulder high, and the world was a jungle for a fireman to escape from. 'No, no, see,' Martin said, and Newton was full sized again, ashamed, as the toy was taken from him and made to sit in a dirty carriage clearly made for some other toy, now lost. 'No, see, he rides in here and goes around, see, he's in charge of looking out for bats.' And indeed two rubber bats were taken out of the box and jiggled in the air menacingly. Like a TV show – like everything, in fact – Newton had stumbled upon a long-running story whose beginning he would never be able to deduce. He was given another fireman, who wore his vest backwards and no hat. 'You be the princess.' This was only fair. In time, at Newton's own house, Martin will himself be forced into minor roles, talking animals and sidekicks. And eventually Martin will relinquish even his own heroes to Newton, the better storyteller. But this is probably why they became friends: because Newton, in the first few moments of their meeting, rather than snarl and complain, accepted the shame of playing the girl. At other meetings, Martin revealed that these toys were minor, like a preamble set before the curtain rises, or the series of people who interview you before you are shown into the executive office. Newton was shown into Martin's bedroom, where a hopeful puppet theater sat on folding feet, striped and painted with an elaborate foreign announcement (German, it turned out, meaning: 'The next performance is at . . .,') drawn above a clock with real cardboard hands, set to 4.30. It was 4.00. The performance – scheduled by optimistic Martin – never came. Instead, Newton was drawn to a tableau of paper knights, each only two inches high, in a magical woodland setting. Martin explained he had punched them out of a book, but he did not explain his problems with their paper half-moon stands, how they bent in his eager sweaty hands, or why his favorite one – the Black Knight – had a mangled stand and had to be leaned against a wall or a bedpost in order to take part in battle. Once they were in the fur of the rug, of course, it didn't matter. They could be pushed down into the pile and made to sit there forever. The bunkbed became a tower, the sheets became a mountain, the underbed a cavern, and, while they kept to realistic roles for a while, eventually each was granted one wish: to fly. Soon the knights did battle from bookshelf to bookshelf. The bats were brought up from downstairs. Nobody had to play the princess.

There was also a secret cache of cars, gold-and-red metal, with real turning wheels that got carpet fluff caught in them and wouldn't go anymore, except it didn't matter because Newton and Martin couldn't be bothered rolling them along the carpet but ran them almost anywhere else, up and down the bunkbed and the little blue desk with a matching chair (both glossy from a repainting) – all the while imitating each other's noises that went from Martin's antique 'burton burton burton' to Newton's futuristic 'vvvvuuuh' – until they ended up, magically, backstage at the puppet theater, where

Martin parted the curtain to reveal (as in a comedy) the headlight-eyes of the cars staring out unexpectedly at the audience. Then, with a scream, they plunged to their doom.

There was a pet, as well, a hermit crab in a shoebox (crayon-decorated with the coral-hands and seaweed boas of the ocean), and the two boys would set the striped shell on a table and wait patiently for it to emerge like a celebrity from a limo: first the filament feelers, then the dainty little legs, and then at last the great brown claw that meant Hermie was feeling bold. As soon as its eyes appeared, one boy or the other (the honor was shared) would poke the thing in the claw or the legs, and the creature would withdraw, suddenly, creepily, with just the tips of his toes showing in the orifice of the shell. But the stupid thing would never learn; another wait, and again the sensual nudity of his legs would tap one by one against the tabletop.

Martin, like any child, also had unplayable toys. Either broken, like the legless horse who rode only in Martin's solitary playtime, or out of sync with his age. There were, of course, the puppets themselves, lovingly donated by a rich aunt. These included hand-made finger puppets, representing a family, and a trio of knitted hand puppets: a tiger, a cop and a wizard. What scenario these three could enact was a puzzle. In the very back of his closet was a marionette of a small boy with a cap, something the old childless woman must not have been able to resist, though it was compli-cated, and too precious for the boy until he was much older, when he would probably consider it girlish or haunted. There was a dour, eyeless collection of animals housed in a hinged barnyard. Each was badly made of colored plastic, and long tabs from the extrusion process showed along their backbones, like the spines of dinosaurs. One was forever coming across them hidden in the carpet, yelping barefoot and retrieving a little pink pig with sharp feet and no smile at all on its face, though you felt it deserved one. They were too featureless to be loved – no child's mind could fold itself small enough to fit inside – and there were so many of them, a hundred, perhaps, that one could only imagine a child lining them up dutifully along the barnyard wall, species by species, like a slaughter of innocents.

They were at the age when every movement was as incredible as a spacewalk. Leaping from the front step could entertain them for hours, even though the step was identical to every step they'd ever seen in their lives. The stunted San Francisco backyard, though – so much better than Newton's own precipitous one – could telescope from an ant-kingdom in the grass to an interplanetary realm below the sadly unclimbable eucalyptus trees. But mostly they were so young that they needed nothing more than to run in circles among the trees, slipping now and then on the sickle-shapes leaves, finding new and yet newer hiding places for their tiny bodies among the bushes and the few patio chairs, waiting with a tiny beating frog-heart in the darkness of the woodpile until either the other boy leapt upon him with his own squeal of terror or the game went on too long, with the seeker beginning to cry beneath the scent and the surf-sound of the trees, and the hider jumping up, nearly in tears himself at having been lost for so long. At those times, an adult had to go outside to comfort them. They were for some reason incapable of comforting each other.

That was during the day. At night, their bodies still longed to run in circles, and, though it was clearly forbidden, they did it anyway. It was amazing to them that Martin's mother could sense immediately if they were jumping on his bed; they both stood with wide-eyed looks of wonder as she ran in, clairvoyant perhaps, and scolded them for ruining the bed, telling them to find something else to do. Sometimes there were spankings; if Newton's own parents weren't there, Martin's mother did not pause to spank him as well. For instance for standing on a stool and reaching into the cookie jar, fearing it was empty, and having the exhilarating sensation of feeling, among the ocean of crumbs, the half-raft of a cookie . . . before bringing the ceramic jar crashing to the floor. Or for getting into Martin's mother's closet and making a mess of things, rooting through her exotic paraphernalia like pirate treasure and tossing long rosy satiny things onto the floor in search of diamond buckles and pearls, which Martin, at that age before a boy knows better, would wear around his own neck. But mostly Martin's father believed in letting them be wild, and if he were around, they could take the sofa apart and make the most astounding fortress out of it, and even – on the best of all possible days – be allowed to eat dinner inside and watch, through the cracks of the cushions, an hour of blessed television. That was life until thirteen.

There are a thousand kinds of thirteen, more than there are kinds of fifty, or eighty. There is Oddly Childlike Thirteen, and Worried and Obsessive, and Alarmingly Manly, and Girlish, and Gothic Horror, and Scapegoat, and Something Happened to Him as a Child, and Beatific and Despised, and Lonely, and Just Plain Stubborn. There is Manic and there is Depressed, still leading separate lives. There is Loves Adults and there is Steals Dad's Antique Pornography. There is Steals Everything, Period. There is Already Smokes and Already Drinks and Already Screws. There is Weeps Alone. And Misses Childhood. And Hates the World. He was none of these; he was less than these. He was the kind of boy who had been a prodigy at six and faded by seven, the kind who would be handsome by twenty and show his old yearbook photos to girlfriends, unable to feel joy when they'd exclaim how hopeless he used to be. Somewhere in between those points was where he lay, and somehow – and this was the hopelessly sad part – he knew it. If you asked him, on a test sheet, to name his own type of thirteen, he would write in his seismographic hand: 'Waits for Time to Pass'.

Pictures, also, reveal very little. There is one of him at that age, in 1984, standing by the fireplace in a navy blazer and gray slacks his father had helped him pick out, clearly dressed for some acquaintance's bar mitzvah, his hair parted and set with a wet comb, dried into long lines like grass when it's been raked of leaves – possibly also sprayed with a canister of his father's Commander, it's that solid. It's a shame that photos, like children, remember only rare moments and never the everyday, for he has never looked like this in his life. A look of guilt, of surprise. Eyes a deep blue, the blue of a baby's eyes that will eventually turn to brown, wide open.

Eyebrows raised, perhaps in his first failed try at posing, at elegance. Or perhaps he has set his face this way as he waits. For his father to adjust the lens; for the sweat to trickle into the pits of his new shirt; for the terrible moment when they have to go. A dismembered hand floating in the ink of navy. One gold button, the only proud thing in the room.

The photo has captured nothing. Not the glow from the flowers on the mantel behind him, a present, which in this picture might as well be fake, or the evaporating droplets on the windowpane. Not this boy's beautiful, desperate love, tamped-down inside him like brown sugar in a measuring cup, which should fill every corner of the frame. Which should make that sad house plant beside him burst into flower. You would never guess that he is not looking out of a picture at all but is standing in a room looking at a grown man, at his own father, and what he thinks of that man we, looking at the picture, will never know. His is not the first photo not to capture these things, but for the viewer they might as well never have existed.

Contributors

DANIEL CLOWES was born in Chicago in 1961 and now lives in Oakland, California, with his wife, Erika, their son, Charles, and their beagle, Ella. His books include *Ghost World*, *David Boring*, *Caricature* and *Ice Haven*.

EDWIDGE DANTICAT was born in Haiti and moved to the United States of America when she was twelve years old. She is the author of several books, including *Breath, Eyes, Memory*, *Krik? Krak!*, *The Farming of Bones*, *The Dew Breaker* and, most recently, *Brother, I'm Dying*, a memoir.

DAVE EGGERS is the editor of *McSweeney's* and the author of four books, including *What Is the What*. He is the co-founder of 826 Valencia.

JONATHAN SAFRAN FOER was born in 1977. He is the author of *Everything Is Illuminated*, which won the National Jewish Book Award and the *Guardian* First Book Award, and *Extremely Loud and Incredibly Close*. He is also the editor of *A Convergence of Birds*, a tribute to the work of the American assemblage artist Joseph Cornell. He lives in Brooklyn, New York.

ANDREW SEAN GREER is the author of three works of fiction, most recently *The Confessions of Max Tivoli*, a national bestseller. He is the recipient of the California Book Award, the Northern California Book Award, the NY Public Library Young Lions Award, and a fellowship from the National Endowment for the Arts. He lives in San Francisco.

ALEKSANDAR HEMON was born in Sarajevo, and moved to Chicago in 1992. Upon his arrival in the US of A, he had all kinds of lousy jobs, including, but not limited to, canvassing for Greenpeace and teaching English as a Second Language to the people who suddenly found their First Language nearly perfectly useless. He acquired an MA degree in English from Northwestern and dropped the pursuit of a PhD the moment he sold his book *The Question of Bruno*. Then he wrote *Nowhere Man*. His stories have appeared in *The New Yorker*, *Granta*, *Esquire*, *The Paris Review* and in the *Best American Short Stories*, among others. He writes a column in Bosnian, under the unfortunate title *Hemonwood*, for the Sarajevo magazine *Dani*. He is a Guggenheim, MacArthur and decent fellow. When he lives, he lives in Chicago.

A. M. HOMES is the author of the acclaimed memoir, *The Mistress's Daughter* and the novels, *This Book Will Save Your Life*, *Music For Torching*, *The End of Alice*, *In A Country of Mothers*, and *Jack*, as well as the short-story collections, *Things You Should Know* and *The Safety of Objects*, the travel book, *Los Angeles: People, Places and The Castle on the Hill*, and the artist's book *Appendix A:*.

NICK HORNBY was born in 1957. He is the author of four novels: *High Fidelity*, *About A Boy*, *How To Be Good* and *A Long Way Down*, and two other woks of non-fiction: *Fever Pitch* and *The Complete Polysyllabic Spree*. In 1999 he was awarded the E. M. Forster Award by the American Academy of Arts and Letters. He lives and works in Highbury, north London.

HEIDI JULAVITS is the author of three novels, most recently *The Uses of Enchantment*. She is a founding editor of *The Believer* magazine and the recipient of a Guggenheim Fellowship. She lives in New York and Maine.

MIRANDA JULY is a filmmaker, performing artist and writer. Her collection of short stories, *No One Belongs Here More Than You*, was published earlier this year. She lives in Los Angeles.

A. L. KENNEDY has written four collections of short fiction and four novels, along with two books of non-fiction – many of these have won awards. Her latest novel is *Day*. She produces a variety of journalism and also writes for the stage, radio, film and TV and performs stand-up comedy. In 1993 and 2003 she was listed among *Granta*'s Best of Young British Novelists.

HARI KUNZRU is the author of *The Impressionist*, *Transmission* and the short story collection *Noise*, and was named one of Granta's Best of Young British Novelists in 2003. He is a contributing editor of *Mute* magazine and sits on the executive council of English PEN. He lives in East London.

JONATHAN LETHEM is the author of six novels including *The Fortress of Solitude*, as well as two collections of short stories. He lives in Brooklyn and Maine.

TOBY LITT was born in 1968. He is the author of *Adventures in Capitalism*, *Beatniks*, *Corpsing*, *deadkidsongs*, *Exhibitionism*, *Finding Myself*, *Ghost Story* and *Hospital*. In 2003, he was named one of *Granta*'s Best of Young British Novelists. His website can be found at www.tobylitt.com.

DAVID MITCHELL was born in England in 1969. He is the author of four novels. He lives in Ireland with his wife and their two children.

ANDREW O'HAGAN lives in London and his latest novel is *Be Near Me*.

ZZ PACKER is the author of *Drinking Coffee Elsewhere*, which was a finalist for the PEN/Faulkner Award and a *New York Times* Notable Book. A graduate of Yale, she has been a Wallace Stegner-Truman Capote fellow at Stanford University, where she is currently a Jones lecturer. She lives in the San Francisco Bay area.

GEORGE SAUNDERS, a 2006 MacArthur Fellow, is the author of five books of fiction including the short story collections *CivilWarLand in Bad Decline*, *Pastoralia*, and *In Persuasion Nation*. He teaches at Syracuse University.

POSY SIMMONDS was born in 1945 in Berkshire. She studied at the Sorbonne University, Paris before returning to England to attend the Central School of Art and Design in London. She has contributed to the *Guardian* since 1972 and has also drawn for the *Sun*, *The Times* and *Cosmopolitan*. Her bestselling children's books include *Fred, Lulu and the Flying Babies* and *The Chocolate Wedding*, and her books for adults include *Gemma Bovery* and *Literary Life*. She lives in London.

ZADIE SMITH was born in north-west London in 1975. She is the author of *White Teeth*, *The Autograph Man* and *On Beauty*.

ADAM THIRLWELL was born in 1978. His first novel, *Politics*, was published in 2003. A book about novels, *Miss Herbert*, is out this year. 'Nigora' is from a novel in progress.

COLM TÓIBÍN is the author of the five novels, including *The Blackwater Lightship* and *The Master*, and a volume of stories *Mothers and Sons*. He lives in Dublin.

VENDELA VIDA is the author of two novels, *Let the Northern Lights Erase Your Name* and *And Now You Can Go*. Her first book, *Girls on the Verge*, was a journalistic study of female initiation rituals in America. She is the co-editor of *The Believer* magazine, the editor of *The Believer Book of Writers Talking to Writers*, and a founding board member and teacher at 826 Valencia. She lives in Northern California.

CHRIS WARE lives outside of Chicago, Illinois, and is the author of *Jimmy Corrigan – the Smartest Kid on Earth*. He is currently serializing two new graphic novels in his ongoing periodical *The ACME Novelty Library*, the 18th and 18½ issues of which will be released in late 2007.

Acknowledgements

Thanks to Ted Thompson and Sarah Vowell for suggesting the project, to Linda Shaughnessy and Georgia Garrett for ensuring publication in many territories, and to Nick Laird for the title.